WHAT I'M NOT

A Porter Brothers Novel

Written By:

D.H. Renfroe

Edited By:

LeShawndra Johnson

What I'm Not

First Edition: May 2026

Paperback ISBN: 979-8-9956501-0-2

Hardcover ISBN: 979-8-9956501-1-9

Permissions & Acknowledgments

Select chapter headings in this book include quotes from films. These quotes are the property of their respective copyright holders and are used for literary and illustrative purposes only. Full credit is given within the text, including the film title and year of release. No infringement is intended.

CONTENTS

To the beautiful souls whose skin defies narrow definitions of beauty—your scars are stunning. You are worthy of a love that sees you, honors you, and holds you gently. I pray when it finds you, it arrives soft and certain, kissing every mark of your journey with a reverence so deep it echoes for generations.

Playlist

Spotify

Apple

AWESTRUCK

My Black Vortex. Pulling me, dragging me, forcing me into your mystery.
Not just physically, but you are stealing my very thoughts, all of my creativity.
For there is nothing I can imagine past you
For there IS nothing past you
You are the limit
The measure of whom all beauty must come for approval.
My Black Vortex pulling me into your world unknown.
Is it Heaven?

—Lawrence Baldwin

PROLOGUE

NINE YEARS AGO

Sophomore Year of High School

Aniyah's fingers drummed against the oak desk, each tap sharp enough to echo. Her teacher's voice floated somewhere above her—a monotone buzz blending into the hum of the radiator—the scrape of pencils and the soft snores coming from the back row. Nothing made sense today. Or maybe everything made too much sense, and she was tired of pretending it didn't.

She wasn't confused by the lesson, she could probably teach it. Aniyah was in the top ten percent of her class with a full AP course load, and a GPA that made guidance counselors beam with pride. She was so good that she could almost touch the hem of Yale's skirts, even with only being a sophomore. School was supposed to be her one guaranteed win.

But today?

Yeah, today wasn't her day.

If anyone dared to ask her what was wrong, she'd probably spit out an answer so sharp it would slice the "*sweet, innocent Aniyah*" image people loved to wrap around her like some pretty ribbon. The girl who didn't curse. The girl who didn't talk back. The girl who always did what she was told.

She scoffed under her breath and tugged at the sleeves of her navy sweater, yanking them over her hands like armor. Irritation buzzed beneath her ribs, tight and hot. The clock on the wall mocked her, its minute hand creeping like it had all the time in the damn world. Only an hour had passed. There were still thirty minutes to go.

She wasn't sure she'd make it.

"I hate this place," she whispered, not caring if anyone heard.

High school was a prison, and AP Statistics was solitary confinement. Not because it was difficult, she could recite probability distributions in her sleep, but because it was mind-numbing repetition. Five days a week of the same routine. The same expectations. The same silence from her parents, unless it was to remind her not to mess up.

Rodger Henderson, her father, believed in discipline. "*Do what you have to do, in order to do what you want to do.*" He said it so often she heard it in her dreams. He quoted it like he'd coined the phrase himself. Her mother, Patrice, echoed him like a shadow. And the result?

No social life.

No sleepovers.

No phone past eight.

No boys.

No friends if they weren't on the honor roll.

Nothing "unproductive."

The only person who ever told her differently was Papa Earl.

Her chest loosened at the thought of him. Earl Henderson, was 75 years old but didn't look a day over 60, and he was Aniyah's world. Her safe space. Of course he came with a sharp tongue and a softer heart. He was one of those old men who called everyone "baby" and meant it. He smelled like peppermint and aftershave, wore flannels year-round, and believed that a kid deserved at least *one* thing of their own. He snuck her candy when Rodger wasn't looking. He taught her how to play spades. He praised her for existing, something her parents never learned how to do.

"Don't let them steal your spark, Firecracker," he always says. "Life is bigger than their rules."

She missed him today. She hadn't seen him in two months, not since her dad forbade her saying that Earl was making her "lazy". She needed him today. Because the spark he talked about felt like it had dimmed to a flicker under all the obligations and restrictions her life currently held against her.

Aniyah tugged her hood over her head, letting her long black hair spill forward like a curtain. Maybe if she was lucky she could sleep until the bell rang. But the moment she let her cheek hit the desk, her chest tightened instead of relaxing. Restlessness clawed at her ribs.

She was wound too tight and moving like a restless, trapped animal.

And then came the sound.

Giggling.

It was high-pitched and *very* obnoxious. The kind of sound people made when they were flirting too hard or trying to get attention by laughing extra loud at someone's corny ass jokes. Aniyah lifted her head and looked across the room and her eyes landed on the culprit.

Katelyn Castello, the sophomore class's "Puerto Rican princess"(that was an inside joke that made Aniyah laugh every time she snuck to watch Love and Hip Hop when her parents weren't home). Aniyah was surprised that the girl passed any classes the way she was always sniffing behind someone's son.

And here she was perched on someone's lap like the chair beneath them didn't exist, twirling a curl of glossy brown hair around her finger, her baby tee clinging for dear life and her mini skirt doing nothing to protect her from the February cold settling over Brooklyn.

Katelyn wasn't shivering though. Not when she had Trevor Porter's arms around her.

Aniyah's stomach clenched.

Trevor leaned back in his seat like he owned it. Like he owned the oxygen in the room. His fade was perfect, every line crisp. Smooth almond brown skin. Thick brows. Dark, sharp eyes that always looked amused or lustful or both. His mouth curved with that stupid, dangerous charm that had half the girls in school ready to risk their GPA for him.

Those dimples were weapons, really. He used them like he knew the damage they caused.

And, okay...he was fine. Annoyingly fine. The kind of fine that made other girls lose their minds, which only made him worse. Pretty boys always thought the world spun around them. Trevor Porter was Exhibit A.

He was spoiled, too. The youngest Porter brother. Rumor had it his older brothers, Jackson and Angelou, did everything for him. Protected him. Covered for him. Sacrificed for him. So, naturally the girls lined up for him and the boys envied him. Teachers forgave him for things they'd crucify other students over. Typical.

If anyone hesitated to give him what he wanted, all he had to do was smile and he got his way. He was just that good.

Aniyah rolled her eyes.

Boys like him were her father's worst nightmare and her secret weakness. Not because she wanted a boy like Trevor, but because she wanted the freedom to make her own mistakes, like he could do so easily. She wanted to be able to want what she wanted, even if it wasn't "appropriate" without having to be ridiculed and disrespected for it. She wanted to be a writer. Her father said it was the stupidest thing he'd ever heard. There was no future in it.

When she expressed that she was interested in teaching, her father didn't speak to her for a week because that wasn't the future he planned. She was supposed to be a doctor, like him. Her mother didn't ignore her, but Aniyah wished she had. The way her nose stayed in the air anytime Aniyah was in the room let her know that her mother absolutely felt the same way as her father. She just wanted to be herself even if it didn't make sense. That's what Trevor had and that's what she craved.

She tried to look away, but Trevor's laugh carried across the room. It was loud, confident and easy. Like he didn't have a care in the world. Joy surrounded him everywhere he went. And here he was, flashing those pearly whites pretending to be amused by whatever Katelyn was whispering.

Even though Aniyah knew—everyone knew—he got bored easily. Katelyn was the girlfriend of the month, maybe the week. Trevor treated girls like seasonal trends. He bragged about it. Bragged about his brothers' advice.

She could practically hear it now, that ridiculous line he parroted from his brother Angelou: "*A girl is only as good as how far her legs will spread.*" Disgust curled in her throat at the memory of Trevor stating those words during their first week of freshman year. All his homeboys laughed in response and dapped him up.

Typical mannish behavior.

She was about to drop her head back onto her desk when Trevor's gaze slid over to hers slowly. A deliberate sweep like he'd felt her looking. When their eyes connected, she could feel the jolt of electricity travel down her spine as if she was listening to her favorite ASMR creator. They stared for a beat too long before his plush lips turned into a full-blown smirk.

The hair on Aniyah's arms raised in response, she had always told herself she was immune to Trevor. They had been in the same classes since the 4th grade. But moments like this proved that there was a small, very small, part of her that could feel the charm he should everyone else. The moment would've been sweet, if Aniyah didn't know any better, but she did. And because Trevor was the kind of boy who couldn't resist adding gasoline to a spark, he spoke.

"Take a picture," he drawled, dimples on full display. "It'll last longer."

Mrs. Hillstrom, the middle-aged teacher, halted mid-sentence. Her chalk froze against the board, she turned to see that it was Trevor speaking to Aniyah. She immediately geared up to go in defense mode because Aniyah was too sweet to be bullied in her class. The rest of the class fell into that delicious hush students lived for when they knew something was about to go down. The kind of hush that meant drama was on the rise.

Aniyah sat up straighter, her annoyance spiking into something sharp. How dare he try to play in her face, as if they weren't the reason she was distracted. Normally she would let it go. But after the morning she had battling it out with her parents, getting caught in the rain and having to walk to school because her dad was pissed, and currently dealing with an HS flare the size of a golf ball under her breast while having to act like she wasn't in extreme pain every time she moved—yeah, she was over everything. Today was the wrong day. And she was the wrong girl.

She stared at him coolly. "Maybe you should take tutoring," she said, voice smooth as glass. "It might actually help your dumb ass pass this class."

A collective gasp rippled across the room.

Trevor's mouth parted like he wasn't sure what to feel. He had not expected Aniyah to respond to him. She was always so quiet and mild. The laughs that bellowed throughout the room didn't help his conflicted feelings either. Should he be offended or impressed or...turned on? His eyes narrowed, but there was heat there. A small flicker. Something he wasn't used to feeling from a girl he'd been baiting. He reached to move Katelyn out of his lap. However, before he could respond, the intercom crackled.

BZZZT.

The long-awaited tone buzzed through the speakers.

Class was dismissed.

Aniyah didn't wait. She stuffed her books into her bag, slung it over her shoulder, and walked out like she hadn't just shocked thirty students and a grown adult.

She didn't look back.

But Trevor kept his eyes on her.

"Babe!" Katelyn called out to him, rolling her eyes because he seemed entranced by Aniyah. Her call went ignored.

He watched her until the door swung shut behind her. Watched the sway of her auburn ponytail, the roll of her shoulders, the deliberate way she didn't give him her attention.

And something unfamiliar curled low in his stomach.

Because for the first time in a long time, a girl hadn't melted under his smile. He gave and she returned it as naturally as breathing. She didn't shy away or blush in front of him. She stood her ground and that was appealing. She didn't look at him like he was the sun. No, she'd looked at him like he was a nuisance–an inconvenience.

A boy too beneath her to give the time of day.

Trevor Porter didn't know if he hated it...or if he wanted to chase that feeling all the way down.

ACT 1

The Mountain

CHAPTER ONE

WHAT SILENCE SOUNDS LIKE

PRESENT DAY:

"Love shoulda brought your ass home last night..." - *Angela, Boomerang* (1992)

The alarm buzzed at six a.m., stubborn and shrill, dragging Trevor out of the kind of sleep that never really rested him. He slapped at the nightstand until it went quiet and lay still for a moment, eyes on the ceiling.

Automatically, his hand reached across the bed.

Cold sheets.

Her side of the bed was empty. Again.

Trevor sat up slowly, scrubbing a hand down his face. Katelyn had not come home last night. The silence of their bedroom had become a familiar kind of ache, the kind that dulled over time but never disappeared. He told himself not to look at the clock, not to imagine what she was doing, or who she was doing it with. Those thoughts would unravel him, and he could not afford that. Not today. It was Zara's first day of second grade. Trevor had hoped that Katelyn would have enough sense to come home and see their daughter off. That thought now, in the quiet of their room, seemed stupid. He did not know when they had gotten to this point. Katelyn was the love of his life, but as of late, he was questioning whether it was ever truly love.

That thought made his heart drop. That couldn't be the case. He had been with Katelyn for so long that this recent distance felt like losing a limb. They had been together through all their milestones in life: graduating high school, first baby, first job, graduating college. This newfound distance was tearing him apart. Some days he wanted to just walk away and start over with Zara but most days—every day—he wanted to convince his wife to come home. He wanted to convince her to love him again, to be his again. It couldn't be too late, but as the silence danced around him—he felt like it was.

Trevor's gaze continued to drift around the cold room until they landed on his worn leather binder, a gift from his late mother, sitting open on his desk. Pages of scribbled notes, shot lists, and drafts spilled out of it. Proof of how far he had come in his craft.

At twenty-six, Trevor Porter was no longer just Della's youngest boy, or the cocky kid people thought would coast on his brothers' shine. As the youngest, he always felt a need to prove that he had the same grit and talent as his older brothers, so he worked extremely hard to achieve his goals. Even as a teen parent, he made sure not to slack off when it came to learning cinematography.

Nearly a decade had passed since he first dreamed of telling stories that looked like his own life. Black love in all its complicated, beautiful, tender forms. And he had done it. His debut feature, *A Sunday Kind of Love,* a romance as delicate and raw as anything he had ever felt, had premiered at Sundance a year prior. Then at the Martha's Vineyard African American Film Festival, where he had stood in the back of a packed theater while strangers wiped their eyes and applauded. The critics compared it to the Netflix hit movie *Really Love.* For the first time, Trevor felt seen as an artist, not just the youngest Porter brother.

A *Sunday Kind of Love* opened doors for him. Suddenly execs were interested in what he had to say and what other stories he wanted to create. And thanks to Jackson's persistence and Mackenzie's faith, Netflix came knocking. *Making Love: The Art of Us* was his now. A docuseries that blended art and intimacy, with Jackson and Mackenzie at its heart. He would be showcasing the passion of Black creatives across the world and how their work translates into what love means to them. His name was on contracts that once felt impossible, his seat at the table undeniable. He could not wait to begin. He was building his future at a fast pace.

But as his career soared, Katelyn had slipped further and further away.

It started two and a half years ago when she landed a position as an executive assistant at Whitmore Global Holdings, one of those slick Manhattan private equity firms that thrived on long hours and endless coffee. At first, Trevor had been proud. Katelyn wanted something for herself outside of being a mom and wife, and he supported her. He could tell not having something to call her own was taking a toll on her happiness. He was the one to suggest she go to work and sent her the link to apply to her current job. He remembered her excitement and them making love for hours that day in celebration of her fresh start, of their fresh start. That all seemed like a distant dream. Soon Katelyn was having late nights at work.

Then the late nights turned into missed dinners for client events. The client events turned into skipped school plays. Birthdays, teacher conferences and bedtime stories. Things that once lit her up became obligations she brushed off. The girl who used to sit across from him quizzing flashcards for film school while he rocked Zara to sleep was now coming home at three in the morning, if at all.

At first, she promised it was temporary. *Just until I prove myself*, she had said, pressing a quick kiss to his cheek on her way out the door. Months passed, then a year, and instead of easing up, it got worse. The job gave her an out. A new world. And Trevor was beginning to realize she did not want to come back from it. This couldn't be it because Katelyn was the love of his life, he had to fix it. He had to-

The alarm buzzed again, snapping him from his thoughts and preventing him from spiraling. He sat in the quiet for another long moment, reaching for a woman who no longer came home.

He sent a text to Katelyn with just three question marks. Her response was almost instantaneous:

Long night. Be home soon. Love you.

Trevor wondered when his significance in her life dwindled down to seven word responses. His chest burned at the realization.

A soft knock broke the silence.

"Daddy?"

The door creaked open, and Zara padded in barefoot, bonnet bouncing, her stuffed brown bunny—Lola—dangling from her hand. She climbed onto the bed with all the determination in her little body and landed in his lap.

"Today is the first day of school," she announced, grinning wide, the gap where her baby tooth had been only making her smile brighter.

Trevor wrapped his arms around her and kissed the top of her head. "Yes it is a big day! You're going to Kindergarten, right?"

She pulled back, eyes gleaming. "No, Silly! Second grade."

"That's right! How could Daddy forget," he said. "Are you ready for it?"

"I'm always ready, Daddy." She hesitated, then tilted her head. "Where is Mommy?"

The question cut deeper than any alarm clock ever could. Trevor smoothed a hand over her braids, careful with his words. "Mommy had to work early, baby. She left before we woke up this morning. But I'm here. And I'm walking you in."

Zara studied him for a moment, then nodded like that was enough. "Okay. But she better come next time."

Trevor's throat tightened, but he forced a smile. "Yeah. Next time. Let's get you ready for your big day!"

An hour later, the kitchen smelled like butter and syrup as Trevor flipped pancakes at the stove, his curls pulled up into a high bun. He moved around the kitchen in sweats and a T-shirt, tattoos brushing the edges of his collar, while Zara sat at the counter in her new uniform.

The white polo was tucked neatly into a navy pleated skirt, her sandy brown braids tied back with pink ribbons that matched the shiny new backpack swinging from the back of her stool. Her socks were bunched just above her shoes, and despite Trevor's attempt at neatness, she already had a smear of syrup on her collar, but she did not care. Zara glowed, cheeks full of pancakes, legs swinging to a rhythm only she knew.

Trevor leaned on the counter and watched her. The light sneaked through the blinds and cut soft stripes across the room. In it, the warmth of her skin looked golden. That was the one thing Zara got from him, her complexion. Everything else was all Katelyn down to the slightly crooked big toe they had. Trevor loved that. He glanced over to the floor mirror and took in his reflection. Almond brown skin, burnished at the cheekbones, golden at the temples. His beard was lined neat, his mouth framed by the dimples he had been cursed and blessed with since birth. His neck tattoo showing—Zara, inked along the line of his pulse. It was his eyes that gave him pause, they looked tired. He looked tired. He wished that he could say it was due to his busy schedule, but Trevor wouldn't lie to himself. It was because he needed his wife and she wanted to be everywhere but with him. That's what hurt the most.

Snapping out of his haze, he plated more pancakes and slid the maple syrup toward Zara on the counter. He immediately regretted that decision but was going to stand beside it.

"Alright, baby. Syrup responsibility is on you, take it slowly. No more getting it on your clothes"

Zara nodded at his words but then proceeded to pour the syrup like a contractor laying concrete, heavy-handed. "Oops," she stated when syrup ran on her hand.

"Controlled pour, madam."

She giggled and licked a spot off her knuckle. Then she continued humming, a little off-key rendition of whatever song had crawled into her head from a cartoon or a TikTok dance he did not know. The sound filled the house with something that felt like mercy. Triggering him to remember a time when life was full of light.

There had been a time, back in high school, when he thought life was simple. Katelyn was his everything, big curly brown hair, wide eyes, and that laugh that made him feel invincible. It was no secret that Trevor was sort of a player when he met her, but all of that quickly flew out the window once they got to know each other. Katelyn's home life was rough, to say the least. Her parents were always fighting, often physically. Trevor came in like a knight in shining armor to offer her a place of solace. What started as a casual fling at the beginning of their sophomore year in high school quickly delved into real young love. The two became inseparable, and Trevor knew they would be together for the long haul.

When she told him she was pregnant two months before graduation their senior year, he had not flinched. He had sworn they would figure it out together.

"Katelyn, you're my everything, real talk. Yes, this baby is unexpected, but she is made from love, and I promise I will be here for you every step of the way." He had stated it with a shaky confidence. Even at the young age of eighteen, he knew he would do whatever he had to provide for his new family. Telling his parents was the hardest part. After their shock wore off, they immediately went into action setting up steps to help the young parents. Trevor and Katelyn moved into the basement of his parents' brownstone, their first apartment (even though it was rent-free).

After graduation, Trevor worked during the day with his dad for the city. At night, he was taking film classes. Katelyn helped his mother with her art workshop classes, before their lives changed, before Della knew she was sick. Though life was busy, it worked for them.

Zara was born on a cool September day, screaming to the heavens and the most beautiful little girl Trevor had ever seen. Once they were in their private room, he quietly asked Katelyn to marry him. She looked at him, her hazel eyes full of love, and said yes immediately. After her six weeks in the house–due to Della's insistence–the couple was married at city hall. It felt like forever. It felt like they got it right.

For a while, they did. Late nights with Zara in his arms, Katelyn quizzing him before exams, the three of them piled on a couch too small for their new family.

He thought that was forever.

Now, sitting across from his daughter in her too-big backpack and her gap-toothed grin, Trevor knew he had gotten one part of that promise right. Zara was his forever. She was the only thing in his life that felt unshakably complete.

"Are you nervous?" Zara asked suddenly, mouth sticky with syrup.

"Me? Why would I be nervous? You are the one starting the second grade."

"But you always get nervous when I do new things."

Trevor laughed and handed her a napkin. "Maybe a little. But I know you will be amazing. You are the smartest kid I know."

"Smart like Mommy?"

The words landed heavy, but Trevor pushed the weight down where she could not see it.

He smiled softly. "Yeah. Like Mommy."

"Can I wear the pink jacket Auntie Nina bought me?"

That was also a new addition that Trevor loved about his life. His brothers were settled down with amazing women who immediately took him in as their younger brother, so naturally, Zara was spoiled. Every time he turned around, she was having a "girls' day" or sleepover with her aunties. Trevor knew they were helping fill the hole that Katelyn was beginning to leave with all her work trips and events, and he could not thank them enough. He just wished they never had to do it.

"Of course."

"And the sparkly lip balm that Auntie Mackenzie bought me?"

"That is a house-only lip balm. You can wear it to the car, then it goes in your backpack."

She groaned. "School is so unfair."

"Wait until you see taxes."

"I heard Papa talk about them before. He said they made him bald. I do not want to be bald. I do not want to see taxes."

"Me either," he said, and they both laughed.

When it was time to hit the road, Trevor had traded sweats for jeans and a crisp button-down. In the backseat, Zara hummed happily, feet kicking against her booster seat with her new backpack propped beside her like a badge of honor.

The drive from their quiet Long Island block stretched out before them, tree-lined streets giving way to the morning rush. Trevor had chosen to settle here on purpose. Close enough to the city for work, but far enough for peace. He wanted Zara to have space to ride her bike, neighbors who knew her name, air that felt like a break from the grind of Manhattan. Softer than the Bronx apartment he and Katelyn once crammed themselves into when Zara was ten months old.

The phone buzzed on the console. It was a Group FaceTime call. Trevor tapped it, and suddenly the car was filled with the Porter chorus.

"Yooo, you ready for the second grade?" Jackson grinned into the camera, Mackenzie perched beside him, Matthew in her lap repeatedly saying, "mama eat-eat!" Behind them, canvases leaned against the wall of their brownstone, strokes of color waiting to be loud.

"Zara." Nina's voice carried through next, Kennedy tugging at her earring while Angelou wrangled Imani in the background. The twins were chaos personified. The project triplets were two years old and already determined to keep their parents on their toes.

Zara squealed and waved. "Hi, everybody."

Trevor laughed and angled the phone so they could see her. His chest tugged at the sight—his brothers with their wives, their kids, their lives loud and messy and whole. How his family used to be.

"Do not cry at drop off, little bro," Angelou teased, smirking while Nina tried to free Kennedy's hand away from her curls. "Zara has this."

"I'm not going to cry," Trevor said, even as Mackenzie and Nina burst into laughter.

"Yes, he will," Zara chimed in, eyes rolling. She had so much fire for a seven year old.

The car erupted with laughter, the kind that filled in the cracks of a quiet morning. For a moment, Trevor let himself laugh too.

Then Angelou's voice cut through, quieter and sharper. "Yo, Trev. Where is Katelyn? She not coming with you?"

The question lingered, heavy in the air, even as Zara kept waving at her cousins. Trevor's jaw tightened, eyes flicking back to the road.

"She had to work early and left before we got up," he said finally, steady like rehearsed.

Jackson's smile faltered. Nina and Mackenzie exchanged a glance. No one pushed, but the silence told Trevor what he already knew. His family saw the cracks too.

So, he forced another laugh, loud enough to smooth the edges. "Anyway, let me get my Superstar to school before she is late."

"Go kill it, Z," Mackenzie and Nina cheered in unison.

Trevor ended the call. The car quieted. Zara went back to

humming, her little feet swinging like nothing in her world had shifted.

Trevor wished he could say the same.

He reached for the radio and let the oldies station find them. Al Green sang about love and happiness, words wrapping around the car like a promise someone else made. Zara tried to sing along and missed half the words. He sang the other half and missed on purpose. They pulled into the school lot on the last note.

The parking lot was buzzing, parents juggling cameras and coffee cups, kids clutching backpacks and balloons. The air carried the first bite of September, cool enough to hint at fall but still soft with late summer warmth. Maple trees that lined the lot had begun to shed their leaves, a few golden and russet ones skittering across the asphalt as the morning breeze picked up.

Trevor parked and took in the scene. P.S. Johnson stood tall in front of them, a sturdy red-brick building trimmed in white stone. Blue and gold banners with the school mascot fluttered from lampposts, and a balloon arch framed the front doors, where staff waved and cheered every new arrival. It was the kind of school he wanted for Zara. Vibrant. Safe. A place that felt like learning was endless.

He unbuckled her seatbelt and Zara all but leapt from the car, her braids swinging down her back, backpack bouncing against her shoulders. She clutched his hand tightly, eyes wide as she drank it all in.

"Ready, Superstar?" he asked.

"Ready," she whispered, her grin bright.

They climbed the steps and stepped inside, and the energy

doubled. The hallways pulsed with life, walls plastered with bright student art, welcome banners in every color, the faint smell of fresh paint mixing with crayons and new books. Teachers knelt to greet students at eye level. Parents leaned in for last hugs. The hum of chatter made the building feel alive.

Trevor squeezed Zara's hand tighter, pride and nerves tangling in his chest as they followed the signs to the first-grade wing. His camera brain kicked in without permission. The light in the hallway was soft and even. The yellow in the bulletin boards warmed the area around them. The hum in the air felt like a movie score.

Room 107 was a cheerful space. Walls painted a sunshine yellow. Cubbies lining one side already labeled with names in neat handwriting. Sun catchers in the windows tossed little squares of color on the floor. A reading nook in the corner with a tiny navy rug and pillows that looked like clouds. Kids chattered at their desks while parents hovered near the doorway. The first day buzz vibrated in the air.

Then a voice cut through the noise.

"Zara Porter?"

Trevor turned at the same moment Zara lit up.

A woman approached, crouching a little to meet Zara's eyes. Her skin glowed, rich umber, the kind of brown that had its own light. Long auburn hair fell in waves that caught the sun and shifted between cinnamon and wine. Winged liner framed wide, intelligent honey-brown eyes. Her lips were full and glossed, and when she smiled, it hit tender and commanding at the same time. Pearl studs glinted at her ears. A soft white blouse tucked neatly into tailored slate slacks set the tone. She was petite, but her body still held soft curves. There was no question who ran this room.

Aniyah Henderson.

It hit Trevor like a punch of memory. The girl who once sat two rows over in Statistics sophomore year. The girl who told him off in front of the whole class and did not blink. The girl he had not thought about in years. Only now, she was not a girl. She was a woman who owned every inch of herself.

"Good morning," she said gently, extending her hand to Zara. "I'm Ms. Henderson, your new teacher."

Zara beamed, slipping her tiny hand into hers. "Hi."

"Hi," Aniyah said, her smile deepening. "I am so happy you are in my class. I saw on your sheet that you like science experiments and graphic novels. That makes two of us."

Zara's shoulders shot up to her ears. "Do we get to do the volcano with the bubbles?"

"Maybe not today," Aniyah said, "but we will make a mess very soon."

Trevor was still staring. His chest tightened, not just with surprise but with something else he was not ready to name. The auburn waves, the eyes, the way her mouth curved. She looked like a memory that had embedded itself in his skin. He took in her hands too. Neat, almond-shaped nails in a nude that made her skin look even richer. A small gold band on her middle finger. No other rings. He did not realize he was cataloging details until she looked up at him. He quickly blamed it on his cinematographer's eye.

Her gaze flicked to his face, then to the tattoo peeking from his collar. The cursive Zara along his neck. Recognition swept across her features. A beat. Then another.

"Trevor Porter," she said slowly, tone edged with disbelief and a hint of amusement. "Well, isn't this something?"

Trevor managed a smile, dimples cutting deep, though his mind scrambled. He felt suddenly aware of everything about himself. The length of his curls. The clean line of his beard. The way the light caught the tendons in his forearms where his shirt stretched. The way his heart had picked up.

"Yeah," he said. "Guess it is."

She took him in making an assessment of his appearance. After almost a decade, one thing was obvious: the man was still fine as hell.

"Can I show you your cubby, Zara? We are color coded. You are blue this week."

Zara nodded excitedly and slipped her hand into Aniyah's. Trevor watched them cross the room. He noticed the small things he always noticed. The quick glance Aniyah gave the timid boy at table three. The way she used touch sparingly and with intent. A hand to a shoulder to ground, not to move. A quiet word that made the anxious girl at the window relax her jaw.

Trevor hung back near the door and tried to get out of the way of other parents. His phone buzzed. He checked it out of habit. More production emails. Nothing from Katelyn.

No new messages.

He tucked the phone away and let his eyes roam the classroom again. A laminated sign near the library corner read *You belong here*. Another above the whiteboard said *Mistakes mean we are learning*. A basket of red apples sat on the back counter next to a stack of name tags. He could see Aniyah in a different room in his head. Off duty, hair down around her shoulders and a mischievous smile, holding an apple at the curve of her palm, teasing someone out of their cool. The image startled him with how fast it came.

He shook it away and looked for his daughter.

Zara had found her desk and was neatly aligning her pencils in a row, tongue poking from the corner of her mouth in concentration. She looked up and flashed him a thumbs up and a bright smile that nearly split his chest.

"You can head out if you want, Mr. Porter." Aniyah had returned to his side without him noticing. Her voice was warm but professional. "We like to give them space to make their own goodbyes. I will send a class newsletter later this afternoon with our schedule."

"Trevor is fine," he said. "And thank you. She is excited. You have already made her feel safe."

"That is the job," Aniyah said. "Safety first, then everything else."

He nodded and started to step back. Then stopped. "It is good to see you."

"It is good to see you too." Her eyes flicked briefly to his left hand. "Congratulations."

He let out a breath he had not meant to. "Thank you."

Her mouth softened at the edges, like she had heard all the things he did not say. "Have a good day, Trevor."

"You too, Ms. Henderson."

He walked back to Zara and crouched beside her desk. "You good, Superstar?"

"I'm good, Daddy." She leaned in for a quick hug and whispered, "Do not cry."

He choked on a laugh. "No promises."

He kissed her forehead and stood. At the door, he looked back. Aniyah had already moved to the front, hands clasped, eyes bright. The room settled like water in a glass. He pushed into the hallway with the other parents and let the river of them carry him outside.

The morning sun had climbed higher. He stood on the steps for a second and tried to regulate his breathing. He told himself the feeling burrowed in his chest was just nostalgia. That it was just the surprise of seeing her again. That she was just an old name in a new room.

But the feeling did not let go right away.

Trevor didn't go straight to the parking lot. He stood under a maple tree just to the left of the front steps and tried to give himself a minute to calm his emotions from dropping Zara off, not hearing from Katelyn and seeing Aniyah again. Kids streamed past with laces untied and shirts half tucked. A father nearby wiped his eyes and laughed at himself for crying at his kid's drop off. A mother set down her coffee and adjusted a collar for the tenth time with a nervousness it seemed she was afraid to let go of. A teacher with a lanyard full of enamel pins shouted, "Welcome to second grade", and the entire sidewalk clapped like the first day of school could save the world.

His phone buzzed. An alert from his calendar about a scout call for secondary locations later in the week. Another buzz. A text from Jackson that was just an eye emoji and a red heart. The message was in response to confirming that Trevor would be on time for their meeting later that day. He sent a thumbs up back.

Trevor opened the messages thread with Katelyn and stared at the last three texts. All the messages in their thread were from him: photos of Zara holding her backpack and the pancake he had cut into a wonky heart. He began to type a message but erased and typed again, then closed the thread without sending anything. He pocketed the phone and went to the car.

On the drive back, silence rode in the passenger seat. He needed the quiet to help ease the ache in his chest.

At the first red light, he caught his reflection in the rearview mirror. He thought about the way Aniyah had looked at Zara first, not at him. He thought about the apple on the back counter and the way imagination messed with a man who lived inside film.

Because here he was with his heart at war, but thoughts of Aniyah lingered.

He put the car in gear and told himself to get a grip.

He had a meeting this afternoon.

He had a story to build.

He had a daughter to pick up at three.

And he had a marriage to figure out, even if the figuring looked more like goodbye.

CHAPTER TWO

THE THINGS WE DON'T SAY

"At some point you have to let this love shit go, and you have to think about respect." — *Shadow Henderson, - Mo' Better Blues (1990)*

When Trevor pulled into the driveway of their Georgian-style home, the determination he had clung to all morning had started to unravel.

He had bought the house three years ago, his first big purchase after his mother's estate was settled. The kind of home that made him feel grown and financially stable.

Columns framed the porch, ivy creeping up the side. Katelyn had fallen in love with it instantly. "It feels like a movie," she had said, spinning barefoot in the foyer when they moved in.

Now, it just felt empty.

The remodel they had planned together stalled after the first coat of paint. Her Pinterest boards went untouched. The bedroom walls echoed. Every inch of the house looked beautiful, staged even, but it did not feel lived in. It did not feel like love.

Katelyn's car sat in the driveway, parked without a care in the world.

Trevor brushed his hand over the hood. It was still warm. She had just gotten home. At nine in the morning.

What. The. Fuck.

He unlocked the door, the smell of lavender candles and expensive perfume hitting him instantly. The house was too clean, too still.

Their home was all sharp edges and gloss, white oak floors, a marble island, gray walls lined with framed photos from a life that felt far away. Pictures of birthdays and beach trips, all smiles and sunlight. Lies preserved under glass.

Trevor followed the faint sound of running water. The bathroom door was cracked, steam curling out into the hallway.

He pushed it open.

Katelyn stood beneath the showerhead, eyes closed, water gliding down her skin. She looked extremely relaxed. As if she had not been gone for nearly twenty-four hours.

"Good morning, sunshine."

Katelyn jumped, a small gasp escaping her lips. She had not heard him come in. Her face flushed as she reached for the soap, trying to mask the panic flickering behind her eyes.

"Morning, baby," her voice was syrupy and sweet, the same tone that used to undo him. Now it scraped against his nerves.

Trevor folded his arms, leaning against the doorframe. His jaw was tight, his stare unmoving, "Where the hell have you been, Katelyn? You missed Zara's first day of school. But I guess you don't care, right?"

Katelyn turned off the water and wrung out her hair, avoiding his eyes, "Do not start, Trev. I told you I had to stay late. The Whitmore event ran over."

"An event that ends at nine a.m.?" His tone was sharp, his restraint slipping. "You did not text me. You did not call. Zara kept asking where you were. Do you know how that felt?"

"No actually, we had rooms at the hotel where the event was hosted. It wasn't over until almost one in the morning. I stayed in the room and came home as soon as I woke up. I know I should have called, and I'm sorry for that baby. I was just working so much that it slipped my mind to check in. It won't happen again." Her hazel eyes pleaded with Trevor. He felt the first of his defenses start to crumble. Katelyn was his person and at least she was trying. His heart was at a tug-of-war.

The pair stared at each other until her hand grabbed his arm, causing the towel she was holding to drop. Trevor couldn't even remember the last time they had made love. The sight of his wife's naked body immediately sent a spark traveling down his body.

Katelyn continued to move closer until she was flush against him. Eyes filled with lust. Her plump pink lips ajar slightly showing her desire.

"I've missed you baby. I've been so busy. Let me make it up to you..." she drawled before dropping to her knees and pulling the button of Trevor's pants open. He should say something. Stop her. Anything. But this was the closest he's felt to Katelyn in a long time, and he didn't want to mess it up. Was he a fool? Probably, but he wasn't going to stop. Her lips lightly kissed the mushroomed head of his dick, causing Trevor to groan and his eyes to roll back.

"I missed you Lyn," he moaned out as she took his length into her mouth. Katelyn moaned in response causing him to shiver from the vibration. She released him with a resounding "pop".

"I missed you too, Trev. Let me show you how much." As she

licked the length of him before swallowing him whole. Trevor saw stars. *This* is how he was supposed to start his mornings. Not alone in a cold bed and empty room. His eyes looked down at Katelyn as she kept working him over. He loved that she had no gag reflex. She could easily deep throat him, even with his size. She was making it count right now, but Trevor wanted to be inside his wife. It had been too long. He gently pulled her hair back signaling her to stop.

"Come here baby, I need you," Trevor's roughened voice spoke. He picked her up like she weighed nothing and walked them to the bedroom. Kissing Katelyn deeply as he positioned himself between her legs.

"You love me?" He asked as he entered her.

"Yes, I love you." Katelyn moaned in response.

"Good because I have some frustrations I need to let out, and I just wanted to make sure." Trevor pulled Katelyn to the edge of the bed, they purposely got it high for this reason. One hand gripped her hip bruisingly the other hand wrapped around her neck. Katelyn's eyes rolled in response. She loved when Trevor got like this. His stroke changed from slow and shallow to deep and hard.

"We haven't fucked in almost three months, Lyn. You think that's a good thing?" He spoke as he continued with the punishing strokes.

"Fuck baby, please don't stop," Katelyn whined.

"That's not what the fuck I asked you. Answer me."

"No, no, no, no. I don't think it's a good thing. I promise-"

"Nah, don't make promises you won't keep. Just take this dick and cum for me." He demanded. He was so mad but turned on at the same time, he couldn't control what was coming out of his mouth. He felt Katelyn's grip around him tighten around him. Soon she was calling out his name while orgasming. He looked down at her and that's when he saw *it.*

A small purple mark right below her ear. One that he did not put there.

He immediately went flaccid inside of her and pulled out.

"What is that mark on your neck?" Katelyn, still hazy from her recent orgasm, looked at Trevor shocked.

"Trev, you were just squeezing the hell out my neck. You know I bruise."

"So now you're trying my intelligence. Katelyn, what the fuck is that mark behind your ear? Who put it there." Katelyn walked, on wobbly legs, to their floor length mirror and turned her head to see the mark Trevor was referencing. She let out a nervous chuckle.

"Boy you're tripping, that is a burn mark. I curled my hair for the fundraiser yesterday and got myself because I was listening to Taylor Swift and dancing. You know I love her." Trevor stared at his wife for a long moment trying to look for signs of deceit. He knew she was bullshitting but his mind did not want to comprehend what the mark meant. What that mark symbolized for his marriage. For his love.

So, he simply nodded his head and walked off to the bathroom to take a shower, he would need to be heading in the city soon. Katelyn being home threw him off his schedule. Somehow, he didn't feel better now than he did when he got home. The thought of his wife laying up with another man brought this burning sensation to his chest. One he would have to ignore for the time being.

He quickly showered and got out. When he walked back into the room, Katelyn had on her pants and bra. He saw her phone light up on the nightstand. She quickly looked at it reading who the contact was and snatched it up. After reading the contents of the text, she suddenly began to move at hyper speed. Trevor just observed with the towel wrapped around his hips. When he opened his closet door it was as if Katelyn just remembered he was in the room.

"I have to go," she said, eyes still on the message only she could see. "I won't be home until late."

"You won't be here to get Zara from school? Is this job worth missing your daughter's milestones?"

"I'm doing this for us," she snapped, finally meeting his gaze. "For our future. You think everything is about you and your perfect little film projects. Some of us have real jobs."

Trevor's laugh came out humorless. "Do not do that. Do not twist this like you are a martyr and I'm the one playing pretend. You are gone every night. You don't come home until the sun is up. When you do, you act like being here is the chore."

She pulled on her shirt quickly, defensive movements. "You have no idea the pressure I'm under. The things I have to do to keep my position."

"What, sleeping your way to the top?"

The words were out before he could stop them. The air snapped between them, charged and ugly.

Katelyn froze, shirt clutched tight, her expression hardening into something unreadable, "Wow. So that's what you think of me now?"

Trevor raked a hand down his face, voice low and weary. "I think you do not look me in the eye anymore. I think our daughter is starting to notice you're never around. And I think," he stopped, breath catching. "I think I don't know who you are anymore."

For a moment, neither of them spoke. The only sound was the steady tick of the clock down the hall.

Finally, Katelyn turned away, "This conversation isn't going anywhere and I'm late for work."

She brushed past him, leaving a trail of perfume and resentment in her wake.

Trevor stood in the doorway long after the front door shut, water still running down the tile, wondering when love had started feeling like loss. He didn't want to lose the life he worked so hard for, but every day it felt like Katelyn was drifting past the point of no return. She said that bruise was a burn mark, but he knew what a fuckin' hickey looked liked. It took an additional twenty minutes for Trevor to get out of his head and continue to get dressed for his meeting.

Later that afternoon, Trevor was parked in front of a sleek glass building in downtown Manhattan, a world away from the silence he had left behind. The mirrored doors of Studio 64 swung open, and a different kind of noise rushed him, this was where he was meant to be.

The conference room had floor-to-ceiling windows and a view of the river that made the city look like a backdrop. A row of framed festival posters lined one wall. Someone had scattered multicolored sticky notes down the table like confetti. A PA wheeled in a cart of drinks and a bowl of clementines. Trevor set his camera bag on a chair and breathed.

Jackson already stood near the head of the table with Mackenzie by his side. He wore paint on his hands like jewelry. Mackenzie's curls were even bigger now, coming to her waist; she was constantly checking a live view to see what Matthew and his nanny were up to. They both looked like the version of happy that got earned.

"Bout time, lil bro," Jackson said with a grin. "You look like hell."

Trevor smirked and tugged his chair back, "Appreciate the warm welcome."

Jackson's smile softened, eyes narrowing a little, "You good?"

Trevor nodded. "Yeah. Just a long morning."

Jackson did not push. He only gave him a small nod that said everything without a word.

After a few moments the producers began to filter in. Alicia, who handled budgets like a magician and never raised her voice. Reed, the supervising producer with a documentary pedigree and a faded tattoo of a camera on his wrist. Laila from music supervision,. gold hoops and a playlist for every mood. Callie from locations, who smelled faintly of sunscreen all year and kept a binder of permits thicker than a dictionary.

Once everyone settled, Trevor stood and flipped open his notebook. His energy shifted instantly. The weight he carried at home fell away the second he started talking about the work.

"*Making Love: The Art of Us*," he began. "This is not just a docuseries about art. It is about intimacy. How Black artists capture love in all its forms; romantic, familial, spiritual and communal."

He paced slowly, his hands were loose and his eyes bright. "I want the camera to feel like an extension of the artist. We open on a craft sequence before we hear their voice. I want to be able to hear the sound of brushstrokes, shutter clicks and charcoal dragging across toothy paper. I also want details such as fingertips pressing clay until it takes a breath. The audience should feel their passion before they understand it."

Heads around the table began to lift. Someone set their pen down. The room grew quiet.

"Conversations happen in motion," Trevor continued. "We do not sit the artist in a sterile chair to interview them. We walk and talk in their studios. We will ride in the car to pick up supplies. We will cook dinner while we talk about the first time they fell in love. I want to capture the small things. The way an artist hums to themselves. The pause in thought before they take a risk. How silence can say more than words."

He turned toward Jackson and Mackenzie, his expression softening. "For you two, I want to show what collaboration looks like when love and art are the same language. Not a highlight reel. The raw stuff. I want to display the disagreements, the laughter and the parts where you cannot find the shape and then you do."

He flipped a page, "Visual language. Warm light. Close-ups that humanize the person behind the art. We lean on natural sound and let music rise from the world. The city has music from so many unexpected sources. A saxophone through a window. The radiator ticking in a studio. The whisper of canvas when a hand drags across it.."

He paused and drew an arc in the air, "We need to have structure. Each episode anchors in one artist and the following question: What does devotion look like in your practice? Where do you put grief? How does the body know when a piece is finished? We intercut their answer with a thread from the work of another artist to keep the world connected. This series is a chorus, not a solo. I want to center all Black creatives. Painters, photographers, sculptors, filmmakers, singers, rappers, and poets. There is so much flow in Black love, and I want to show it in all facets and fonts."

He stopped. He had not noticed how still the room had become. Every producer, every assistant, even Mackenzie sat with eyes fixed on him.

When he finally looked up, the silence caught him off guard.

Jackson broke it first, a slow smile tugging at his mouth. "Damn, Trev. You just sold me on our own story."

Laughter rippled around the table, breaking the spell, but the energy lingered. Reed leaned forward with his elbows on the table. "We can schedule studio days around natural light to keep that warmth. I can get you a second camera for the walk and talks."

Alicia nodded. "If we keep our company moves tight, we can afford the extra day with the sculptor and still get the rooftop sequence you spoke on."

Laila tapped her notebook. "I already have a list of ambient tracks and a newbie drummer who builds soundscapes from breath."

Callie slid a folder toward him. "Rooftops, loft spaces, a ceramics studio in Bed Stuy, and a Harlem brownstone that still has the original molding. Permits are not a problem if we lock by Friday."

Trevor took a breath, his shoulders lowering slightly as he realized they had all been hanging on his every word. For the first time that day, the ache in his chest eased.

This was where he belonged. In creation. In vision. In purpose. Here, he could still believe in love.

They moved into logistics. Budget lines, hold dates, insurance. Trevor stayed precise and steady, but a lighter current ran under his voice. He could feel Jackson watching him in the in-betweens, not with worry now, but with pride.

When the meeting wrapped, chairs scraped back and the room dissolved into small knots of conversation. Mackenzie squeezed his arm on her way out. "Thank you for how you see us," she said quietly.

He smiled. "You make it easy."

Jackson lingered. "You want to walk out with me?"

They stepped into the hallway. Studio posters glowed in glass frames. A PA hustled past with a coil of cable around his neck. The elevator pinged and opened. Inside, it was just the two of them.

"You do not have to tell me anything," Jackson said, voice filled with only the intuition an older brother would have. "I just want you to know I'm here."

Trevor stared at the brushed metal doors and let the words sit. "She came home at nine this morning," he said finally. "Completely missed Zara's first day. She apologized saying that the event wrapped so late she ended up staying in one of the company-sponsored hotel rooms. At first, I accepted that explanation. Then...then while we were having sex, I saw a hickey on her neck. She said it was a small burn from curling her hair. Come on J, I'm not an idiot. Fine, I let that go, then she gets a text and starts moving like the house is on fire which pissed me off. Who the fuck has her moving like this? I said something I should not have. I don't know if I meant it or if I'm just tired of pretending. I just want my wife back, man. It feels like I'm in a losing game."

Jackson nodded. "Being fed up will make you say the truth in a way that sounds like a weapon. But it is the truth, nonetheless. I don't like this Trev. I'm gonna be honest, this past year, it's like you've been a shell of yourself when it comes to anything outside of dealing with Zara. You don't deserve that. You're a good man who should have a good woman by his side. I don't want you getting lost in Katelyn, if it's the end, it's the end."

Trevor huffed feeling his eyes pool with tears, an emotion that he didn't want to show. "That's the thing, J. I don't want it to be the end. I want my little girl to have the mother back that looked at her like she was the moon. I want the woman back that promised to love me forever. There is this ache in my chest that won't go away. I thought today was going to be a step in the right direction, but then...I saw that mark...I–I don't know what to do."

Jackson let out a deep sigh in response. It pained him to see his little brother hurting this way. Trevor had always had a special place in his heart, being the baby of the family. The man standing in front of him was broken, and that made him want to go to war. Unfortunately, this was not à battle he could shield his little brother from, and that shit? Hurt as much as a dagger to the heart.

"You take this one day at a time. You're not going to have all the answers, Trev. But I want you to remember that you are a Porter man and that you can and *will* overcome this. If Katelyn gets left behind it's because she doesn't deserve you. And if she doesn't get better with Zara, you make sure to make that decision as her father, that she never goes without, okay? If you need to cry, you know I'm here, Angelou and Dad are too. You are not alone."

The elevator opened. The street noise met them like a wave. Trevor's phone buzzed in his pocket. He glanced down.

> Katelyn: Tried to get out of here early.
> Couldn't. Staying late. Do not wait up

No apologies about not coming home, once again. Like she didn't care about the fight they had early. What was the point?

He slid the phone away. "Man, fuck this! Katelyn just let me know that she would be late again." Trevor saw a mask of anger come over Jackson's face. His brothers have always been protective of him. Something that was a blessing and a curse growing up. He couldn't breathe without one of them commenting on it as a teenager. But here, now? He was so thankful. Something told him that he would need Jackson's quiet strength to get through whatever storm was coming.

"Don't go anywhere, I need to make a quick call." Trevor watched his brother put his phone on speaker. Soon the voice on the other end caused Trevor to laugh.

"Jack, why is your father at my office for the third time this week to take me to lunch? Ain't that many gyros in Manhattan for him to be here this much." Angelou's voice boomed on the other end. Jackson and Trevor both laughed in response despite the tension in the air.

His brothers may not pick up on it, but Trevor saw how soft his dad spoke with Lou's assistant, Ms. Teri. She was a widow and a sweet lady, and definitely the motivation behind all the lunches.

“I have no clue what dad is doing, but just go with it.” Jackson responded. “I was calling for something important. You still have that P.I. on the payroll?” Trevor‘s head snapped in Jackson’s direction.

“Why does Angelou have a private investigator on payroll? The fuck he got going on? Architectural Design is not dangerous.” Trevor added.

“Mind your business, T-Money. And yes, I do, why?” Angelou asked.

“Trevor needs him to follow Katelyn for a while, see what she‘s been up to.”

“I do?” Trevor asked.

“You do,” both brothers responded simultaneously.

“I’ll reach out to him now. He’ll have something by the end of the month. This guy is good.”

“Okay, yeah then...get him. I have to go get Z.” Jackson could see Trevor’s anguish that he tried to hide.

“Bring her by the house if you want,” Jackson said. “Matthew needs someone to show him how to share.”

Trevor put on a small smile that didn’t reach his eyes. “Text me. I might take you up on that.”

P.S. Johnson at dismissal was a happy kind of chaos. Kids spilled into the sunshine in lines that fell apart instantly. Backpacks bounced. Teachers stood with clipboards and called names over the sound of after-school plans.

Trevor found a spot near the gate and scanned the crowd.

There. Zara, marching out with her class, arm in arm with a little girl who wore two different socks like it was on purpose.

When she saw him, she forgot all about lines. She barreled over and wrapped herself around his waist.

"How was your first day?" he asked, hugging her back.

"It was the best! We did stations. I'm in the blue group. We read a book about a bear who does not hibernate because he wants to be a chef. We get to bring a book from home on Friday. Ms. Henderson said my printing is neat," Zara responded, speaking a mile a minute.

"Of course she did. Did you make any friends?"

"Jada. She likes mangoes. Ms. Henderson showed us the class plant. She said if we take care of it, it will grow. Can we get a plant at home?"

"We can get two plants at home."

Zara beamed, "She also gave everyone an apple because it is the first day. But we have to wait to eat it until we get home because it needs to be cut up."

Trevor laughed happy about how excited his daughter was about school, "That sounds exactly right."

He glanced up and there she was. Aniyah stood beside the door with her clipboard. The sleeves of her blouse were rolled to the elbow now, and there was a soft glow on her skin from the afternoon heat. She held a red apple at the curve of her palm while she spoke to a parent, nodding and smiling. The image pricked him with a strange sense of déjà vu, like he had seen it framed somewhere—the color graded to gold, the apple bright as a stoplight.

She looked over and found him. For a second, the crowd thinned in his mind. She lifted the apple a little, a half wave, a simple hello.

He lifted his hand in return.

Zara tugged his sleeve, "Can we get ice cream?"

"We can get ice cream."

"Ms. Henderson says you have to ask me about my three highlights."

"Three?"

"She says three makes your brain think harder."

"Then I definitely want three."

Aniyah reached them as a last student was claimed by their parents, "Zara was a dream," she said, voice filled with warmth and calm. "She helped a classmate zip their backpack and remembered every routine."

Trevor felt the words land somewhere deep. "Thank you. For taking care of them. For taking care of her."

Aniyah's smile softened. "That is the job." She handed Zara a small half sheet of paper. "This is our class newsletter. It has the weekly schedule, what to bring for show and tell, and my contact if you need anything. We do a family photo wall. If you email a picture, I will print it."

Zara bounced. "Can we send the one of Papa and me in the park with the bubbles."

"We can," Trevor said.

Aniyah nodded. "Perfect."

For a heartbeat, it was just the three of them. Then another parent approached with a question about dismissal, and the moment dissolved.

"Have a good evening," Aniyah said as she turned, an apple tucked against her clipboard.

"You too," Trevor said.

He held Zara's hand through the crosswalk and felt steadier than he had that morning.

They stopped at Mr. B's Ice Cream Shop with the chalkboard menu that he changed daily and the bell on the door. Zara got strawberry flavored ice cream with rainbow sprinkles. Trevor got coffee and pretended it was not because he needed something that would keep him present in the moment. Coffee had a way of doing that for him.

On the drive home, Zara listed her three highlights.

One. Blue group.

Two. Jada.

Three. Ms. Henderson says mistakes mean we are learning.

"Good list," he said.

"What are your three?"

He thought of the meeting. He thought of the way a room can lean in all at once when they are hanging onto your words. Of Jackson's quiet in an elevator being his pillar of strength in a moment drowned in melancholy. Then his mind flashed to an apple in a teacher's hand.

"One. My meeting went well," he said. "Two. Your hug at dismissal. Three. I remembered why I love what I do and again my meeting went really well."

"That is four," Zara said, thrilled to catch him.

"Keep my secret."

She zipped her lips and tossed the imaginary key out the window. He caught it and put it in his pocket. They both grinned like they had invented joy.

Evening fell slow. Trevor made pasta while Zara did her reading log at the counter, legs swinging. He checked his phone twice. No message from Katelyn. He typed again and erased it again. He hated the version of himself that begged for the bare minimum. But he was stuck, for all intents and purposes, Katelyn was his person. She was his heart. He couldn't understand why she wanted to continuously hurt him like this. Hurt Zara like this.

After dinner, they watched a nature show about coral reefs. He tucked Zara into bed and sat on the floor beside her while she fell asleep. Before she could close her eyes, a question fell from her lips.

"Daddy?" Her sleepy voice questioned.

"Yes, Superstar?"

"Does Mommy still love me?" Trevor felt his stomach drop to his ass and his heart began to pound.

"Why do you ask that, baby?" He was impressed that his voice did not come out as shaky as it felt.

"She never likes to do things with me anymore. She doesn't tuck me in anymore. When I asked if she wanted to watch Princess and the Frog with me, she said she didn't have time and walked away." Trevor watched Zara intently as she took a moment to get her thoughts together, then he saw the tears begin to fall. He quickly sat on the side of her bed and pulled her into his lap holding her tight.

"Hey, hey, hey Superstar. Of course, Mommy still loves you. She has been busy, but it isn't right that she hasn't made time for you and hurt your feelings." He rocked his baby—his life—his world as she continued to cry.

"I'm sorry! If I did something wrong, I promise I won't do it again, Daddy!" Those words set his world on fire. The heart that ached for his wife back hardened at the evidence of her neglect on their daughter.

"Listen to me, Zara," he began, pulling her back from his chest so she could look at his face.

"You have done absolutely nothing wrong. Do you hear me? You are the greatest gift Mommy and Daddy could ask for. We love you so much. I will make sure to talk to Mommy okay?" He brought her back to his chest and felt her head nod in response. Soon her whimpers turned to soft hiccups. He listened to her breath even out. It steadied him knowing that she had found peace amongst her pain.

His phone lit on the nightstand.

> Katelyn: Event preparation taking longer than expected. I'm going to crash at the host hotel. See you in the morning. Sorry.

He stared at the single word at the end. Sorry. It felt like a sticker slapped on a cracked window.

He typed.

> We need to talk tomorrow. I'm not doing this absent shit anymore.

He hit send before he could soften it.

In the quiet after, he walked down the hall and stood in the doorway of their bedroom. The bed looked too big. The house hummed with the small sounds old houses make. He picked up a blanket from the armchair and went to the couch in the living room instead.

He lay down and stared at the ceiling. The shadows on the plaster looked like maps. He traced a route that led somewhere new.

He did not know yet if the map would take him out of a marriage, or through it, or back to himself. He only knew something had to change.

When sleep finally came, it found him on the couch with one arm over his eyes and the word tomorrow beating in his chest like a drum.

CHAPTER THREE

THE LIFE I BUILT

"My mother wasn't very good at love. What if I'm just like her?" - *Sara, The Photograph (2020)*

Aniyah took attendance while the kids colored their name plates. She kept her tone light and warm, and her focus tight on the moment. That was how she did everything here. It was why the room always felt like a place kids wanted to return to.

Still, her mind drew a quiet circle around Trevor Porter.

"Lord," she thought, *"if life did not have a sense of humor."*

She remembered him in flashes more than scenes. The sound of a laugh that came from the chest. The way light liked his butterscotch skin. The dimples girls wrote about in group chats. That ridiculous swagger he wore like it was sewn into his jeans. She had rolled her eyes and taken notes. She had told herself he was not her business. Then senior year came and went. Years had folded over the memory like sheets.

She glanced toward the door and saw the empty space he had left behind. She exhaled and pressed her palm against the desk. Focus.

"Alright, scientists and authors," she said, clapping once. "Let us talk about what we need to feel safe and brave in this room. Who has an idea?" Hands flew up. The day had officially begun.

The classroom emptied in waves after dismissal, the last echo of tiny sneakers fading down the hallway. Aniyah erased the day's objectives from the whiteboard and stood for a second with the marker poised in the air, letting the quiet settle. She loved this part. The soft after of a room that had been loud with possibility all day.

On her desk sat a basket of apples, this had been her thing since her first year of teaching three years ago. Her friends had joked on her first day that she needed to have apples to fit the "Teacher Bae" aesthetic. What started as a joke was now a daily tradition. She had handed the apples out at the end of each day with a smile and a reminder to wash them at home. One rested on a stack of handwriting sheets now, perfect and red, catching the late light like it knew it was being admired.

She capped the marker and reached for her water. The cool hit her tongue and pulled her mind to the current state of her life. After the amazing day she had, she wished there was someone—outside of her friends—that she could call.

Her relationship with her parents was estranged, at best. It began with her initial diagnosis of Hidradenitis Suppurativa at twelve—after she got her period, that was the first chip in the perfect picture they had of her. A daughter with a disease they couldn't control, one that left horrible scars behind. Aniyah spent years as a child hating her body and its imperfections because of how they treated her. She quickly progressed from Hurley Stage One to Hurley Stage Three between the ages of thirteen and fifteen. She still remembers the nights she cried herself to sleep because the pain from the boils was so bad and all she had to take was Tylenol.

Looking back, she should've left then to be with her Grandpa. Even now, dealing with keloids throughout her body and the occasional flare, she still remembers the insecure teenager who just wanted to hide.

As an adult, she loved her body. She loved her scars. There were over seventy-five of them hidden on her breasts, beneath them, across her lower abdomen, thighs, and ass. She was a walking masterpiece of the pain she endured. That only made her love herself more.

When she decided she wanted to be a teacher instead of a doctor like her dad, he all but lost it. That was the final straw. Her senior year of high school was rough. She ended up moving in with her grandpa, Earl Henderson, the light of her life, after a particularly nasty argument with her parents where her father, in his no-nonsense tone, stated that if she did not want to be a doctor, she was cut off. Imagine being a fresh eighteen and your parents already disowning you, even after overworking yourself to be the perfect daughter and student. None of that mattered because she desired something different from the life they had planned for her.

It didn't take Earl any time to come get his granddaughter, curse his son out, and change Aniyah's life forever. During the short time she had with her grandpa, she quickly regretted not leaving her parents' house earlier. Earl was her gentle giant. He had been a bus driver for forty years and had recently retired when Aniyah moved in with him.

He cheered her on during the rest of her senior year, throughout her college years, and was the loudest person at her graduation. Her parents didn't even attend. Whenever she had a flare, Earl was diligent about taking care of her and making sure she had everything she needed. There was a time she had a flare so bad under her arm that she couldn't lift it. Earl would fuss whenever he saw her trying to raise it to complete her usual chores. He would also speak life into her whenever she felt down because of it.

"Firecracker, this only adds to your beauty. You are perfect. Plus, dealing with this pain now? You'll be ready to kick life's ass when you're outta my house. I already know you won't let some bullhead boy try to run over you, but if it happens, let him know your Grandpa Earl will whoop his ass."

Aniyah went on to get her MEd directly after and received that degree a year later. She landed a job at P.S. Johnson a few months after graduation and it felt like everything had fallen into place. Moving from her grandpa's house to a studio on Long Island felt like moving across the country and she felt worried about leaving him alone. Earl quickly shot down her fears letting her know he had been alone for decades before she was even thought of, and he would be just fine. Even so, she made sure they kept their Saturday movie and dinner date standing. She loved her grandpa with everything that was in her and he adored her just as much.

It was Aniyah's first Christmas break as a teacher, and she had decided she was going to spend a few days over her grandpa's. When she walked up the stoop late in the afternoon, there was a churn in her stomach that let her know something was wrong. She had just talked to him that morning, but that did not put her at ease. She walked in to see her grandpa laid out on the floor and immediately went to help him, but it was too late. Hours later she would find out that he suffered a major heart attack, it was quick, he wouldn't have suffered.

That did nothing to bring Aniyah any comfort. The days that followed felt like they all rolled together. Earl was a very particular man, so he already had his funeral arrangements done. All Aniyah had to do was show up. That's when she saw her parents for the first time in six years. They were haughty and ready to leave but stuck around to settle Earl's estate. To everyone's surprise, a year prior he changed his will and left everything to Aniyah, which pissed her father off. A small smile graced Aniyah's face as she thought about Earl continuing to be her savior from beyond.

That had been two years ago, life had since changed drastically. She sold the brownstone because she couldn't bear to be there any longer without her grandpa. She went through and made sure to get the items from him that she wanted to cherish for the rest of her life, records, artwork, his lucky tie, sweatshirts, jewelry and an evergreen bucket hat that he adored. Everything else, she sold in an estate sale.

Then she did the most reckless thing, bought a condo on Long Beach, a barrier island off of Long Island's South Shore. It sat high over the boardwalk, floor to ceiling windows framing the ocean like it had been put there for her alone. She had bought it with a chunk of the inheritance Grandpa left her, the rest tucked away because he taught her to be steady in a world that was not.

Her place was earth tones personified and brought a sleek comfort that made Aniyah's body relax every time she stepped through the front door.

Plants crowded her living room now. Monstera with leaves as big as dinner plates. A rubber plant in the corner. Trailing pothos that had figured out how to flirt with sunlight. She watered them on Sundays. She read them poems sometimes, not that she would admit it. She wrote her own too. Lines that came at midnight and refused to leave until she set them down.

Her mind snapped back to the present taking in her empty and quiet classroom. On its own her mind trailed to Trevor, she was still in shock about seeing him yesterday. She was sure it would wear off as time went by. Her next thought was to him being married. Just by looking at Zara, she knew that Katelyn was her mother. The thought of that woman took her mind to another place, toward the city summer just past, hot air and rooftops, and a face she had *not* expected to see again...

It was August in the Lower East Side. A rooftop party where the dress code read carefree and the DJ understood that R&B at sunset could fix most things wrong in the world. Aniyah did not always say yes to invitations, not since Grandpa passed and the quiet got into her bones, but Mya had dragged her out with promises of tacos and a view.

She had been leaning on the railing, taking in the skyline when she saw her. Katelyn, in a slip dress the color of champagne, laughing with a tall white man who wore his shirt too tight and his confidence even tighter. No ring on her finger. The kind of laughter that made other people look and wonder what joke they had missed.

They drifted close during a circuit around the bar. Katelyn's gaze slid over Aniyah, then back again like she was trying to place her.

"Hi," Aniyah said, because she was raised right.

"Hi. Long time no see!" Katelyn's smile was swift and cool. "Did you become a doctor?"

"No. I teach."

"Oh," Katelyn said, like the word had flavors she did not like. "How sweet."

The man squeezed Katelyn's waist and leaned in to say something low. Katelyn's laugh came out sharp. She offered a nod the way some people tipped at valet, then moved on without another word.

Cold could be beautiful. That was true of the weather and people. Katelyn fit that description. She wasn't one to hold a grudge against someone she hasn't seen since high school, but Katelyn had always rubbed her the wrong way. It was her attitude and the way she was always smiling condescendingly at the women around her like she was so much better than everyone else. That may work with folks that didn't grow up with her, but Aniyah knew the truth. Katelyn wouldn't be shit if she didn't have Trevor Porter and his family. They literally changed her life, and she had the nerve to talk down on anyone else.

Aniyah told herself to let it go. She had no reason to care who that woman was now or who she was with. The city was full of small collisions that meant nothing.

She did not know yet that their worlds would touch again in a yellow classroom with a reading rug and a wall that said, "You belong here."

Now thinking about the little girl who was so full of light but still had a sadness hovering not too far behind made Aniyah angry. Zara was a delight to have in class. She was intelligent, a sweetheart and always helping her peers. Aniyah felt a fierce protectiveness over Zara and wanted to help shield her from anything that was hurting her. It was clear that Katelyn was cheating on Trevor and that could possibly be what is triggering Zara's sadness. She prayed that they would both be free from that torment, so that they could find the peace that she found in her condo every night.

A week after school started, Mya and Stephanie, Aniyah's two best friends, decided it was time for her to stop taking herself on dates to the plant nursery in Freeport and get back to dating actual men. They were her sisters by choice, loud where she was quiet, brave where she was careful. They did not play about her, and they did not accept her excuses.

"He is normal," Mya said on the three-way call. "A unicorn. Has a skilled trade that brings in good money. Owns a toolbox. Not allergic to commitment."

"His name is Robert," Stephanie added. "He is an HVAC tech. He fixes things for a living. That's symbolism, Niyah. He's a good man, Savannah."

Aniyah laughed, "Kenneth was a terrible fucking man, Steph. You two are ridiculous."

"You will thank us when he installs a new thermostat for free," Mya said.

The date was at Yardie Kitchen, the Jamaican spot three blocks from the school where the oxtails fell off the bone and the plantains tasted like sunshine. Aniyah wore high waisted jeans, a white cropped button up, and small pearl studs. She left her hair down. Auburn waves fell to her shoulders and made the melanin in her skin glow. .

Robert stood to greet her when she walked in. He had kind eyes, a clean fade, and work strong hands. He also had breath that could kill a plant which instantly killed the little attraction she had felt for him.

Aniyah powered through. She ordered ginger beer and tried not to breathe through her nose when he leaned forward to ask questions. He was sweet. He told stories about his nieces. He loved his mother. He had just finished a weeklong job in a brownstone where the radiators were older than he was. He was, by all measures, a good man.

His breath was not.

She nodded and smiled and kept her answers short. She ate her rice and peas like they were a mission. She made a joke about the Yankees that landed well enough, then glanced at her phone and lied about an early morning. When the date ended, she hugged him quickly and promised to text, then slid into the backseat of an Uber with the speed of someone escaping a small, polite fire.

The driver headed toward Long Beach. Aniyah tipped her head back and let the city slip by outside the window. A billboard rose above the expressway, black background, warm gold lettering that looked expensive but felt intimate.

Making Love: The Art of Us.
Directed by Trevor Porter.

The words hit like a tap on her shoulder from a hand she used to know. Curiosity pulled her forward in the seat. The name rested heavy and bright at the same time. Trevor, not the sophomore in high school, but the grown man. The dad. The man with dark eyes that seemed to follow her every movement in the mornings he dropped off his daughter. Seeing his name on that billboard made her stomach flutter. He went after his dream and *got* it. That brought about a feeling in her that she didn't want to name. Trevor was off limits, but she would enjoy the view.

At home, the elevator opened to a wall of glass and water. She kicked her heels off, opened her laptop, and called her girls on FaceTime.

"First of all," she said when their faces lit the screen, "how dare you."

Mya threw her head back and laughed. "He was bad?"

"I think his breath is fighting demons."

Stephanie clapped a hand over her face. "No."

"Yes."

"Everything else?"

"Fine," Aniyah said. "Nice, even. I cannot get past the breath assault. How do you take a woman out with your mouth smelling that bad?! As bad as that shit was, he had to have been able to smell it himself. I should fire y'all from the blind dates."

Mya wiped tears. "I'm sorry. I really am. Maybe he had a rough day and forgot."

"Forgot to brush his teeth?!" Stephanie exclaimed.

"A toothbrush would have had a rougher one," Aniyah said.

They devolved into the kind of laughter that felt like medicine. When it faded, Stephanie sobered first. "You okay for real?"

"I'm okay," Aniyah said, softer now. "It is just the quiet. Sometimes it is loud. I know I made the right decision to move out here, but every now and then I miss Papa so much I forget how to breathe. For now, I'm okay."

They nodded. They knew the sorrow she dealt with on a daily basis. They were the only people who did. Aniyah's grief from her parents and losing her grandfather sometimes made her hate her solitude. It was crazy how her sanctuary could become a prison cell when things got too still.

While they traded stories about work drama and Mya's auntie who had just discovered how to make Instagram reels, Aniyah typed Trevor Porter into the search bar of her computer. The screen filled with links to interviews and festival photos. There was even a clip from Sundance where he stood in the back of a theater, jaw tight and eyes glassy, while a room full of strangers clapped for a love story he made loosely based on his parent's love story, according to Google.

Porter Brothers Foundation, she read. A cancer foundation owned by Angelou, Jackson and Trevor. They started it after the passing of their mother. She clicked through to a foundation site and saw Della's name on a scholarship. The press release mentioned her passing in clean, careful language that made grief look tidy. Aniyah closed her eyes for a second and saw Della as she really was. A warm spirit who showed up at school field days with a trunk full of juice boxes. The mom who knew every child's name by the second week. A hug and a laugh that made you feel like you had done something right just by being there.

Aniyah scrolled and learned more than she meant to. The documentary series he is releasing soon following artists all over NYC with his brother and sister-in-law at the forefront. The artist profiles he'd completed as a new filmmaker. The photo of Trevor on a rooftop, curls pulled back, holding a camera the way some men held babies. Aniyah remembered the billboard said "Directed by Trevor Porter" in bold like the billboard. Success looked good on him. The kind of good that came from hard work and not just luck.

"Okay," Mya said, narrowing her eyes. "Who are you cyber-stalking?"

"No one," Aniyah said too fast.

Stephanie leaned into the camera. "Do not lie to me, girl. I can see that concentration wrinkle in the middle of your forehead."

Aniyah sighed and shared her screen so they could see what she was looking at. Their twin gasps made her laugh.

"Trevor?! Those dimples," Mya groaned. "They survived."

"Of course they did," Stephanie said. "The devil made them."

Aniyah shook her head and closed the tab. "It is nothing really. I saw a billboard on my way home from that disaster of a date that said he has a docuseries dropping. My brain went on a field trip. That is all."

"Uh huh," Mya said. "Field trips have chaperones. We are them. Be careful."

"I'm always careful," Aniyah said. She looked at the glass, the water beyond, the reflection of herself small in the window. "That is the problem."

"He's still with what's-her-face? Katie?" Stephanie asked dead serious.

"Katelyn, girl!" Mya laughed in response. "I hope not, because Niyah and I def saw her at a rooftop party over the summer with Arnold Schwarzenegger."

"Mya! That man was not Arnold Schwarzenegger! Why would you say that?!" Aniyah was crying laughing at this point.

"Shit, that's what he looked like. If she is with Trevor, then she's cheating for sure. Which is crazy because who cheats on fine ass Trevor Porter?"

"Well, considering the ring on his finger and the little girl that is her mini me, I'd say they are married." Aniyah added.

"Bitch what?! Married? And she's out her popping her coochie for the Terminator? Get out!" Stephanie responded.

"I'm not doing this with y'all!" Aniyah continued to laugh.

"I have an early morning. Goodnight sisters!"

After they hung up, she sat on the couch with her knees pulled to her chest and wrote in the notes app because the poem would not wait.

What I'm not, she typed,

is a ghost in my own life.
What I want is a hand at the door
that knocks and does not run.

She read it twice, then tucked the phone under a pillow like that would keep the words safe.

Before Aniyah knew it, the first month of school had passed. October in the classroom came with sweaters and colorful boots. The light changed. Mornings came in darker and slid across the floor with a slower stride. The kids brought in leaves and announced that the trees were *falling* with a kind of eager excitement in innocence that made her heart warm.

During the past month, her friends had also set up on three more disastrous dates. She promptly fired them from the job because the last guy was the worst. He had the nerve to sit across from her and ask if she wanted to have a quickie in the bathroom with a sleazy smile. She promptly got up from the table and never looked back. She was done with blind dates for the foreseeable future. In the meantime, she would concentrate on her students. There is always a shift when fall comes. Either chapters opening or closing. Aniyah was always good with spotting the sign when change was coming.

It happened on a Thursday. Zara walked into the classroom quietly, which was not like her at all. She hung her backpack on the blue hook and moved slower than usual. During the morning meeting, she pressed her palm to her stomach and winced.

Aniyah knelt in front of her. "Are you okay, love?"

"My tummy feels hot," Zara whispered.

Aniyah put the back of her hand to Zara's forehead. Warm. Not scary, but not right. She guided her to the reading nook and had an aide bring a small trash bin just in case. She called the office for a thermometer and hit the number listed for emergency contact on Zara's file.

Katelyn answered on the third ring. The background sounded like a lobby with heels on marble.

"This is Ms. Henderson, Zara's teacher." Aniyah said. "Zara has a fever. It would be best to pick her up."

A pause. Then a bright voice that did not match the news. "Call Trevor."

"I called the first number listed. If you are unable, I can reach out to him next."

"Do that," Katelyn said. "And Ms. Henderson.

"Yes?"

There was a smile in Katelyn's tone that did not feel warm. "This is friendly advice. Mind your business about what you saw over the summer."

Aniyah pulled the phone back for a second to look at it, like the screen might explain why Aniyah's first conversation since that rooftop would have her coming out the side of her neck. "My business is your daughter. That is all. Maybe you should be minding your home so you wouldn't be out here giving thinly veiled threats."

"Call Trevor," Katelyn repeated, and the line went dead.

Aniyah exhaled slowly and hit the second number.

Trevor picked up on the first ring. The sound around him was different. Metal and shouted cues and the roll of cart wheels.

"Hello."

"Hi. It is Aniyah Henderson from P. S. Johnson. Zara is not feeling well. She has a fever. I think it would be best to take her home."

"Where is she right now?" His voice was steady and low, all urgency tucked under control.

"In the reading corner, resting. She is with me."

"I'm on my way," he said. No hesitation. No explanation about where he was or why it was hard.

"We are actually shooting at a location nearby. It shouldn't take me more than ten minutes to get there, fifteen at most."

After that he ended the call. Aniyah sat beside Zara on the rug and read in a whisper about the hungry caterpillar. Ten minutes later the office buzzed to say a parent was here.

Trevor came in with wind still on his coat. He crouched beside Zara and touched her forehead with the back of his hand the way Aniyah had. His eyes softened. He spoke to her like the room had shrunk to just the two of them.

"Hey, Superstar."

She blinked at him, relieved. "Daddy."

"We are going home," he said. "Soup, cartoons, naps. Order of your choice."

"Cartoons, soup, nap," she murmured.

"Done." He looked up at Aniyah. "Thank you."

"You are welcome," she said. "She will be okay. It is a low fever. Tylenol, fluids and rest."

He nodded and reached for the backpack on the blue hook. The tattoo on his neck moved when he swallowed. Aniyah took in the artistry of his tattoos, not only Zara's name but flower vines. They were beautiful. Seeing Trevor being such a caring dad landed in a way that was unexpected.

Aniyah felt something warm unfurl in her chest, slow and unfamiliar. It surprised her with how simple it was. Seeing the way his love shows up for Zara. His little girl was worried and like Superman, Trevor came to her rescue. That kind of presence that is grounding. The tension that eased from Zara's shoulders when she saw her dad landed straight to Aniyah's heart.

He helped Zara into her coat and lifted her with the ease of long practice. She tucked her face into his shoulder and went soft. The room changed shape around them.

He paused at the door. “Ms. Henderson.”

“Yes.”

He looked like he wanted to say something else. Then he only said, “Thank you again,” and was gone.

The air settled. Aniyah stood in the doorway for a second, watching the hallway where they had disappeared. She felt the ghost of the rooftop summer and the sharp laugh of a woman in a slip dress. She felt the cool of glass against her palms at home and the weight of words she wrote in the dark. She felt steady and unsteady at once.

She went back to the reading rug and picked up the open book on the floor and placed it back on the shelf. She hoped Zara would be okay.

After school, she sent the class newsletter and included a small note. Zara went home feeling under the weather. She is loved and in good hands.

She watered the plants by the windowsill. She stacked the pencils. She turned off the lamps. On her way out, she took an apple from the basket and rolled it in her palm. It shone.

Outside, October had sharpened. The wind lifted her hair and brought the ocean to mind even this far from the shore. She thought of a billboard on the expressway. She thought of a name in bold. She thought of a man who left a set like it was nothing and a little girl who let herself rest because he was there.

The feeling that spread through her was not dramatic. It was not even loud. It was a small, clear yes in the center of her chest.

She put the apple in her bag and walked toward the train.

CHAPTER FOUR

THE BEGINNING OF THE END

"Get your shit! Get your shit! And, get out!" - *Bernadine, Waiting to Exhale (1995)*

Trevor carried Zara through the front door, her body had gone heavy with the kind of sleep that fever brings. He nudged the door closed with his heel and held her a second longer than necessary. Her breath warmed the curve of his neck. The house felt colder than it should.

"Alright, Superstar. We're home."

He eased her onto the couch, took off her shoes and tucked a throw around her. The thermostat clicked when he raised it two degrees. He set the kettle on. He filled a bowl with cool water and found the soft washcloths in the linen drawer. He moved on autopilot. Checks and balances. Ginger tea, broth, acetaminophen dosed by weight, the blue humidifier that puffed like a train in a children's book.

Zara stirred. "Daddy?"

"I'm right here."

He pressed the thermometer under her tongue and traced the Z in her name along her back with a fingertip. She could always feel even half asleep. The thermometer beeped. 101.8. Not terrifying, but still not good.

He called the pediatrician's line and spoke to a nurse who had the calm voice of a person who had heard every worry in the world. Fluids. Rest. Call back if breathing changes. Come in if the fever spikes past 103. He wrote it all on a sticky note and stuck it to the fridge like it was a contract. He washed her up and put on her favorite Lilo pajamas. He tucked her in the bed with a kiss on the forehead and a promise of soup.

As he traveled back to the kitchen, he saw the call sheet for tomorrow's studio day was pinned to the cork board with a bulldog clip. Reed had made it look like he knew what it was doing. Trevor stared at the list of times. Lighting test. Camera rehearsal. B roll of paint mixing. He swallowed against a grind of guilt that tasted like metal.

He texted the group thread.

Trevor: Zara has a fever. I will still make call if needed, but I may have to remote in.

Alicia: We got you. I can shift the camera rehearsal and push coverage

Reed: We can send you a feed. Stay with her.

Mackenzie: Do not worry about us. We are good.

Jackson: We will send soup.

Trevor smiled at that and set the phone facedown on the counter. He put on a playlist of soft jazz and let it fill the kitchen like it could smooth the corners of the day. He ladled broth into a mug and carried it to the bedroom. Zara cracked an eye and took a sip without complaint. She was brave like that.

He put on *Carl The Collector* at low volume. The characters moved through bright problems and brighter solutions. He adjusted the humidifier and remembered the first time he did this. Zara was four months old, and the fever had landed without knocking. His mom had sat with him on the bathroom floor while the shower ran hot and turned the room to cloud.

"*You will not break*," she had said. "*Your girl needs you calm. So, breathe.*"

He breathed now, in through the nose, out through the mouth. Over and over until the drum in his chest softened.

As the afternoon faded, he opened his laptop and pulled up the lookbook for *Making Love.* He typed notes for the new structure and flagged two sequences for color tests. He wrote a paragraph about how silence should be allowed to sit inside a frame like a guest you want to stay. He felt the engine of his brain catch and run. He watched it with one eye while the other stayed on his daughter.

The sun slid behind the houses across the street. Lights jumped on, one window at a time. Trevor reheated broth, dosed medicine, rubbed her back in circles until her breath levelled again. He texted Katelyn.

Zara is sick. Picked her up at school. She is resting.

The message marked delivered. No reply. They had been walking on eggshells around each other since that morning she ran off. She had been home more, but somehow always missed Zara's pick up or drop off. Trevor had let it slip that Aniyah was Zara's new teacher and he could've sworn Katelyn froze before rolling her eyes and saying, *"After all that work? I thought she was supposed to be a doctor?"*

That statement left a bad taste in his mouth. Considering Katelyn's profession, he did not know why she felt haughty towards Aniyah. They slept in the same bed, but he hadn't touched her since he found the hickey she tried to play off like a burn. On his brother's advice, he also went and had an STD panel done, thankfully everything came back clean. He was due to meet with Angelou and his P.I. by the end of October, and he was nervous about what he would find out.

He couldn't deny that there was a part of him that wanted the PI to find nothing. For this just to be the rough patch married couples who have lasted talk about and for him and Katelyn to be the couple they once were. From the distant look in her eyes every morning, the smile that she always has when looking at her phone and the nonchalant way she handles Zara, those days are long gone. Still... he hoped.

At eight, he went upstairs to check on Zara. She blinked at him when the light from the hallway entered her room. He brushed her hair off her forehead and read one book about a pig who wanted to fly and another about a train that chose to be brave. He tucked her in and set the trash bin and a glass of water within reach. He kissed her temple and stood for a second longer than needed. He listened to make sure the rhythm of her breath did not change.

Downstairs, he cleaned the kitchen. The hum of the refrigerator and the low saxophone on the speakers held the silence between them like a blanket that had gotten too thin. He thought of Aniyah saying, "She is loved and in good hands," in today's classroom newsletter. He held that sentence in his mouth for a full minute because it fit.

The front door opened at ten forty-three.

Katelyn stepped into the foyer like she was entering a party. Heels clicking. The kind of perfume you could name by brand if you cared about that sort of thing. She slid her coat off her shoulders and draped it over the banister. She looked good. She always did. The city had put a shine on her that made strangers stare.

"You are home," she said, like he had been away. She looked past him into the living room, then at the stairs. "Where is Z?"

"Asleep, she is still fighting her fever."

Katelyn paused for half a second. "She will be fine."

He nodded. "She will."

Katelyn's eyes moved back to him. She let them travel the length of him like a new idea. He was broader than he used to be. Gym mornings had carved his shoulders without his permission. The serious switch was on his face, and she had always liked that. She walked toward him slow and deliberate, hips a suggestion inside a pencil skirt and silk that caught the kitchen light.

"Hey," she said softly. "You look good."

He did not move,"It has been a day."

"I can make it better." She stepped close enough for her perfume to find his throat. Her fingers slid up his chest and hooked at his collar. Her mouth tipped toward his jaw. She laughed low like they were sharing a joke in a quiet theater.

Trevor pulled back, "No."

Katelyn frowned at his rejection. She couldn't believe it, "You are serious right now?"

"I'm serious every time I'm standing in our kitchen wondering why I'm alone in this house. I'm serious when our daughter asks where you are and I make something up because the truth sounds like I hate you. I'm serious when I say we cannot keep doing this."

Her chin lifted, "I was at work."

"You were somewhere," he said. "It has been *months* of somewhere."

She rolled her eyes, "I'm sorry! Do you want a cookie because you handled a fever?"

He stared at her for a long beat, "I want a partner who comes home."

Silence settled for half a second. She broke it with a sound like a door shutting.

"I am home!" Katelyn shouted.

"Aye, watch your tone when you're talking to me. Our daughter is finally sleeping peacefully, I'll be damned if you walk your triflin' ass up in here and wake her up." Trevor's voice was a whisper but it was so hard. Katelyn had never heard him talk to her like that. She had been dodging this conversation since he sent that text message last month.

"Why are you talking to me like this?!" She screeched.

"Do you know our daughter asked if you still loved her? She apologized for whatever she did wrong and wanted her mother back," Katlyn's eyes began to water as Trevor continued, "She asked what she had to do to get her mom back. You always come home after her bedtime, if you're coming home. You've missed taking her to school and her fucking birthday, Lyn! Do you know how fucked up that is?" Trevor paused because he felt himself being overcome with sadness thinking about his little girl.

"I get it, if you've fallen out of love with me, but Z" —he points up, signaling where she is sleeping in her room— "Does not deserve any of this. Either you're in or you're out."

Would it be dumb that there was a large part of him that

wanted her to say that she wasn't done, that she still loved him and her daughter and they would work on this. The pair locked eyes for a moment. That's when he saw it, her resignation.

"This was not the life I pictured for myself, Trevor." Her confession came out tired as she sat on the arm of the couch.

"When we met, my life was terrible. I was broken watching my father beat my mother. It felt like I was trapped with no way to escape. Then you came...The school's most wanted. You had the *perfect* life, with your *perfect* parents and your *perfect* brothers that would do anything for you. And...you let me in."

"What are you saying, Katelyn? You only got with me to escape your family?"

"No! No. I loved you. I did." *Loved.* The words cut through Trevor like a knife. He felt all of the air leave his body.

"Loved. Wow. You don't love me anymore?" He hated the way his voice pleaded with her to change her mind, but Katelyn's back went ramrod straight as she doubled down on her admission.

"Somehow along the way, while helping you chase your dreams and forgetting mine, the love I felt changed."

"I never asked you to forget your dreams! I begged you to go to school and to get into nursing like you wanted. My family was here to help you. You decided to stay home."

"I know! Don't you think I fucking know that?!" She yelled.

"Aye, watch who the fuck you're talking to. You may be getting dicked down by those white boys at that firm, but I'm still your husband. Treat me with respect."

"I never wanted this," she said solemnly. The words came out swift, sharpened by a year of regrets.

"I didn't want this life. I didn't want to be a mom. I didn't want to be someone's wife doing pancakes and school newsletters. I'm twenty-six with nothing to show for it. I thought getting pregnant was cool because you were the hottest boy in school and

I one upped every girl. But that hype is played out now. I don't want this." The confession stung, but the smug look on Katelyn's face showed she meant every word.

Trevor's body went very still. Then it was colder than still. He didn't move his face, it held in place like a camera on a locked off tripod.

Katelyn kept going, "I have been seeing someone. The Finance VP at Whitmore. He makes my life make sense. I feel alive with him in a way I never feel here. I want a divorce." The last word dropped to a whisper.

The whisper did not matter. It traveled the hall like a shout. Trevor let out a laugh, the pain in his heart did nothing to quiet the humor that burned through him.

"You know, for one of your favorite movies to be *The Family That Preys*, you cannot be that gahdamn dumb. But you know what? Maybe you are. I cannot wait to see how this story plays out."

Trevor saw the shape in the doorway first. A small shadow inside a larger one. He turned and found Zara in the archway with the blanket from her bed wrapped around her shoulders. Eyes wet. Nose pink. Lower lip tucked inside her teeth the way she did when she was trying not to cry.

His heart slammed. He moved before his brain could catch up.

"Hey." He went down on one knee, so his eyes met hers. He kept his voice level even though his pulse had broken every rule. "You couldn't sleep?"

"I heard voices," she said. The wobble in her words cut him in half. "Are you and Mommy mad at each other?"

Trevor breathed. "We are talking. Grown up talking can sound loud sometimes. You're safe, Baby."

Her tears fell harder. "Are you leaving?"

He swallowed. He drew her into his chest and felt the heat of her fever through the blanket and his T-shirt. "No. I'm not leaving you. I'm not leaving you, ever."

She nodded into his collar and sobbed twice like her body had to let it out before it could believe him. He picked her up. She curled against him with the heavy trust of a child who loved without calculation.

He carried her upstairs. He set her down in bed and stroked her hair back from her damp forehead. He talked to her about silly things. The cartoon pig who wanted to be a pilot. The plant she wanted for the living room. Ice cream after the fever broke. The quiet spells you could cast with your breath when your heart was loud. She listened. Her tears slowed. He handed her tissues and a glass of water. He wiped her nose and kissed her temple.

"Daddy's right here," he said. "Right here."

"Right here," she repeated, more to herself than to him.

He sat on the floor beside her until her eyelids fell and stayed. He counted a full sixty breaths. He stood and tucked the blanket around her. He blew out a slow breath and let it empty him of the last of his restraint.

Downstairs, Katelyn had poured herself a glass of wine. The liquid clung to the side of the glass and looked like it wanted to climb out.

Trevor walked to the hall closet and pulled out the navy suitcase they used for weekends at his father's place. He set it on the runner and unzipped it with a sound that felt like a choice. He went to the bedroom and opened drawers. He did not throw. He did not toss. He folded with a precision that bordered on reverent and then put the folded things into the suitcase like evidence into a box. He added shoes. Toiletries. The little black dress that had probably seen every rooftop this summer. He took the jewelry box from the dresser and set it inside. He zipped the case closed and wheeled it to the top of the stairs.

Katelyn stared at him like she did not recognize the man moving through her life. “What are you doing?”

“Getting you out.”

“You cannot kick me out of my house.”

“This is not your house,” he said in a calm voice. “It’s mine. My name is on the deed, thanks to Angelou‘s insistence. I should thank him for that. You are free to call a lawyer tomorrow. Tonight, you can go to your boyfriend. Or a hotel.”

“You are out of your mind.”

“I’m fed the fuck up,” he said, and it came out quiet. “You said you did not want this life. You said you wanted him. You said you wanted a divorce where our daughter could hear you. I will not let you set fire to this house and then take a nap in my bed.”

Her mouth opened. Closed. Then opened again. She looked around like the furniture might agree with her, “You cannot. You cannot do this.You are the one that asked for honesty. You can’t kick me out just because you did not like the answer!”

“That’s exactly what I’m doing.”

He rolled the suitcase down the stairs and out to the porch. The night air wrapped cold around his bare arms. He set the suitcase beside the door and walked back in. He grabbed her coat from the banister and held it out. She did not take it. He draped it over his arm and carried it out too.

When he returned, she stood in the foyer like a statue asked to move. The wineglass looked ridiculous in her hand. He reached past her and opened the door.

“Katelyn.”

She flinched at the sound of her name said like a period.

“Go.”

She stared at him for a long time. Something in her eyes shifted. Not anger. Not guilt. Something like calculation finally accepting it had been outmaneuvered. She set the glass on the console without looking where it landed. She walked past him. She picked up the suitcase and did not look back.

He closed the door. The latch clicked. The sound went through him and left a clean ache.

He stood very still in the foyer. He listened for Zara. He heard the humidifier. He heard his own heartbeat.

He locked the deadbolt.

He turned off the kitchen light. He washed the wineglass and set it upside down on the rack. He put the house back into order with small movements. He went upstairs and checked on his child. Her breath sawed softly. He touched her hair and the fever felt a little less sharp.

Back in the hall, he leaned his forehead against the wall and let his shoulders shake once. Just once. Then he straightened. He pulled his phone from his pocket and opened a new note titled To Do.

- *Call a lawyer in the morning.*
- *Call the bank to change the accounts*
- *Change the locks*
- *Call Alicia about remote directing plan.*
- *Pick up electrolyte pops.*
- *Text Dad.*
- *Text Jackson.*
- *Text Angelou, Need P.I. info ASAP*
- *Email the school a doctor's note if needed.*
- *Buy a plant for the living room.*

He saved the note and slid the phone away. He walked to the bedroom and stopped in the doorway. The bed looked wrong. He took the pillows and shook them out like they had collected dust from a life that was over.

On the dresser, the framed photo of the three of them at the beach smiled at him with teeth that looked like lies. He turned it face down.

He went to the couch and lay there with a blanket and the house breathing around him. He stared at the ceiling and counted backwards from one hundred. Somewhere around seventy-one, he imagined a classroom washed in yellow and a teacher rolling a red apple in her hand. He did not know why that image came to him now, only that it felt like the opposite of a door closing.

He slept.

ACT II

THE FALL

CHAPTER FIVE

WHEN TRUTH GETS LOUD

"Life is like a disco: no matter how the music changes, you just keep on dancing." - *Mrs. Watson, Jumping The Broom (2011)*

It was the second week of November and Long Island looked caught between seasons, bare branches tangled against a pewter sky, lawns carpeted in brittle leaves that hadn't made peace with falling yet. The air had that clean sharpness that hinted at winter, but not the glittering kind. It was the sort that made you tuck your hands deeper into your pockets and breathe slow, like the whole world was holding itself together.

Trevor liked this time of year. He liked the quiet before the holidays swallowed everything whole. He liked the way the neighborhood smelled like damp earth and chimney smoke. And lately, he liked that stillness meant less space for pretending.

It had been three weeks since Katelyn left his house and filed for divorce. One since the court date that rearranged the shape of his life.

The Porters had made it their mission to keep him and Zara from sitting too long in the silence. Angelou and Nina showed up with takeout containers from every corner of Manhattan, the twins taking his home by storm. Jackson and Mackenzie brought fresh canvases for Zara and a box of markers that bled through paper but made her smile anyway. His dad came armed with patience, tools, and stories that started with "back in my day" and ended with laughter Trevor didn't know he still had in him.

The house smelled like roasted apples and nutmeg that night courtesy of Nina's mix on the stove and it had the kind of warmth that fought the chill outside. The trees in the yard were bare now, except for one stubborn maple that clung to its red leaves like pride.

Zara had built a fort out of couch cushions and blankets, her dolls arranged in a perfect semicircle around her. A movie hummed in the background, the kind she never finished because she'd fall asleep halfway through, head on her dad's arm, hand clutching his shirt like it was a promise. After an hour he gently removed himself to finish working.

Trevor watched her from the kitchen table, laptop open, camera equipment stacked by the wall. The emails had slowed down since the separation became official. People were nice about it in that way polite people are when they're curious but don't want to sound cruel. He didn't mind the quiet. It gave him room to breathe.

He thought about the hearing again. He'd tried not to, but the mind is its own thief. This was their new normal. A life without Katelyn—for him—finally felt peaceful.

"It's going to be okay, Trev. You can get through this," he spoke to himself entering the thick wooden doors.

The courthouse smelled like paper and coffee that had been reheated too many times. Everything was gray: the floors, the walls and the sky outside. Even the lawyers wore gray. He'd never hated the color more.

Angelou had shown up early, leaning against a column near security with a manila folder under his arm and a jaw that said he was prepared to burn the world if he had to. Trevor didn't ask what strings his brother pulled to get the hearing expedited. He didn't want to know. He only knew he couldn't have survived waiting another month.

Katelyn arrived fashionably late. She acted like she was stepping into a fashion show instead of a divorce proceeding. Her coat was camel wool, her perfume the same one she used to wear when they were happy. She didn't look at him right away. Just adjusted her cuffs and smiled at her lawyer.

He remembered when that smile used to be for him.

Her attorney started talking about equity, assets, compensation, the kind of language that made love sound like inventory. The house. The car. Spousal support. Future royalties. She wanted half of everything, and Trevor tried to sit still while the words landed like stones on a frozen lake.

His lawyer leaned forward, calm but cutting. "Before we discuss division," he said, "there's a matter of infidelity."

That was Angelou's cue. He slid the manila folder onto the table like a move in chess.

Katelyn's attorney frowned, opened it, and went pale by

degrees. There were photos, screenshots, hotel invoices, receipts, dates and most importantly–names. A pattern that told the truth with painful precision: Katelyn had been cheating on him for a while now and not just with the swanky VP guy. The thought was another kick to the gut.

Trevor didn't look at the images. He'd already seen enough when Angelou brought the evidence to him that morning, voice low, expression unreadable. He'd only said, "I'm sorry, little bro, but you deserve to know the truth."

The judge took one look at the folder and shifted tone entirely. Suddenly "equitable division" turned into "custodial stability." Her lawyer's voice lost its gloss. The judge's pen scratched, steady and deliberate.

Then came the sentence that broke something he hadn't realized was still holding.

"I would like to terminate my parental rights," Katelyn said with absolute certainty. No regret in her voice.

The room went still.

Her words didn't shake. They didn't crack or stutter. She said them like she was declining a dessert menu with an air of nonchalance and not deserting her child.

Trevor felt his chest cave in slow motion. The air thinned. The sound left the room. He could only hear his pulse and the faint hum of the ceiling light.

He saw flashes of her at eighteen, barefoot on the cheap couch they'd bought with their first paycheck, laughing as they came up with baby names. He remembered her drawing hearts in the steam on the bathroom mirror. He remembered her hand, warm on his back, when they'd talked about forever.

He could not reconcile that girl with the woman sitting across from him now, signing her name to something no mother should.

His lawyer asked if he wanted to respond. He didn't. What

was there to say to someone who had already left before the door closed?

He only said, "I'll take care of our daughter." And the word *our* caught in his throat like glass.

After the gavel fell, he walked out into the cold, his brothers flanking him. Angelou's eyes were hard and dark. Jackson kept running his hands over his face like if he stopped moving, he'd break too. Leon didn't say anything. Just put his arm around Trevor's shoulders and held tight.

"I'm here," His dad said quietly. "We all are."

Trevor nodded, though he wasn't sure he believed it yet. The world looked too sharp. The light too thin. The hole in his heart seemed to overtake his entire body. Katelyn being gone was necessary, but all that ran through his mind was when they first moved into their apartment with a 10 month old Zara. Time warped at an alarming rate reminding him that his past was just that, his past and the reality he was living in is not changing. He didn't remember going to pick up Zara, didn't remember signing off on shooting material, didn't remember what they ate for dinner. His world was just as grey as that courtroom.

That night, he sat by Zara's bed, watching her chest rise and fall, the innocence of her sleep cutting him open. Every now and then, she'd sigh in her dreams and reach out, hand searching for something. He let her find his. He would be exhausted when the sun rose, but oddly, he was at peace. There was an immediate urge to make a change. This led him to texting his family group chat:

Trevor: Lou, give me the name of your barber. I want a haircut.

Angelou: I'll give you more than that, we have a meeting at my favorite strip club soon. No backing out

Leon: Am I invited?

Jackson: Dad, you don't even text and THAT'S the first thing you say?

Leon: I may be your father but I'm still a man first.

Trevor: Maybe next time, big fella. I need you to watch Zara for me. I plan to get extremely drunk.

Leon: Nina and Mackenzie busy? I have some extra ones to throw. I'm retired after all.

Jackson: DAD

Angelou: You know it don't matter to me dad. That's why I'm your favorite.

Leon: You're something alright

Trevor locked his phone because he knew they would be going back and forth for at least another hour. Just as he leaned his head back against the side of Zara's bed, he felt her stir.

"Daddy?" Her tiny voice questioned.

"Yes, Superstar?"

"Is mommy never coming back?" Trevor sat for a moment, trying to still the thoughts clouding his mind.

"No, baby. She isn't. Look at me," He went to hold her as soon as the tears began to flow. "Daddy loves you so much and I'm not going anywhere. Your family loves you. Mommy just needed a new life. She still loves you, okay?" Zara nodded as she continued to cry. Trevor let her have this moment. What more could he say? That this was his fault? That he didn't love Katelyn hard enough to keep her? That he should've moved to fix what was broken when he first noticed the cracks instead of hoping that it would mend itself?

There were plenty of ways that he was blaming himself even though the logical part is telling him that this was Katelyn's fault. He couldn't stop from feeling like shit. So in that moment while his little girl was crying in his arms, he let himself break with her. The tears began slowly and then started to fall more rapidly. In the night, he let himself release the hurt that had been burdening him for the last two years. That night, he slept in Zara's room. Grief from the past lay along his frame like her down comforter. They would have a better future. He would make sure his little girl's light returned to her eyes.

The week after the hearing was a blur of structure and survival.

He woke before dawn, made pancakes even when he didn't want to eat, packed lunches with sticky notes that said *You got this* in uneven handwriting. He learned how to braid tighter, how to get toothpaste stains out of sweaters, how to keep a house running on less energy but more purpose.

Zara adjusted in her own quiet way. She asked fewer questions about her mom, but he could feel the ache in her drawings —stick figures of two people holding hands, the space between them filled with color where Katelyn used to be.

She'd taken to sitting by the window after dinner, chin on the sill, watching the streetlights blink on. "It looks like stars down here," she told him once. He nodded, too full to speak.

It was Jackson that told him he was still wearing his wedding ring a few days after the divorce, then told him to take as long as he needed to take it off. That evening after wrapping filming, he took it off and immediately threw up afterwards. The knots that settled into his stomach about beginning the unknown made sleep evade him that night.

A few days later he had Angelou's barber cut off the hair he had been growing since he found out that Katelyn was pregnant. He only trimmed it to keep it shoulder length.

"What are you releasing?" The barber, named Curtis who looked to be in his fifties, gruffed out before working the clippers against his curls.

"What you mean?" Trevor questioned in response.

"You had that look when you came in here. You're heavy. Usually when I get those types that means they are cutting to let go of something."

"Damn, you're good. I just got divorced. Been married since I was nineteen."

"Been divorced myself. I'm remarried now." Trevor sat up, intrigued.

"How was that experience?" Curtis paused his work to think for a moment.

"I will always have love and respect for my first wife. She is the mother of my kids. Our ending wasn't great. I definitely could've handled it better. I realize now, we were two people that were never meant to go past the first date. We got pregnant early in our courtship and I knew I had to make it right. Had two more kids before it really started showing we shouldn't be together anymore."

"That sounds like my story. How did you end up remarried?"

"I met my second wife unexpectedly. I was pushing 40. And I was picking up dinner from the Chinese place right by my place. They accidentally switched our orders. Thank God she checked her food before leaving. I looked at her and her smile pulled me in. A simple conversation had us finding a place to eat our dinner while continuing the conversation. Before we knew it, it was one in the morning and I didn't want to leave. So, I didn't. It's been twenty years and I know that she was meant for me."

"Damn, that's dope." Trevor didn't stop to think about the pang in his chest from thinking about if he would ever meet someone like Curtis' wife.

"When it's time, young blood, you'll know." Curtis responded with finality, before concentrating on his work. Trevor's mind continued to go into overdrive. He sat with feelings heavy on his chest as strands of his hair fell to the ground. Was he still truly in love with Katelyn? This time alone, he was starting to see the cracks in their foundation. He loved her once, but he certainly was not in love with her today. He hurt most for his daughter. She was quieter these days and that made his chest hurt more than being single.

When Curtis was finished with his taper fade, Trevor almost didn't recognize himself. A weight that had been on his shoulders seemed to lift with the sight of his new haircut. He quickly paid Curtis, promising to be back in two weeks and then made his way home to get ready to go out with his bros. The quiet house made his mind drift to Zara. He missed her. Even though she would only be gone for a night and he never had to worry about her on Saturday nights.

The Porter men dinners became anchor points. The first Saturday of every month, no matter what.

Sometimes it was Brooklyn, sometimes his place. Sometimes it's his dad's. They'd cook, talk trash, argue about sports, then end up reminiscing about Della until the laughter turned soft. Though, he knew tonight was to check on how he had been holding up

Zara stayed with her aunties on Porter dinner nights. Mackenzie spoiled her with crafts and warm cookies. Nina made playlists and built pillow forts taller than the couch. Zara usually came home on Sundays glittering and exhausted, curls frizzed, cheeks flushed, heart lighter. Trevor lived for those nights because they gave her pieces of womanhood that he couldn't.

Since Nina and Mackenzie would keep Zara that night, when Trevor got home after leaving the barbershop, the silence returned heavier than before. He'd fall asleep on the couch more often than not because the bed held too many memories, laptop on the table, a half-finished drink beside it. The ghost of his mother's voice reminding him he was still her boy, still capable of joy.

In that moment though, he felt as if joy was the furthest thing from his reach. These were the times he missed his mother the most. She would know what to do and how to navigate this new existence that had been thrusted upon him.

"Trevor, baby. You have to slow down!" Della used admonish about him running through their home because he was always prone to trip and fall. The words wouldn't change as he got older because he was the type to rush into something without taking the time to think about if it was something he truly needed. The last time his mother had told him to slow down? When Katelyn went into labor. He had come to his mother to tell her his plans of asking Katelyn to marry him. Her response was one he didn't expect, but now, sitting in the aftermath of his marriage they were always playing in a loop in his head.

"Trevor–baby–I always told you to slow down. Katelyn isn't going anywhere. Are you sure this is what you want? You can take your time..." Her voice drifted as she looked deep in thought. The look on her face, the empathy she had for his naiveté haunts him till this day. Maybe if he would've listened...

You can take your time

You can take your time

You can take your time

"Stop!" Trevor voiced to his thoughts. Praying his mother's

voice would go quiet for the night and his regrets wouldn't swallow him whole. Just as he finally got his mind quiet, his phone binged.

Angelou: Get your ass up. We are going out tonight. Meet me here 43 E 75th St at 10pm don't be late

Jackson: You know you put this in our group chat right? Is this invite extended to everyone??

Angelou: Don't you have a commission to finish?

Jackson: Don't you have twins to take care of?

Leon: Boys, you two just can't stop. I'll see you there at 10. This is the booty club right?

Trevor cackled reading his dad's message. He was constantly reminded that he hit the jackpot when it came to family.

Trevor: Dad, no one calls it the booty club anymore. I will be there at 10 pm sharp.

Trevor locked his phone and got up to get ready. In the shower he let his tears fall. He felt like a failure. How could he have been so blind to everything? He doesn't regret Katelyn because Zara was the best thing that has happened to him, but he does regret marrying her. Regrets keeping her around his daughter because now he had to pick up the pieces to his daughter's heart that Katelyn shattered. Zara never deserved that. He finished getting ready in his all black fit, with his black Timbs. He would wear his signature chain, but it was from Katelyn and he didn't want that bad energy around him.

Getting into the city already had Trevor on edge when he pulled up to the valet. He tossed the keys and proceeded into the unmarked building. The bass met him before the door fully closed behind him, low and steady, like a second heartbeat humming beneath the floor. The hallway was narrow and dark, washed in amber light that made every shadow look intentional. A man in a fitted suit gave him a once over, nodded, and stepped aside. When Trevor rounded the corner into the main room, the space opened up like a secret.

The club was drenched in red and gold light, velvet booths curved along the perimeter, glass tables catching the glow of chandeliers that shimmered like they were dipped in honey. Black bodies filled the room, every shade from deep onyx to warm caramel moving in rhythm with the music. Laughter rolled across the space, thick and easy. The air smelled like expensive cologne, brown liquor, and something sweet burning slow in the background. It felt less like a club and more like a sanctuary for release, a place where Black men and women came to exhale without explanation.

On the main stage, a woman with skin the color of dark roast coffee climbed the pole with the grace of someone born without fear. Her thighs flexed as she inverted herself, legs splitting wide before she spun, hair cascading toward the floor. The crowd roared as she transitioned seamlessly, flipping upright and sliding down in a controlled descent that made it clear she owned the stage and every eye fixed on it.

Trevor stopped mid step.

She moved like gravity did not apply to her, like she had made a private deal with the laws of physics. When she hooked one leg and arched her back, the lights kissed the sheen of her skin, and he felt something in his chest shift. It had been a long time since anything purely physical had caught his attention without guilt attached to it.

He dragged his eyes away before he could get caught staring too hard and scanned the room for his family. Angelou's laugh cut through the music first, deep and reckless. Trevor followed the sound to a corner section roped off with black velvet. Jackson leaned back with that quiet observant posture he always carried, locs pulled back, eyes tracking everything like he was sketching the room in his mind. His dad sat between them, sharp in a tailored blazer, a glass of dark liquor resting comfortably in his hand like he had been born knowing how to hold it.

Angelou spotted Trevor and stood, arms wide. "Look at this man," he announced as Trevor approached. "Fresh fade, fresh papers, fresh start."

Trevor rolled his eyes but couldn't stop the smile that crept up anyway. He slid into the booth and clasped hands with Jackson first, then leaned in to hug his father. Leon's embrace was firm, steady, the kind that said I got you without needing to speak it aloud.

Angelou was already waving down a server. "Two rounds of your top shelf whiskey. We are not easing into anything tonight."

The first round arrived quickly, dark liquid in chilled glasses. Angelou lifted his in a toast, "To freedom."

They clinked. The burn hit Trevor's throat fast and hot, settling into his chest like liquid courage. The second round came before the sting had even faded. Angelou insisted they run it back. Trevor did not argue. He welcomed the blur at the edges of his thoughts.

Leon set his glass down slower than the rest of them and turned toward his youngest son. The music swelled around them but in that booth it felt quieter somehow, contained.

"How you doing, son? Really doing."

Trevor inhaled, stared down at his hands. The new fade felt

foreign when he dragged his palm over it. "I don't know," he admitted. "Some days I feel light. Then other days I hear Ma in my head."

Jackson's posture shifted, attention sharpening.

"She kept telling me to slow down," Trevor continued, voice rough. "I thought marrying Katelyn was me stepping up. Doing the right thing. I didn't think about whether it was the right thing for me. Now all I can hear is her saying I could take my time."

Leon's jaw tightened at the mention of Della. For a moment his gaze drifted somewhere else, somewhere years back.

"Your mother," Leon said slowly, "believed in you more than anybody. She also knew you had a habit of running toward responsibility like it was a finish line."

Angelou leaned forward, forearms on his knees. "You were nineteen, Trev. You did what you thought a man was supposed to do."

"I hurt Zara," Trevor said quietly. "She's the one that pays for it."

Jackson shook his head locs flowing from side to side. "Zara has you. She sees you showing up every day. That's what she'll remember."

Leon reached across the table and gripped Trevor's shoulder. "Regret can either teach you or trap you. You don't get to rewrite the beginning. But you get to choose what this next chapter looks like."

Angelou lifted his glass again, softer this time. "This ain't the end of your story. It's the beginning of you being happy on purpose. If you want it."

Trevor let those words settle. Happy on purpose. The idea felt unfamiliar, almost indulgent. He had spent so many years trying to prove he was good enough that he had never stopped to ask if he was fulfilled.

Before he could respond, the crowd erupted again. The dancer he had noticed earlier finished her set in a split that drew another wave of applause. She rose slow, chin high, eyes scanning the room like she was selecting her next destination.

And then she looked straight at him.

Even from across the club he felt it, that deliberate focus. She hopped off the stage, heels clicking against the floor, hips swaying with unhurried confidence. The closer she got, the more striking she became. High cheekbones. Full lips glossed to perfection. Long legs that seemed engineered to command attention. Rhinestones traced the curve of her bodysuit, catching the light with every step.

"Sapphire," Angelou greeted, grin widening.

She slid into their section like she belonged there, because she did. Her perfume wrapped around them, sweet and intoxicating.

"Angelou Porter," she purred, running a manicured finger along his shoulder. "You been hiding from me."

"Been busy," he shot back easily. "But I had to bring my family to see the best in the city."

Her gaze shifted to Trevor, slow and assessing. "And who is this fine specimen looking at me like I'm the eighth wonder of the world."

"That," Angelou said, clapping Trevor on the back, "is my little brother. Just signed his divorce papers. He deserves a proper welcome back to the streets."

Sapphire's smile deepened, wicked and playful. She leaned closer to Trevor, close enough that he could see the flecks of gold in her brown eyes.

"Congratulations," she murmured. "You celebrating or you mourning?"

He swallowed. "Still deciding."

"Well," she said, straightening, "I specialize in helping men make up their minds."

Angelou laughed and pulled out his wallet. "Private dance. On me."

Sapphire's brows lifted in approval. "Paradise room's open."

She extended her hand toward Trevor. For a split second he hesitated, aware of his father sitting a few feet away, aware of the shift this represented. Then Angelou slipped two condoms into his palm, subtle but firm.

"Handle business," Angelou whispered.

Trevor stood, pulse thudding in his ears. Sapphire's fingers intertwined with his, her grip confident as she led him through a hallway bathed in purple light. The music softened as they moved away from the main floor, replaced by a slower rhythm that vibrated through the walls.

The private room was intimate, walls lined with black leather, a mirrored panel reflecting dim light back at them. A plush couch curved beneath a spotlight that cast everything in a sultry glow. The air felt warmer here, heavier.

Sapphire closed the door behind them and turned, eyes locking on his again. Up close she was magnetic, every movement intentional. She stepped into him slowly, palms sliding up his chest, testing the terrain. He could feel his body responding before his mind caught up, heat pooling low, breath turning shallow.

"Relax," she whispered, guiding him to sit.

She took a step back, giving him a full view of her. Then the music shifted and so did she. Her hips rolled in controlled circles, arms lifting above her head as she began to move with deliberate precision. She climbed onto his lap for a moment, just enough to let him feel the warmth of her body without granting more, then slid away again, leaving him reaching for air.

Every spin, every bend, every arch of her back was a study in control. She wasn't just dancing for him. She was studying him, watching the way his jaw clenched, the way his hands flexed against his thighs. She leaned down until her lips hovered near his ear.

"Tonight," she breathed, "you don't have to be anybody's husband. Anybody's son. Or anybody's father. Just be a man."

The words settled into him like a spark hitting dry wood.

Trevor exhaled slowly, eyes darkening as he reached for her waist, ready to stop watching and start feeling. Sapphire sat in his lap and started to grind against him.

"It's okay, Daddy. You can touch me. I want you to touch me." Her voice was the perfect mix of a whine and moan that shot straight to Trevor's dick. His hand tightened on her waist guiding her movements. A whimper fell from Sapphire's full lips. He felt her juices on his pants. Her smell permeated throughout the air. She smelled delectable. Her brown eyes locked with his and in that moment, they knew what this was. Before he lost his nerves and got back in his head, Trevor had his dick sheathed in the condom his brother was smart enough to give him and he was pushing into Sapphire's walls.

"Fuck, this pussy feels so good. Work that shit for me, ma." His rough voice commanded.

"You stretching me out so good, where the fuck have you been?!" She asked while bouncing in his lap.

"I was wasting time elsewhere, but I'm here now and I'm fucking you good. Keep working that shit." Trevor met Sapphire thrust for thrust. His thumb found her clit and began to rub in slow circles. If this wasn't a quick fuck, he would've definitely loved to have taken his time with her. The hand that was gripping her waist came up and wrapped around her throat. Her pussy gripped him tighter from the sensation. He could feel her start to flutter around him. He moved his thumb faster across her clit and gripped her neck tighter. Sapphire's hands gripped his legs as she continued to bounce on him.

Watching a woman come undone was a fixation for Trevor.

Seeing the ways she could use his body to bring her the ultimate pleasure also turned him on. In this moment, seeing Sapphire orgasming on him pushed him over the edge and he came harder than he had in a long time into that condom, which he had to thank Angelou for, because there was enough cum to definitely make another baby. Trevor gently lifted her off his lap. A lazy smile appeared on his face. He felt lighter already.

"Thank you, this was amazing." Trevor said while pulling the condom off and tying it up. He would flush it in the bathroom.

"Shit, I should be thanking you, baby face. That dick is gold. I wouldn't mind seeing you again." Sapphire replied, fixing her clothes. She was glad she was done for the night after this because she just came hard enough to go to sleep.

Trevor smiled in response, his dimples peeking out, "We'll see, if I'm back here, I'll definitely want to see you." He gave her a nod before leaving the room and heading to the bathroom to clean up. When he walked back to their section it was Angelou that noticed him first, a wide grin spread across his face.

"That man is walking lighter already." Angelou stated, capturing the attention of Jackson and Leon. Leon was getting a lap dance which threw Trevor all the way off.

"Angelou, did you get our father a lap dance?!" Trevor asked, sitting back down in his seat. Leon seemed to be having a great time putting $20s in the women's thong.

"Why is it my fault? That was actually Jackson." Trevor's eyebrows shot up in surprise. "Yeah, the prodigal son is out here buying lap dances for his Daddy." Angelou snickered before sobering.

"You good?" He looked pointedly at Trevor searching for any crack in his armor.

"Yeah," Trevor said, for once believing it, "I'm good."

"You sure?" Jackson questioned, his eyes knowing. Trevor could never hide from Jackson.

"Yes, Jac. That was the reset I needed."

"His ass is already coochie whipped and it's only been one night," Angelou laughed out while taking a sip of his drink. Leon snapped his head around.

"Son, just what were you doing back there with that young lady?"

Trevor answered, "You don't want to know." While Angelou answered, "Getting close to her on a spiritual level."

"Lou, shut the fuck up, you talk too much," Jackson barked trying to hold back his laughter.

"I raised a bunch of hoes. Wow. Thank you, young lady." Leon dismissed her with a kind smile. His face turned serious as he looked at his youngest son.

"Trevor, don't go starting something if you're not ready to handle it," Leon warned. Trevor finished off his whisky and looked at his father.

"Dad, I'm not starting something. I just needed something new. I have been, excuse my language, fucking the same woman since I was a teenager. It was time to feel some new walls. And wonderful they were. Neither one of us was looking for love, just release...and man, I got it." Angelou choked on his wing at Trevor's candidness. Why did the youngest always have the slickest mouth?

"Just because we are in a strip club doesn't mean you get to talk to me like you don't have any damn sense...I get it though. Glad you got your shit off. Now eat your wings." Leon gruffed back. "You deserve every bit of happiness that's coming your way, Bunny. When it comes, don't run." Trevor groaned at his dad calling him his childhood nickname because he used to love to hop everywhere and get on his mother's nerves.

"Yeah, *Bunny,* you deserve every win that's coming your way." Jackson said.

"Y'all annoy me so much, but I love you," Trevor gritted out.

He wouldn't admit it aloud, but tonight loosened a part of him he didn't know he needed. He would forever be grateful for his family and the love that surrounded him even if he was struggling with romantic love. Just as he finished that thought a flash of auburn hair and honey-colored eyes flashed in his mind.

Parent-teacher conferences came the third week of November right before fall break, right as the temperature dropped enough to make the air bite.

The school parking lot was full of bare trees and crunching leaves. The hallways smelled faintly of paste and pencil shavings. Construction paper turkeys decorated the doors, the kind where kids traced their hands for feathers. A bulletin board read *Thankful for Our Class Family* in crooked letters.

Trevor waited outside Room 107, hands shoved into his coat pockets. He could hear laughter inside, a soft, genuine sound that carried warmth even through the door.

Then it opened, and Aniyah stood there as a couple left hand in hand.

The light from the hallway caught in her hair, deep auburn curls that brushed her shoulders and framed her face. She wore a fitted turtleneck, slate gray, tucked into wide-leg trousers that looked effortless but intentional. A thin gold chain rested at her throat. Simple pearl studs. Calm poise in every movement.

"Mr. Porter," she said, smiling. "Come on in."

Her voice had a steadiness he hadn't realized he needed until he heard it.

He followed her inside. The classroom felt lived-in, walls lined with watercolor self-portraits, bookshelves packed with paperbacks and plants. The windows fogged faintly from the difference between the cold outside and the hum of warmth within.

They sat at the small table by the reading nook. She opened a folder with Zara's name written neatly across the top.

"First, the good news," she began. "Zara is kind. She helps her classmates without being asked. She's reading above grade level. She loves and excels at mathematics. She even volunteers to read during circle time, and the other kids listen when she does."

Trevor felt his shoulders ease, the tightness he'd been carrying softening a little. "That sounds like her," he said, voice low.

Aniyah smiled while her eyes lit up. "She's a joy to have here. Truly."

Then her tone gentled. "I have noticed she's quieter lately. More reserved than when school first started. She still participates, but she prefers the quiet corner more often and she's not as lively in class. It's not cause for alarm, but I wanted you to know I see it."

The words opened something in him. He hadn't realized how much he'd been waiting for someone else to notice, to confirm that it wasn't just in his head.

He exhaled, long and unsteady. "Her mom... left," he said finally. "She filed for divorce last month and—" he hesitated, looking for language that didn't hurt as much. "She decided she didn't want to be involved in Zara's life anymore. It's only been two weeks, but it feels like Zara is holding on by a thread and I hated having to tell her that mommy moved away and won't be coming back."

Aniyah's expression softened as she took in Trevor's stricken expression. She didn't interrupt. She didn't try to fill the silence with noise. She let it breathe until he could keep going. He knew he had word vomit at the moment ,but it was the way Aniyah looked at him with concern, not pity, that made him feel like it was safe to share.

He told her what he could, what had happened and why Zara was more reserved. He spilled the details about the hearing and Katelyn signing away her rights. He told her about Zara sleeping on the couch some nights because she was still hopeful for her mom to come home. About how Zara had started asking to stay home instead of going to her classmate's birthday party because she missed mommy. He didn't vilify Katelyn's choices because he didn't need to. The facts were heavy enough on their own and painted her in the cruelest light.

When he finally stopped talking, Aniyah reached for a glass of water and took a small sip. Grounding herself before speaking because rage overtook her and she wanted to be careful when speaking on a student's mother.

"I'm so angry for her," she said softly. "And...I'm proud of you."

He blinked. "Proud of me? For what?"

"For showing up and remaining Zara's foundation," she said simply. "For giving her steadiness when her entire world has tilted with Katelyn's sudden departure. For not making her your reason to break. You two have been together since we were kids, I can't imagine how that feels. Yet, you show up every day and not missing a beat when I know it's hard. That takes guts, Trev. Give yourself grace for breaking down."

Her words landed slow and deep. He felt something in his chest unclench.

Aniyah reached across the table and placed her hand over his. It wasn't dramatic, just warm, steady contact. Human contact, something he tried to act like he didn't need, but he craved. For all his bravado, Trevor was a teddy bear when it came to love, he loved to love on his woman...something he hadn't done in years. It's the reason he had been back to see Sapphire three more times since their first encounter. A habit he would need to break soon because they were both becoming attached to a routine that could not last. Feeling Aniyah's hand against him made him feel vulnerable. Tears that refused to fall pooled in his eyes.

"You're doing an excellent job, Trevor."

He closed his eyes for a moment, letting the words settle in the space that had been empty for weeks. When he looked up again, she was still watching him, not with pity, but with respect. Maybe even admiration.

"Thank you," he said quietly. His voice sounded different in the room, softer, truer. "You don't know how much I needed to hear that. I know we got off on the wrong foot all those years ago. But you're not so bad." That last remark made them both laugh.

"I was never bad. That was always you trying to be a smart ass just because you're fine." Aniyah said without thinking.

"Oh you think I'm fine?" Trevor's voice deepened at the weight of Aniyah's admission.

"I wasn't-"

"Nah, baby. It's too late now. You admitted it. For the record—you—Ms. Henderson, are fine as *hell.*"

"You were literally just lamenting about your divorce, now you're in here being fresh?"

"Duality. Two things can be true at the same time." Trevor's voice gave finality to the incoming excuses.

Their hands lingered longer than necessary, neither of them rushing to move. When they did finally pull back, it was with the same small, nervous smile that acknowledged what had passed between them without naming it.

Aniyah cleared her throat, opening the next folder. She was sure her face was red and the way Trevor's eyes watched every move she made? Her panties were good and finished.

"Here are some things I've been using to help her in class. A feelings chart, a sensory break schedule, and a fidget spinner for her to play with when she is feeling anxious."

He nodded, listening, grateful for the details that gave him something to hold onto.

"Would you like a copy for home?" she asked.

"Yes," he said. "That would be great."

They went over reading goals, math units, and the upcoming Thanksgiving showcase where Zara would perform a short poem about gratitude.

When the meeting ended, the hallway was nearly empty. The light outside had dimmed to that soft November gray that comes before evening. Trevor insisted on walking with Aniyah outside. Waiting on her by the door and watching her shut down her classroom felt natural. He didn't want to think about what that could mean.

Trevor hesitated by the door. "Do you have a ride?" he asked. "It's getting cold."

"I have my car," she said with a small smile. "I'll be fine."

He nodded, adjusting the strap on his bag. He should've left then, but something held him there.

"Aniyah," he said, his voice lower now.

She looked up.

"Thank you for seeing her," he said. "And for talking to me like... this."

"No need to thank me," she said, smiling gently. "It's part of my job to see her. And it's easy to talk to you." She let slip out before she could think about it.

He smiled, small but real. "That's good to know. I thought I might have scared you off."

"Absolutely not," she said, and the corner of her mouth lifted just enough to make the air between them shift.

He stepped into the hallway. She walked him to the door, her heels quiet against the linoleum. They stopped beneath the frame, the faint hum of a heater filling the silence.

"I'll walk you to the car." His voice was deep enough to send a shiver down Aniyah's spine. She absolutely would *not* think about what that meant.

"Let me find out Trevor Porter is a gentleman." Aniyah teased as they walked across the parking lot.

"I'm just being the man my parents raised me to be." When they got to her car Aniyah leaned back on her door facing Trevor.

"I wanted to say sorry...about your mom. She was a beautiful woman." Trevor nodded at the words he never got used to hearing. He stepped an inch closer to Aniyah without thinking. It was like a gravitational pull surrounding them without their knowledge.

"Thank you for that. I appreciate it." In that moment they stood there, rooted in place, eyes locked. Aniyah knew she needed to get her ass away from Trevor and out that parking lot. Trevor leaned in and wrapped his arms around Aniyah pulling her in for a warm hug. He felt her body tense and then almost instantly relaxed. Her arms wrapped around his waist and pulled him in closer. Something told Aniyah he needed this hug just like she did.

They stood embraced longer than what was considered normal. Aniyah had been touched deprived for so long this felt like a welcomed release so she burrowed her face deeper into Trevor's chest and released a deep breath. Trevor rested his cheek against the top of her hair, the scent of jasmine invading his nose.

"I needed this," His raspy tone admitted.

"Me too," Aniyah replied. Holding her felt spiritual and that scared the hell out of Trevor. The peace he felt suddenly evaporated and he was pulled back into the present. Slowly he let Aniyah go and backed away from her. Her face was flush, eyes bright. They looked at each other for a beat longer before she turned to open her door.

"Good night, Trevor," she said.

"Good night, Ms. Henderson." He closed her door once she

was situated inside and walked off ignoring how fast his heart was beating.

He made it all the way to the other side of the parking lot before he let himself breathe.

The cold hit first, sharp and clean. He glanced up, the sky was the color of steel, clouds heavy but not yet ready to break. His breath came out in small ghosts. For the first time in weeks, the cold didn't bother him.

Because somewhere between the quiet of that classroom where Aniyah made him feel seen and then the hug outside of her car where she made him feel cared for, there was a change in how he felt towards her. It wasn't a monumental feeling. Not yet. But it was a spark, a flicker in the ashes, that told him maybe the world could still feel warm, even in November. That was a feeling he was scared of diving into, because it was too soon.

He unlocked his car and sat for a while before starting the engine, letting the feeling linger. Inside, the heat built slowly, and outside, the leaves rustled like applause in the wind. He was grateful that his dad was cooking dinner at home with Zara so he could sit in this moment and revel in how perfect Aniyah felt in his arms.

For the first time since everything fell apart, he didn't feel broken. Just open and that felt like an answered prayer.

CHAPTER SIX

THE WAY YOU LOOK AT ME

"I'm so glad you're here. I need you. I really need you." - *Ma Bell, I'm Gonna Git You Sucka (1988)*

The car door closed with a quiet finality that felt louder than it should have.

Aniyah sat inside her car longer than necessary, her fingers still curved around the staring wheel. Trevor's footsteps moved away across the asphalt, measured and steady. He did not rush. He did not look back. He carried himself like a man who had learned how to survive in public.

She could still feel him.

The imprint of his arms around her waist. The weight of his cheek resting against the crown of her head. The moment his body softened against hers like he had finally allowed himself to exhale.

It hadn't been flirtation.

It hadn't been casual.

It *had* been something deeper and more dangerous because it was honest.

Aniyah forced her body to move. The quiet inside the car pressed in close. She stared through the windshield at the dim parking lot, the skeletal trees stretching upward against a bruised November sky.

Her pulse had not slowed.

When he wrapped his arms around her, she felt two things at once. His need. And her own.

That unsettled her.

She did not blur lines. She did not misread trauma for intimacy. She did not cross boundaries she set for herself.

But the way he held her had not felt like crossing.

It had felt like he was grounding her in the moment. For once she didn't feel lost in her body the echo of her loneliness surrounding her. She was present, warm and safe.

She started the engine. The heater breathed to life, warm air sliding across her knuckles. As she pulled out of the lot, she caught a glimpse of him in her rearview mirror, standing beside his car with his head tilted slightly toward the sky.

The image followed her home.

The sky was dark when she reached her condo. She let herself inside and dropped her keys on the entry table without turning on the overhead lights. The glow from the city and the moon was enough.

She crossed the living room and stopped at the window.

There was something about the ocean in winter. It was restless but calming in the same breath which is why she often stood at her windows for hours.

She leaned her forehead against the glass. His voice echoed in her mind.

Thank you for seeing her.

He had meant Zara.

But she knew he had meant himself too. Aniyah closed her eyes. She had spent years building a life that felt intentional. A career she chose. A home she filled with warmth. A quiet that belonged to her. She did not let men walk into that space without clarity. She did not let loneliness dress itself up as connection. And yet...

When he held her, it felt like recognition.

Not of who they were in high school. Not of some teenage love that never happened. It felt like two adults meeting in the wreckage of separate storms and realizing neither of them was pretending anymore. She exhaled slowly and walked to the kitchen. Poured a glass of water she did not drink. Instead, she opened her notebook because the words were waiting.

At the top of the page she wrote:

What I'm Not

She stared at the line until the ocean filled the silence.

What I'm not is
a harbor for borrowed grief
that forgets its own.

Her pen paused.

What I'm not is
afraid of warmth in winter
if it is earned slowly.

She closed the notebook and pressed her palm against the cover. This had to be slow. It had to be.

Saturday night, Mya and Stephanie saw it on her face before she even sat down.

They had been friends since they were five years old. They knew her tells the way other people knew their own handwriting.

Mya was first through the door, tall and caramel-skinned with long faux locs gathered high, her posture relaxed but observant. She wore a tailored camel coat and boots that clicked softly against the floor. Her eyes held humor and assessment in equal measure.

Stephanie followed, deep brown skin glowing under the restaurant's low light, her natural curls shaped perfectly around her cheekbones. Her leather jacket fit like it was made for her, and her gold hoops caught every flicker of candlelight when she turned her head.

They slid into the booth across from Aniyah like they had always done, claiming space without asking.

Mya didn't even wait for the server to walk away before she tilted her head and really looked at Aniyah.

"You're quiet in a different way tonight," she said, not accusing, just observant. "Something is definitely spinning wheels in that head of yours."

Aniyah tried to laugh it off. "I'm always quiet."

Stephanie snorted softly. "Not with that constipated look on your face. You aren't fooling anyone. So spill."

Aniyah glanced between them looking at her expectantly. "Y'all are dramatic."

Mya leaned back, folding her arms loosely. "We went to kindergarten together. I know your faces. That one right there says something got through the armor and shook you up. You've been thinking about it for a while now. Spill."

Silence stretched just long enough to make it honest.

Aniyah reached for her water. "Parent teacher conferences were this week."

"Uh-huh," Stephanie said gently. "And Trevor Porter walked into your classroom." There was no teasing in her voice now. She knew the look Aniyah had now, it was the same one she had freshman year of high school when Trevor showed up from summer break looking like a heart throb. The girl was gone for him then and she was gone for him now.

Aniyah exhaled slowly. "Yes."

Mya's expression softened instead of sharpening. "How is he, for real? You know I'm mutuals with Katelyn and I saw her posting about being on a yacht with The Terminator."

Aniyah took her time answering. "He looks like someone who hasn't had space to fall apart. He's holding it together because he has to for Zara, but you can clearly see he is going through it as well."

Stephanie nodded once. "After putting up with that crazy ass bitch for years? That tracks."

"He told me what happened between them," Aniyah continued, voice lower now. "Katelyn terminated her parental rights to their daughter. Can you believe that? Zara is such an amazing little girl, she doesn't deserve that woman as a mother."

Mya's jaw tightened. "That woman is—" She stopped herself and shook her head. "You're right, Zara doesn't deserve that."

"No," Aniyah said quietly. "She doesn't."

Stephanie watched her carefully. "What did you do when he spilled the beans about it?"

Aniyah's fingers traced the edge of her glass. "I mostly listened. I told him he was doing a good job. When the meeting was over..." She hesitated in responding because she still couldn't name what happened between them.

"Something happened between you two, didn't it," Mya questioned softly.

Aniyah nodded. "He walked me to my car and for a moment, we just stared at each other. Then he pulled me in for a hug and it felt...It was what I needed. It was what *he* needed."

Stephanie's eyes sparked at the glow she saw in Aniyah's face. A smirk graced her lips. "Did you pull away?"

"No," Aniyah admitted. "I thought I would. I didn't."

"And how did it feel?"

Aniyah swallowed, "Like it was everything we needed in that moment and when he pulled away, I missed him. That is fucking crazy! This man is just that, a man. But it felt–."

Mya's voice shifted into something protective, "Aniyah, that's the kind of moment that can mean everything or nothing. The difference is timing."

"I know."

"He's fresh out of something," Stephanie added. "And you don't do casual. You don't dip your toe in water you know you'll drown in. Please be careful with this. I don't want you to lose yourself trying to save his broken heart."

Aniyah leaned back slowly. "That's what scares me. This scares me."

Mya reached across the table and squeezed her hand. "Are you scared of him? Or of how much you feel?"

Aniyah didn't answer right away. Then quietly responded, "Both. And I know it doesn't make sense, after one conversation I shouldn't feel shit. But I do. And I know it's a moot point because he has a lot going on. It's a shame too, because he got a haircut and his face is the perfect seat." She whines.

"Aniyah! Put your pussy on ice!" Mya responds laughing.

"What? I'm being honest. You know I have a thing for the artsy guys."

"That family is full of artsy men," Stephanie replied, smirking.

"Remember Sergio? The drummer?" Aniyah asked, mentioning her ex from four years ago.

"The one that had the hole in his sock so we called him Zero?" Mya replied all the girls burst out laughing that made a few patrons turn their heads, but they didn't care. That was the beauty of sisterhood.

Mya studied her again, "So, what are you going to do?"

Aniyah met her eyes. "Nothing," she said honestly. "He needs time. And I need to make sure what I feel isn't just because of proximity and loneliness."

Stephanie smiled faintly, "You already know it's not."

Aniyah did not respond.

Because she did, but at this moment there was nothing she could do about it. Aniyah would continue her days as she did before Trevor and Zara Porter walked into her life—alone.

Thanksgiving break arrived wrapped in quiet.

Her friends invited her to their family homes. She declined gently. This season she wasn't up for visiting someone else's traditions. She wanted the ocean. She wanted stillness. She wanted to sit with herself and not perform joy for anyone else.

She cooked alone and set the table anyway. She had fixed Cornish hens, collard greens, mac and cheese and dressing. All the recipes she learned from her Papa. It was her way of feeling close to him without grief overcoming her. Once her dinner was done, she placed a small plate by the window.

"Happy Thanksgiving," she whispered softly into the empty condo.

The memory of her grandfather helping her cook dinner at his place five years ago played in her memory like a movie. The way he asked questions that required honesty. The way he never let her shrink. She always regretted not having more time with him. She should've had more time. The rest of her dinner went quietly as she tried to drown her sorrow like the ocean in front of her. Thankfully the urge to nap after she stuffed herself took over and her slumber was filled with peaceful memories.

Her phone rang mid-afternoon, waking her up. Checking her phone Aniyah saw that it was her mother. Her stomach began to knot because she knew this conversation wouldn't be a good one. Her first thought was to ignore it. She should have. Despite those feelings, she answered.

"Hello."

A small pause on the other end, like her mother was choosing her tone. "Happy Thanksgiving," her mother said.

"Happy Thanksgiving." Another pause, longer this time.

"Are you... at work," her mother asked, ignoring the fact that Aniyah was a teacher and she would be off on the holidays

"No. I'm home."

"With friends," her mother questioned, already trying to decipher how she was spending her day.

Aniyah looked toward the window, the ocean dark and steady beyond the glass. "No. It's just me today."

Her mother exhaled, quiet but pointed.

"Aniyah." If Aniyah didn't know any better she would think her mother cared, but Aniyah knew better. The way she said it wasn't with care. It wasn't her name. It was a warning.

"I'm fine," Aniyah said, keeping her voice even.

"You could have come here," her mother replied. "Your father asked about you this morning."

Aniyah didn't answer right away. Her father asking about her didn't always mean he wanted her in his presence, most of the time it was to see if she was still on her wayward path. Sometimes him asking about her just meant he wanted the idea of her nearby, behaving and following the rules he set out for her. She hadn't talked to her father since the day they read her grandfather's will. She remembered him storming out pissed that he didn't get a dime of the money his father had left. If it were up to Aniyah, she wouldn't talk to him for the rest of her days on this earth. Still her mother called periodically to check in on her. The conversations were usually cold and quick.

"I just wanted a quiet peaceful day," Aniyah said.

Her mother's voice softened in a way that never lasted. "Quiet is not the same as peace."

Aniyah's fingers tightened around the phone. "I have peace, actually. I worked hard for it."

There was a beat of silence before her mother responded.

"And you still teach," her mother said, like the word tasted strange. Who knew training the youth would cause such disgust with her parents.

Aniyah closed her eyes briefly. "Yes."

"I don't understand why you insist on making things harder than they need to be," her mother continued. "You were always smart. You had options. You could have had a life with security."

Aniyah sat up from where she was lounging on the couch prepared for the verbal sparring she was about to do with her mother. She should be used to this now, but every time she left the conversation with a broken heart.

"I have security, I love what I do. I have always loved teaching. I don't know why you can't get it through your head. I have a good life. My career is fulfilling and I didn't have to compromise to get it."

Her mother gave a small sound, somewhere between disbelief and irritation. "You live alone in a condo by the water and write little poems on the side like that's a plan. That sounds like a fulfilling life to you? I have news, little girl, you're not living."

Aniyah's throat tightened, but her voice stayed low and steady. "My poems are not little, they are an outlet. You do not have to be disrespectful just because you don't understand it. And teaching is a plan. I'm a good teacher. My students are safe with me. I'm not lost, Mom."

"Your students," her mother repeated in a tone that sounded irritated. Her cadence when she said "students" sounded more like she was talking about stray pets than actual children.

Aniyah looked down at her own hands, fingers twisting between each other as her anxiety spiked. "I'm not doing this today."

Her mother ignored that boundary the way she always had. "You're getting older. Time is moving. I don't want you waking up one day realizing you chose... this. And lost out on what could have been."

Aniyah's chest rose slowly, then fell. Looking outside her window, she wished her relationship with her mother flowed carefree like the ocean. She wished she was protected by the woman who gave her life but knew that would never be the case.

"You mean realizing I chose myself, like I've been doing," Aniyah said quietly.

Her mother's voice sharpened, because when she couldn't control Aniyah, she tried to cut her.

"You always want to make it sound noble. But it's stubbornness. You could have had respect."

Aniyah's grip on the phone loosened. Something in her settled, not because it didn't hurt, but because she recognized the pattern.

"I have respect," Aniyah said, voice steady. "Just not the kind you approve of."

Her mother scoffed softly. "This is exactly what your grandfather filled your head with."

Aniyah's stomach dropped, the way it always did when her mother used him like a weapon.

"Don't. Don't you dare bring my grandfather into this. He was the best thing that ever happened to me," Aniyah said, the word quiet but firm.

"He turned you against us," her mother continued, anger slipping through the cracks. "He made you think you could live without this family. Now look at you! Alone with nothing to show for it."

Aniyah's eyes burned, but she didn't let her mother hear it in her voice. "He gave me somewhere to go when you told me to leave. Don't come on here spewing nonsense that you know is not true!"

Her mother inhaled sharply. She wasn't expecting Aniyah to say it out loud.

"That was years ago, we are past that," her mother said.

Aniyah stared at the water. "And I still remember it like it happened yesterday."

The line went quiet. Aniyah knew her mother was contemplating her words. She wished that her mom would truly understand where she was coming from but Aniyah wasn't dumb. She knew that nothing she was saying would be heard for understanding. When her mother spoke again, her tone was different. Softer, but not kinder.

"I called to see if you were okay."

Aniyah swallowed. "I'm okay."

"And are you... seeing anyone," her mother asked, like that would redeem everything.

Aniyah's mind flickered, just once, to Trevor's arms around her. To warmth. To restraint. To the line she wasn't crossing. She wouldn't give her mother that, they didn't have the type of bond where she would feel comfortable talking about her conflicted feelings.

"No," Aniyah said. "I'm not."

Her mother sighed disappointed, "Aniyah. You can't keep choosing solitude and calling it strength."

Aniyah's voice stayed gentle, because she refused to fight today. "And you can't keep calling my life a mistake because it doesn't look like yours. I have to go, Patrica."

Her mother went quiet again. Aniyah let the silence sit. Let it do what silence does when there's truth inside it.

"You always were difficult," her mother replied.

Aniyah's voice stayed even. "It's funny, for a woman whose whole life is funded by her husband, you sure do have a lot to say about mine."

The call ended without warmth. It was a long while before Aniyah was able to bury the torment in her heart. She stood by the window for a long moment after regulating herself. Then she returned to her notebook.

What I'm not is
the daughter who bends her spine
to be loved.

December entered the school in a rush of construction paper poinsettias and forced cheer. Aniyah stood outside Room 107 with her clipboard and the look of someone who had agreed to something slightly bigger than her capacity. Because she had. She observed all the parents dropping off their kids. She tried hard not to focus on one family in particular, but no matter what, her eyes traveled to them.

Trevor was crouched to unzip Zara's coat. Once he was done, he stood up to hang it in her cubby. Aniyah had to stop biting her lip in response to how good he looked. The hair cut gave him a more mature look that made his face even more lethal. They had not had a moment alone since the parent-teacher conference and Aniyah wanted to keep it that way. The further Trevor was away from her the better for her sense and libido.

"Morning," he said once Zara ran off to get her morning worksheet and sit down in her assigned seat.

"Morning," Aniyah replied, choosing to keep the interaction light, "We are officially a theater company now. I've been voluntold to direct the Christmas program."

Why did she even offer him that information?! It was the way Trevor always seemed to put all of his attention on her when she was talking. He always looked deep into her eyes, throwing her off game.

He smiled and those damn dimples made themselves known, "Congratulations."

"That is one word for it," Aniyah snorted in response. "It's going to be the retelling and age appropriate version of A Christmas Story. Being that I only have two weeks to pull this off, don't expect an Oscar worthy production. Coach Riley had been in charge of it every year prior to this one, but since he is out on leave it fell through the cracks. Now, it's my problem."

"Oh yeah?" Trevor responded, his interest peaked. "Is Zara going to be in it?"

"Of course, she is the ghost of Christmas past. The biggest part is getting production down. Thankfully we have the previous year's costumes." Trevor could see that Aniyah was overwhelmed. He wanted to ease that worry by pulling her into his arms again, but this was not the time and definitely not the place. Instead, he offered up his services.

"I can help you, you know telling stories is my thing," Trevor offered. Aniyah playfully rolled her eyes at this humbleness like he isn't an award-winning director. "I have afternoons free," he said. "My current production pauses after today for the Christmas holiday. If you need lighting, anything technical or just someone to roast these kids with, I'm your guy."

Aniyah laughed in response. She would definitely roast these kids with Trevor. Their eyes locked again as the bell rang signaling the start of the school day. Aniyah felt the electricity crawl up her spine by being this close to him again. He wasn't at an inappropriate distance but she could feel the heat from his body.

"I will take all the help I can get. We start rehearsals this afternoon at 4pm. Zara can stay with me until that time if that works for you?"

"Yes. I can be here by 3:50. Anything you need just let me know." Trevor stood a beat longer than necessary breathing in Aniyah's scent and committing it to memory before backing away to head out the school.

"Thank you, I will see you then." Aniyah promptly turned and went into her classroom, she could not be pulled into Trevor's orbit again no matter how fine and vulnerable he was.

"Everyone have their morning worksheets?" She asked the

class. A chorus of "yes, Ms. Henderson!" filled the room. Time to get the day started.

It was no surprise that Zara was excited to stay with Aniyah once school let out. She had been bouncing off the walls since Aniyah told her she would be staying behind until Trevor came to rehearsals later that evening. They were currently resetting the classroom for the next day. Zara moved with a burst of determination that made Aniyah smile as she watched her line up pencils with careful precision.

"Look, I did it straight," Zara said, stepping back to admire her work.

"You did," Aniyah replied, adjusting a stack of books on her desk before glancing over again. "Better than me."

Zara beamed, shoulders lifting with pride as she moved to the next task without being asked. Aniyah let her, appreciating the way she took to responsibility for completing the task list to straighten up the classroom.

Once the room was set, Aniyah guided them toward the reading corner, where soft pillows had been stacked into something more comfortable than functional. The late afternoon sun stretched through the windows, warming the small space as she settled onto the rug beside Zara, passing her a bowl of fruit and a cup of ice cream she'd ordered earlier through FoodDash.

"I got strawberry," Zara said, already digging in.

"I can see that," Aniyah murmured, opening her own cup, watching the way Zara relaxed into the moment, legs stretched out, the class teddy bear tucked at her side.

Zara glanced around after a few bites, eyes narrowing with curiosity, "Do you live here?"

Aniyah laughed softly, the sound slipping out before she could stop it, "No, baby. I have my own place."

"Where?"

"Out by the ocean."

Zara's face lit up immediately, "I love the ocean. My daddy takes me sometimes." She paused, spoon hovering midair. "I wish he'd take me more."

Aniyah smiled, leaning back against the pillows, "You know what? I think that's a fair request. I'll help you with that. We'll make sure he hears it."

Zara giggled, the sound bright and easy, but it faded just as quickly as it came. Her gaze dropped to her lap, fingers tightening slightly around her spoon.

"The last time we went," she said, quieter now, "my mommy was there too. But she didn't wanna be there. She wasn't as happy as Daddy and I were."

Aniyah felt the shift immediately, the way the air settled heavier around them. She set her cup aside, turning fully toward Zara.

"I'm so sorry to hear that, baby."

Zara shrugged, trying to carry it lightly. Aniyah saw her eyes glisten and that made her want to protect the little girl more than anything, "It's okay. Mommy should be happy now. She went to what makes her happy." She hesitated, then added, softer, "Daddy says it's not my fault, but sometimes it feels like it is. Like... if I didn't make her mad when I asked her to spend time with me, she'd still be around."

Aniyah reached for her without thinking, her hand closing gently around Zara's smaller one, grounding her before the thought could settle too deep.

"Zara," she said, her voice steady but warm, waiting until the little girl looked up at her, "listen to me, baby."

Zara's eyes met hers, wide and uncertain.

"I had a mommy that didn't want to be around me either," Aniyah continued, her thumb brushing lightly over Zara's knuckles. "You know what I found out?"

Zara shook her head.

"It's not you, baby. It's them. Mommy has to heal a boo-boo inside her heart on her own. That's something only she can do." Aniyah held her gaze, making sure every word landed where it needed to. "It's not your fault. It's not your daddy's fault either."

Zara's fingers loosened in her grasp, her shoulders dropping just a little.

"I know your daddy loves you more than anything," Aniyah added, a small smile touching her lips. "I know you're a rock star. Doesn't he call you his Superstar?"

Zara's expression shifted, a hint of her earlier brightness returning, "Yes, he does!"

"I believe that too," Aniyah said softly. "Fully."

Zara nodded, settling into that reassurance, and after a moment, her attention drifted, landing on Aniyah's hands resting between them.

"Miss Aniyah," she said, tilting her head slightly, "Your nails are really pretty."

Aniyah glanced down at her French manicure, the subtle design on her ring finger catching the light. "They are?"

"Yes!"

Aniyah smiled, something lighter weaving back into the moment, "Well, thank you. You know what? I could take you to get a manicure one day. Would you like that?"

Zara's eyes widened instantly, "Yes, I would."

Aniyah laughed softly, "We'd have to ask your dad first."

Zara nodded quickly, "We do have to ask Daddy."

"Of course we do," Aniyah said, her tone warm as she reached for her ice cream again. "But if he says yes, we'll make a whole day out of it."

Zara grinned, already imagining it, and the space between them settled into something easy again. Aniyah was glad she could bring happiness to the little girl who seemed to be carrying the wait of the world on her shoulders because of Katelyn's choices.

For the rest of the time they were together, Zara and Aniyah read, told funny stories and even napped. She was sure Trevor knew it, but he had an Angel for a little girl.

The first full rehearsal for *A Christmas Story* felt like controlled chaos wrapped in tinsel.

PTA parents lined the back of the gym with coffee cups and folded programs, offering suggestions in low voices while pretending they were not offering suggestions. Children zigzagged across the stage with oversized scripts, their excitement louder than the squeak of folding chairs scraping the floor. Someone tested the sound system twice. Someone else asked where the leg lamp prop had gone.

Aniyah moved through it all with quiet authority, clipboard in hand, issuing direction with the kind of calm that disguised the storm under it. She had agreed to something bigger than her comfort, and she would see it through.

Trevor kept himself just off her shoulder, attentive without crowding her. He adjusted light angles and rewired a loose extension cord without being asked. He deferred to her decisions in front of the parents, letting it be clear that this was her production. Her mind kept drifting to earlier.

He had woken them up from their nap when he came back to the school from work. Aniyah let him know the time spent with Zara was wonderful and she'd be happy to do it again any time he needed.

The look that crossed his face was grateful and lascivious. Desire struck like hot coal in her center. This was not what she wanted. So, she kept her distance.

It should have been simple collaboration. It was not simple.

Every time he crossed the gym floor toward her, something in her awareness shifted before she could control it. She felt him before she saw him. She had told herself this would remain professional. She had meant it.

Halfway through blocking the opening scene, a PTA mother approached Aniyah with mild urgency.

"The old Marley chains are still in the back closet," the woman said. "They are on the top rack. I tried to get them but I couldn't reach them. You're a few inches taller than me, could you get them?"

Aniyah nodded. "I'll grab them."

Trevor's head lifted at once. "I'll come with you," he said. The decision had already been made before Aniyah could object.

She could have declined. She should have declined.

Instead, she simply said, "All right," and walked toward the side storage closet near the stage.

The door closed behind them with a soft click that sounded louder than it should have.

The closet was narrow and warmer than the gym, the air carrying the scent of fabric and cardboard and years of forgotten productions. One dim bulb cast everything in a muted amber glow. Racks of costumes crowded the walls. Plastic crowns hung beside velvet cloaks. A pair of angel wings leaned crooked against a box labeled 2019.

Aniyah stepped toward the back rack and looked up. The chains were coiled high on the top bar, just beyond reach.

She rose onto her toes, fingers stretching toward the metal.

Her sweater shifted at her waist. The rack scraped faintly under her weight.

"Let me," Trevor said softly from behind her.

Before she could move away, he stepped closer. His chest aligned with her back as his arm lifted past her shoulder. His presence filled the narrow space in a way that stole the air from her lungs. He reached easily for the chains and brought them down, the metal clinking lightly in his hand. But neither of them stepped away. The chains hung loosely at his side.

Her body was acutely aware of him. The steady rise of his chest against her back. The warmth through layers of fabric. The quiet strength in the way he held himself. The smell of his cologne surrounding her.

Why did he have to smell so damned good?

The silence did not feel accidental.

It felt suspended. He spoke without shifting away.

"I need to say something," he murmured, his voice low enough that it settled along her spine instead of ringing in the air. She did not turn yet. She could not trust her balance or her heart.

"I've been thinking about that night in the parking lot," he continued. "About how you felt in my arms. I walked back to my car and sat there longer than I meant to because for the first time since everything fell apart, my mind went quiet."

Aniyah's breath caught at his confession. Trevor was not dramatic when he said it. He was not fishing for reassurance or empty promises. He needed to free himself of the torment his memory was doing to him with its constant replay of that moment.

"It scared me," he added after a beat. "Not because it was wrong. Because it felt steady and I haven't felt that in a really long time."

Slowly, Aniyah turned within the small space.

The movement forced him to step back only slightly, but there was nowhere real to go. The shelves pressed behind her.

She looked up at him searching his eyes for a hint of dishonesty but found none. They were clear, searching and vulnerable in a way that made her chest tighten.

"You're still healing," she said, her voice quiet but anchored. "You just signed your divorce papers not too long ago from a woman you've been with since we were sixteen. Your daughter is in my classroom. I don't cross the line with my student's parents. And I won't blur them just because it feels good in a moment."

"I know that," he said. "I respect it. I respect you. I'm not asking you to ignore any of that."

"Then what are you asking?" she asked gently. Trevor inhaled slowly, choosing his words.

"I'm asking you to believe that what I felt wasn't desperation. It wasn't me reaching for the nearest warm body because I'm lonely. It was something that felt... grounded. I was finally back in my body, not suspended between time trying to figure out what the hell I was doing." The vulnerability in his voice made her throat tighten.

"This is complicated," she whispered.

"It is," he agreed. "I have work to do. I'm not pretending I don't. I'm not in a place where I can promise anyone anything beyond honesty. I just can't stand here and act like I don't feel this, like I don't feel you." Aniyah knew this was the moment she needed to walk out that closet and away from this man.

Neither of them moved.

The air between them felt charged. She searched his face, looking for recklessness. She didn't find it.

"You don't get involved with parents," he said quietly, reminding himself as much as her.

"No," she replied. "I don't."

"And I don't want to lean on you while I'm still learning how to stand on my own," he added. "I also don't want to walk away from something real just because it doesn't make sense on paper." Her pulse thudded against her ribs at his confession.

"You are asking for a lot," she said. "How do you even know it's something real here and not just two people who are tired of being lonely? We haven't had much interaction since high school and then you show up here all jaded and fine. I'm supposed to believe you're serious?"

"I am," he answered. "I would never rush you into anything. I know what I felt when we were alone together and I know what I'm feeling now. I won't pressure you." The chains slipped from his hand and clinked softly against the rack, forgotten.

The distance between them was barely inches now.

He did not grab her although his hands were itching to do so. He did not corner her. He simply stood there, close enough that she could feel his warmth, waiting for her to decide whether the space would close. Aniyah's fingers rose almost without permission and rested lightly against the center of his chest, his heartbeat firm beneath her palm.

"You make this hard," she murmured.

A faint smile touched his mouth, not playful but knowing, "You make it worth thinking about."

Something in her chest gave way. The lean happened slowly. So slowly it almost felt inevitable. Their foreheads brushed first. Breath mingled. He paused there, giving her one last chance to pull back...She did not. Their lips met softly. The first kiss was gentle, almost reverent, like they were confirming that this was real and not imagined. When she didn't retreat, his hand found her waist carefully, fingers resting there as though asking permission even in contact. She answered by drawing him closer. Their lips touched lightly and Aniyah felt the electricity shoot up her spin.

Why are his lips this damn soft? She thought to herself as she got lost in the feel and taste of Trevor.

The kiss deepened gradually, unhurried but unmistakably hungry. It was filled with weeks of tension. Days of replaying one another in quiet spaces.

Her hand slid into the back of his head, pulling him closer. His breath shifted, breaking against her mouth before he steadied himself and kissed her again with more certainty feeding her his tongue which she eagerly responded by giving him her own. A moan escaped her lips as the kiss deepened. .

The shelving pressed lightly against her back. His thumb traced a slow arc against her waist as though memorizing the shape of her. The world outside the closet dissolved. The hum of the gym. The scrape of chairs. The murmur of PTA parents. It felt suspended. Out of body. Like something that had been building long before either of them admitted it.

When they finally pulled apart for air, neither of them stepped away immediately. Their foreheads still rested together.

"This is reckless," she whispered, though her fingers had not left his sweater.

"Only if we pretend it isn't happening," he replied softly before going back in for another quick kiss. Before it had a chance to deepen a voice cut through the door.

"Ms. Henderson? We need the chains."

Reality returned to Aniyah like a bucket of ice water was thrown on her. They separated quickly, though not clumsily. She picked up the chains. He ran a hand over his fade and stepped back, putting distance between them that had not existed seconds before. When they stepped out into the gym, the lights felt brighter.

Aniyah resumed her role without faltering, directing children and cueing lines with the same composed authority as before like she wasn't just wrapped around that man like a snack moments prior. She worked hard the rest of the rehearsal to not look at him.

Trevor for his part, gave Aniyah space. He did not hover. He did not look for her eyes every few seconds. He understood that whatever had just happened required air because he too was shook by that brief encounter. When he went to the closet with Aniyah, kissing her was not a part of the plan. He just wanted to check on her and make sure she wasn't overwhelmed. Yet...now all that he could think about was her lips on his. But he knew this couldn't be rushed.

During a break, Zara drifted toward Aniyah and leaned against her side while practicing her lines under her breath. Aniyah bent slightly to listen, her hand resting lightly at Zara's shoulder as she offered a quiet note of encouragement. Trevor watched them from across the gym, a feeling of calmness washed over him seeing his little girl be her once animated self. She had been a recluse since her mom's departure. So much so that Trevor was starting her in therapy soon. Watching them now brought joy to his heart.

He knew he was not ready to build something new at full speed. He knew his heart was still tender in places he had not yet examined. But he also knew that what had happened in that closet was not a distraction. It was the beginning. And this time, he would take his time. Their eyes met once more across the gym floor. The spark was still there, waiting to burn bright.

Aniyah for her part tried her hardest to act as if she hadn't just been lip locking with Trevor Porter while on the clock... not even thirty feet away from the kids?! She may have had a crush on him back in the day, but she couldn't let puppy love cloud her judgement. Was the kiss everything she wanted and more? Yes, but it couldn't let happen again. If it did, she would just be setting herself up for heartbreak. She couldn't bear anymore than what she's already endured. From this moment forth, Trevor Porter is just an associate. No more getting to know him as an adult and definitely no more kissing.

CHAPTER SEVEN

THE SPACE BETWEEN US

"Even you, can pull a serious fine honey out of here. All you gotta do is remember one golden rule, which is, the man with the gold —rules" - *Hustler, Strictly Business (1991)*

"Fuck," Trevor moaned out as he came. This was the relief he needed after the last couple of days.

The sheets were still tangled around their legs when the ceiling fan began its slow rotation again, stirring the warmth that lingered in the room. The air carried the scent of vanilla from the candle on the nightstand and the faint trace of sweat cooling against skin that had only moments ago been pressed together without restraint.

Trevor lay flat on his back, one arm folded beneath his head, the other resting loosely at his side. His chest rose and fell in steady rhythm, but his mind had already begun its quiet retreat. Sapphire shifted beside him, her thigh draped over his hip, her fingers moving lazily across the center of his chest as though tracing the outline of a thought she could not quite name.

Their breathing had not yet returned to normal, yet the intensity that had filled the room minutes earlier was already dissolving into something softer. It was not awkward, but the shift in the air was less desirable. This was the space they always reached after the heat subsided, when bodies settled and reality crept back in.

Sapphire propped herself up on one elbow and studied him with an expression that held neither accusation nor insecurity. She had always been perceptive in that way. She did not demand more than what was offered, but she noticed when something shifted.

"You drift fast," she said quietly, her voice still husky from exertion.

He turned his head toward her, blinking once being pulled back into the room from his thoughts. "What you mean?"

She traced a slow line down his sternum with the tip of her nail, thoughtful rather than flirtatious. "You're here until you're not. It's like a switch flips. Post nut clarity? It's almost always instantaneous."

Trevor let out a low breath and stared up at the ceiling. The fan blades moved in patient circles above them, steady and indifferent.

"I don't mean to," he said after a moment. "I have a lot on my mind, and I can only shut it out for so long."

"I know," she replied gently. "That's why I'm saying something." Silence stretched between them. Trevor didn't know what to say to appease Sapphire, hell, he didn't even know her real name. There wasn't a reason to. But he knew the more they met, the more serious things would become and he would end up on the "ain't shit nigga" list if he continued and that was not the man he was.

He had come here tonight with intention to clear his mind of the person who had been ruling his thoughts as of late because he knew she was actively avoiding him. Aniyah had not lingered at drop-off all week. Every morning he had found her occupied with something just important enough to avoid standing close to him. She had become careful in their interactions with one another. There were no more lingering looks or gentle touches. When he walked in the room she made sure she was on the other side. He respected her need to protect herself. Trevor was the first to admit he was not in the headspace to start a relationship or even date someone. Though, with all of that realized, Aniyah avoiding him still unsettled him.

Sapphire rolled onto her back and folded her hands over her stomach, staring at the same ceiling he was studying.

"You don't look satisfied," she said quietly, "For a man that just got his nut off, you look like the world is on your shoulders. You know I'm here to talk if you need a shoulder."

Trevor turned his head toward her again, "I'm okay there is nothing I need to talk about. I'm good."

She smiled faintly at the defensiveness in his tone, "It doesn't look like that from where I'm lying. Whatever you say, Trevor." Sapphire rolled her eyes and looked back at the ceiling. The honesty of what he said landed somewhere deeper than he expected. At that moment, Trevor knew he needed to end things.

He sat up slowly, swinging his legs over the edge of the bed. The sheet slipped from his waist and pooled at his hips. He dragged his hands down his face, grounding himself before speaking.

"I don't want to keep coming here if I'm not fully present," he said at last. "It's not fair to you and I don't want to hurt you, unintentionally or otherwise."

Sapphire did not move right away. She let the words sit in the room before responding.

"That's rich," she scoffed. "What? You found your self-respect? It's not that deep, baby. I'm not some damsel in distress. You don't want to get your dick wet here anymore, cool. Move on to the next bitch."

He nodded once. "It doesn't even have to be all of that, Saph. This was a good time. I needed something new in my life and you were perfect. I just realize that where this started is not where it currently is. The water is getting murky."

"Murky? The fuck do you think this is? For the love of Trevor? Clearly you have been out the game a while, but here is free game, homeboy. Just because I let you hit doesn't mean I want to be your wife. It was fun. I saw something was on your mind, I asked if you wanted to talk. Anywhere in there did I say I wanted to be your girl? Newsflash nigga, I get dicked down because I want to. I don't need anything from you. This was uncomplicated at first but now–"

"Now it doesn't feel uncomplicated anymore."

She pushed herself upright and drew the sheet around her body, studying him with quiet clarity. "Yeah and I don't do complications. Angelou was more chill than this."

He did not deny it, but hearing her compare him to his brother made bile rise in his throat.

"Yeah, it's time for me to head out. You take care of yourself Sapphire." Trevor said quickly, knotting the used condom to flush down her toilet and putting his clothes on. Just because he was the youngest brother didn't mean he would sit there and let a woman "lil' bro" him like he wasn't a grown ass man.

"So what? You offended now?" attitude evident in her voice. Trevor paused, zipping up his pants to look at Sapphire. She was still fine as hell even with the irritation written across her face. To be someone who wasn't bothered by him wanting to end things, her actions weren't proven that to be true.

"Say what you want," He leaned over on the bed, his lips a breath away from hers. "But I just made that pussy cum four times back-to-back ending in a back breaking squirt. You can't little boy me, Sapphire. Because after I'm gone, that pussy is still going to be crying for me. Now," He leaned back up and pulled his shirt back on. "I want you to enjoy the rest of your day. It was fun."

With that he walked out her apartment and out her life. He would just need to think of a new way to distract himself from his thoughts of his failed marriage and that second grade teacher that haunted his dreams.

Divine Expressions, Mackenzie's Harlem studio, carried its own kind of quiet despite the movement inside it. The scent of fresh canvas and hot lights blended with dark roast coffee, creating that specific atmosphere that only existed in creative spaces where art was being taken seriously. Crew members moved in measured rhythm, adjusting tripods and checking sound levels while Mackenzie stood beneath a wash of soft light, her camera strap looped around her neck as naturally as a necklace.

Trevor watched her from a distance, headset resting around his collarbone, hands loosely tucked into the pockets of his jeans. There was something about watching someone operate fully inside their gift that always made him reflective. Mackenzie did not shrink under the lights. She expanded.

Nina stood several feet away, arms folded loosely across her chest, observing everything with the quiet vigilance that defined her. She had that way about her. Always seeing what others missed. That's why for a while after the divorce, Trevor avoided close moments with her because he knew she would see through him with the weird perception of a big sister. He got enough of that from Jackson.

When Trevor glanced in her direction, she caught the shift in his expression immediately. Her eyes softened, and she tipped her chin toward the hallway that led away from the set.

"Walk with me for a second," she said quietly.

He followed without hesitation.

The hallway was cooler, the hum of production fading into a muffled backdrop as they stopped near a large window overlooking the street below. Nina leaned back against the wall and studied him with the kind of gaze that did not miss much.

"You look different this week," she said thoughtfully. "I can't put my finger on whether it's a good or bad different."

Trevor let out a small breath and rested his shoulder against the opposite wall. "That doesn't sound vague at all."

She gave him a faint smile. "I'm serious."

He ran a hand slowly over his jaw, buying himself a moment. "Zara has her first therapy appointment this afternoon."

Nina's posture shifted immediately, concern and relief crossing her face at once. "That's good, Trev. That's really good."

"She's nervous," he admitted. "I tried to keep it light this morning, but she knows it's about her mom. I don't want her thinking something is wrong with her because of what happened."

Nina stepped closer and placed her hand against his arm briefly. "You are doing what fathers are supposed to do. You're not pretending this didn't hurt her. You're giving her space to process it. That matters."

He nodded, but his gaze drifted past her toward the set where

Mackenzie was adjusting her stance beneath the lights, her voice carrying faintly as she rehearsed a line.

Nina followed his eyes and then returned her attention to him slowly. "That's not all."

Trevor let out a quiet laugh that held no humor. "You ever considered becoming a detective?"

"I don't need the badge," she replied calmly. "What else is going on?"

He hesitated, and that hesitation told her more than his words would have.

"Trevor."

He looked at her fully then, and for a moment he was not a director or a single father navigating a public divorce. He was simply the youngest brother trying to sort through something unfamiliar.

"There's someone," he said finally.

If Nina was surprised by that admission, she didn't let it show. The only tell that Trevor saw was the slight quirk of her eyebrow. She did not interrupt. She waited.

"She's Zara's teacher," he continued, and that made her eyebrows lift slightly.

"All right," she said carefully. "Keep going."

"She and I went to school together. I never really talked to her back then, but I noticed her. *Everybody* noticed her. She didn't move loudly. She didn't have to. She had this way of standing in a room like she knew exactly who she was."

His voice shifted when he spoke about it, softening in places without him realizing.

"You liked that," Nina observed gently.

"I respected it," he corrected quietly, then let the distinction sit. "I was already with Katelyn when I started realizing how much I paid attention to her. By then it didn't matter. I was in too deep. Life kept moving."

Nina listened without inserting herself.

"She's Zara's teacher now," he continued. "We had parent teacher conferences, and I don't know how to explain it without sounding dramatic, but she was there in a way nobody else was. She didn't treat me like I was broken. She didn't pity me. She just... saw me."

"That did something to you, didn't it?"

"It steadied me," he admitted.

Nina folded her arms again, thoughtful rather than reactive. "And now?"

"And now I kissed her. She's been avoiding me like the plague ever since. The shit is driving me nuts, even though I understand."

The confession hung between them. Nina's eyes sharpened assessing Trevor in the moment, trying to pick up on what he wasn't saying.

"How long ago was your divorce finalized?"

He let out a breath. "Recently."

"She's right to be cautious," Nina said softly.

"I know that."

"Do you?"

He looked away for a moment, then back at her, "I don't want her to be a rebound. I don't want to use her to prove I'm fine. That's not what this feels like."

"What does it feel like?"

He thought about that carefully before answering, "It feels like something I should take my time with because it will lead to something real."

Nina's shoulders relaxed slightly. "Then take your time."

He gave her a look, "That sounds simple when you say it."

"It *is* simple," she replied. "It's not easy. But it's simple. If you're serious, then court her."

He blinked, "Court?"

"Yes," she said, completely unbothered by the word. "Take her out properly. Make plans. Open doors. Let her see who you are when you're not rebounding. Show her that what you feel is real, Trev."

He rubbed the back of his neck, embarrassed and amused at once. "It's simple but you just made it sound complicated. Like I'm running a campaign for her to get with me."

"It is," Nina said evenly. "You're not running for office. You're trying to build her trust."

He laughed softly, but there was weight in it.

"Don't treat her like a distraction either," Nina added, her tone shifting slightly, protective in the way only someone who loves you deeply can be. "You've been moving a certain way since the divorce. I have eyes. Out here being fast with these hoochies."

He didn't argue with that. Although he had only been with Sapphire, he knew that he was in a delicate state.

"Don't let her be another place you land just because you're lonely," Nina continued. "If you want her, show her you are stable. Show her you're patient. Don't rush her just because your feelings are loud at the moment. The biggest hurdle she is probably trying to overcome with you is trusting that what you're showing her is the real deal and not a band-aid."

Trevor nodded slowly, "I hear you."

"Good," she said gently. "Because she has every reason to protect herself. You have to make it safe for her not to."

Before he could respond, Mackenzie's voice carried more clearly down the hallway as the cameras began rolling.

They both turned toward the set.

Mackenzie stood tall beneath the lights, her face bright and hair wild as she spoke about heartbreak and finding her voice through art. She described how she once believed love had passed her by, how she poured that grief into photographs until she could recognize herself again in the frame. She spoke about meeting Jackson when she was not searching, about how working beside him felt like alignment instead of collision.

"The right love," she said into the camera, her voice steady and sure, "does not chase you. It meets you where you are and builds with you from there. Love is not scarce, it's abundant. Even when you feel like it has run out." Her eyes flicked toward Trevor for the briefest moment.

It was subtle.

It was intentional.

Trevor felt the message settle somewhere deep inside him, not as pressure, but as an invitation.

Nina glanced at him out of the corner of her eye.

"You hear that? Because we both know she said it for you," she murmured softly.

He nodded.

He would make sure that Aniyah knew what she meant to him.

Dr. Sanders' office felt intentionally warm, like every detail had been chosen to soften whatever walked through the door. The walls were painted a muted honey tone, and the late afternoon light filtered in through gauzy curtains that made the room glow without glare. A faint citrus scent lingered in the air, clean but gentle, blending with something sweeter he could not quite identify. The waiting room chairs were cushioned in soft fabric instead of cold vinyl, and a small shelf of children's books curved along the far wall beneath framed artwork drawn by other small hands.

Trevor sat with his knees slightly apart, elbows resting on his thighs, Zara's hand folded tightly in his. She had chosen the seat closest to him and leaned just enough that their shoulders touched. He could feel the tension in her fingers where they wrapped around his.

"Do I have to talk the whole time," she asked quietly, her voice barely above a whisper.

He looked down at her and smiled softly. "You only have to talk about what you want to talk about. Dr. Sanders is just someone who listens and helps you sort out the big feelings that don't fit in your backpack."

Zara considered that, her brows pulling together slightly. "Like when my chest feels tight."

"Exactly like that," he said. "You don't have to carry that by yourself."

The door to the inner office opened slowly, and Dr. Sanders stepped out with a presence that felt immediately steady. She wore a deep emerald blouse tucked into tailored slacks, and her natural curls framed her face in a way that made her smile feel expansive rather than overwhelming. Her skin held a rich cherry tone that caught the warm light, and when she looked at Zara, her attention was complete.

"Miss Zara," she said with gentle brightness. "I'm so glad you're here today."

Zara looked up at Trevor instinctively, searching his face for confirmation.

He squeezed her hand lightly. "I'll be right here when you're done."

Dr. Sanders crouched slightly to Zara's level without diminishing herself. "We're just going to talk and maybe draw a little. Nothing scary. You get to decide what we do first."

Zara hesitated for a breath, then nodded and slid her hand from Trevor's grasp. The release felt bigger to him than it should have.

He watched her small frame walk through the doorway, her

curls bouncing slightly with each step. When the door closed, the quiet returned with weight.

The hour that followed moved differently than time usually did. Trevor tried to read a magazine left on the table, but the words blurred. He found himself replaying moments from the past year, scanning for signs he might have missed, questions he should have asked sooner, comfort he could have given better.

He wondered whether she blamed herself in ways she did not articulate. He wondered whether he had said enough to make her feel chosen.

When the door finally opened, Trevor stood without realizing he had been holding his breath.

Zara stepped out first, and something about her posture had shifted. Her shoulders were not as rigid. Her hand was not balled into a fist.

Dr. Sanders followed, her expression warm but thoughtful.

"Zara did beautifully today," she said, gesturing gently toward a corner where a small art table sat. "She shared more than I expected for the first session."

Zara wandered toward the table and began stacking small wooden blocks without being prompted, humming faintly to herself.

Dr. Sanders lowered her voice slightly as she addressed Trevor. "There is clear grief associated with maternal separation and what we would clinically refer to as attachment disruption. That is developmentally appropriate given the abrupt termination of parental involvement."

Trevor nodded slowly, absorbing each word letting her words sooth him.

"She presents with adaptive coping behaviors," Dr. Sanders continued. "She's observant and eager to maintain stability in her environment. What we will focus on is processing the loss while reinforcing secure attachment with you as her primary caregiver. She looks to you as her emotional anchor."

The phrase settled in his chest.

Anchor.

"Is she going to be okay," he asked, the question leaving him before he could filter it.

Dr. Sanders' smile softened. "She's already okay. She is grieving, and she is adjusting. Those are not the same as broken. The fact that she feels safe enough to express confusion and sadness tells me she trusts her foundation."

"Am I doing right by her," he asked quietly, needing that reassurance because most days he felt like he had no clue how to navigate the day.

Dr. Sanders held his gaze. "You are doing the work. That matters more than perfection ever could."

The feeling of hope didn't flood him dramatically at hearing Dr. Sanders words. It settled gradually, like warmth spreading through cold hands.

In the car, Zara climbed into her booster seat with less hesitation than she had shown entering the building. She buckled herself in, concentrating on the latch before leaning back against the seat.

"She's really nice," Zara said as he started the engine.

"I had a feeling you'd like her."

Zara looked down at her fingers as if she was nervous to say what she felt. "I told her I miss mommy."

The words were quiet, but they did not shatter him the way they once had.

"That makes sense," he said gently. "It's okay to miss mommy."

"She said I can miss mommy and still be okay at the same time," Zara continued. "That sounded weird at first. But then I thought about it, and it kind of makes sense."

"It does," he said, his voice steady even as his throat tightened. "Your heart can hold more than one feeling."

Zara stared out the window for a moment, watching trees blur past. "I'm still the best little girl, right?"

The vulnerability in the question cut deeper than anything else had that day.

He reached back at the next red light and squeezed her knee lightly. "You have always been the best little girl. Nothing that happened changes that."

Her shoulders relaxed further against the seat.

"Ms. Henderson says that too," Zara added casually.

His hand tightened briefly on the steering wheel before he forced himself to breathe evenly. "She does?"

Zara nodded with certainty. "She's the best teacher I ever had. Even when I have hard days, she still talks to me softly."

Trevor listened carefully and tried his hardest to will his heart to slow down at the mention of Aniyah.

"I think she would be a really good mommy," Zara continued, her voice thoughtful rather than excited.

The words landed heavy and light at the same time.

"What makes you say that," he asked, careful not to infuse the question with too much but he noticed his voice go up an octave.

Zara considered it with the seriousness only children possess. "She's nice even when she looks tired. Mommies are supposed to be like that."

Trevor let that settle rather than rushing to correct or redirect because he was afraid he would agree and spark more hope in his little girl. He never wanted to set her up for heartbreak, so instead, he remained quiet. The school came into view ahead of them, the building familiar and steady in the fading afternoon light. He parked the car and turned in his seat to look at her fully.

"You don't have to figure out grown-up things," he said gently. "Your job is just to be Zara."

She smiled at that, satisfied. As he stepped out of the car and opened her door, he felt something shift inside him again. The hope that was there early replaced itself with a heavier feeling, resolve. Whatever the future held, he would build it carefully. Because he had no choice, Zara deserved every bit of softness life had to offer and he would make sure she got it.

"Wow," Zara exclaimed when she and Trevor walked into the multipurpose room that afternoon, the transformation was already underway.

In the span of a week, Aniyah had somehow turned chaos into structure. Paper snowflakes draped from a fishing line across the ceiling. A makeshift fireplace constructed from painted cardboard stood stage left, complete with tissue-paper flames. The long cafeteria tables had been pushed back to create a performance space, and a borrowed spotlight from the high school theater department cast a warm wash over the center of the room.

A hand-painted banner reading *A Christmas Story: A Second Grade Retelling* hung slightly crooked above the stage, which only made it more charming.

They had one week left. And somehow, against all odds, the production was ahead of schedule.

Zara slipped from his hand and ran to join her classmates, her curls bouncing as she announced, "Daddy, today I get to float like a ghost!"

Trevor smiled. "Float responsibly."

Across the room, Aniyah stood near the sound table, clipboard tucked against her chest as she coordinated with two PTA mothers about prop placement. She wore a red sweater dress that fell just above her knees, the knit fabric hugging her in a way that made it difficult for him to pretend he was unaffected. Her boots were low-heeled and practical, but nothing about her felt casual. Her hair was pulled back into a soft puff, gold hoops catching the light each time she turned her head. She caught sight of him for half a second. Then she looked away to maintain her composure:

Professional. Focused. Unavailable.

Trevor adjusted the lighting board, refusing to smile at the fact that she had clocked him just as quickly.

The kids gathered onstage in various states of festive confusion.

"All right, everyone," Aniyah called, her voice clear but warm. "From the top of Scene Three. Remember, we are projecting our voices. We are not whispering secrets to the floor. We want our parents to be able to hear us."

A small boy dressed as Tiny Tim raised his hand. "Ms. Henderson, if I say 'God bless us everyone' too loud, will God hear me faster?"

The room erupted in laughter.

Aniyah pressed her lips together to keep from smiling too wide. "God has excellent hearing, Joseph. Just focus on the audience."

Trevor shook his head, amused.

Two PTA mothers hovered near the prop table, both overly invested in the rehearsal and noticeably under-invested in subtlety.

One of them, blonde highlights peeking from beneath a knit beanie, sidled closer to Trevor as he adjusted the spotlight.

"You're Zara's dad, right," she asked, her tone sliding into familiarity.

"I am."

"I heard you're in film," she continued, crossing her arms in a way that felt strategic. "That must be exciting. Being in the industry and all."

"It keeps me busy," he replied politely.

Her smile lingered longer than necessary. "I imagine it does."

From across the room, Aniyah's pen paused mid-note. She did not look up at them, but Trevor was sure she heard them.

The second PTA mom chimed in, stepping closer. "We were just saying how lucky the kids are to have someone with real experience helping with production."

Trevor gave a courteous nod. "Happy to help."

"Maybe you could give me some pointers sometime," the first one added lightly. "On lighting."

He caught the shift in Aniyah's posture then. The smallest tightening of her shoulders.

He kept his voice neutral. "Lighting is about balance. You don't want to overexpose something that's already bright." The PTA mother blinked, uncertain if she'd just been redirected.

Across the stage, Zara drifted through her ghost cue, arms raised dramatically as she declared, "I am the Ghost of Christmas Past and I remember when you were mean!"

One of the boys playing Scrooge forgot his line entirely and whispered loudly, "What am I supposed to say again."

"Regret," Aniyah supplied calmly from below the stage. "You feel regret."

The boy nodded with exaggerated seriousness. "I regret it very much."

The room applauded.

In one week, they had gone from chaos and costume confusion to actual pacing. Lines were memorized. Cues were landing. Even the paper snow backdrop had stopped falling mid-scene.

Trevor found himself watching Aniyah more than the stage. The way she moved through the room with intention. The way she knelt to adjust a child's scarf without disrupting momentum.

The way she laughed when a line went sideways but never lost control.

They avoided being alone. That had become their silent agreement.

And yet, every time they crossed paths, the air shifted.

When rehearsal finally wrapped, children scattered toward backpacks and parents. PTA mothers gathered their things reluctantly, offering Trevor one last lingering smile before retreating.

Zara wandered over to him, rubbing her eyes.

"I floated good," she murmured sleepily.

"You floated like a professional," he replied, lifting her into his arms.

She wrapped around him easily, head settling against his shoulder as though that had always been her rightful place.

He thanked a few parents for helping out with the production, then waited.

Aniyah moved slowly now, packing up with deliberate care. She knew he was there. He knew she knew. When the room had emptied almost completely, she grabbed her bag and stepped into the parking lot. Trevor followed a few steps behind, Zara heavy and warm against his chest.

The evening air had cooled significantly. He pressed his key fob, and his car engine hummed to life across the lot. He walked to the backseat first, opening the door carefully and lowering Zara into her booster seat with the kind of precision that only came from practice. She stirred slightly as he buckled her in.

"Love you, Daddy," she mumbled.

"Love you more, Superstar." He closed the door gently and turned.

Aniyah stood beside her car, parked directly next to his, keys in hand. She should have gotten in already. She should have left.

She had not.

He walked toward her unhurried, stopping close enough that the warmth between them returned immediately.

"You did good today," he said quietly. "The kids look ready."

Her chin lifted slightly. "They've worked hard."

"And you haven't?"

She hesitated just enough to acknowledge the compliment without accepting it fully, "It's coming together."

A breeze passed between them, lifting a strand of hair near her temple. He reached up instinctively, then stopped himself.

"I know what we said the other day in the closet," he began, his voice lower now, less performative and more intentional. "About the fear of starting something new so soon.vHow the timing of this isn't ideal." Trevor noticed Aniyah's fingers tightened around her keys.

"Yes," She responded lightly.

"I thought about it," he continued. "And I realized we let the worst-case scenario make the decision for us."

Her eyes met his.

"I'm not asking you to leap, I know my situation is a lot to handle. I'm not asking you to ignore any of that," he said. "I'm asking you to let me take you to dinner on Saturday."

The look of surprise that lit up Aniyah's face would've made Trevor laugh if he wasn't so damn nervous. He hadn't asked anyone on a date in ages and this one was on he desperately wanted her to say yes to.

"What happens if I say yes, we go out, and if I don't like who you are right now," she asked carefully.

"Then I step back," he replied. "I will respect your boundaries and you would never have to worry about me pushing up on you again."

He stepped closer then, slowly enough that she could move away if she chose to, but she didn't. His hand lifted deliberately, brushing along her forearm, up to her shoulder, and resting at the side of her neck. He felt the warmth of her skin pulse beneath his fingers. Her breath shifted. Her pupils widened, the reaction immediate and involuntary. Trevor felt a rush of heat come over him seeing Aniyah's reaction to his closeness.

"But we both know," he murmured, his voice grazing the little space between them, "you're going to like who I am now."

Her lips parted slightly in anticipation of feeling his pressed against them again. He leaned in and pressed a brief kiss to her mouth. It was restrained and comforting at the same time. A promise rather than a claim.

When he pulled back, the tension did not dissipate. If anything, he wanted to open her back door and make love until her voice went hoarse from screaming his name loudly, repeatedly. However, this was not the time and damn sure not the place. He thought for a second to will his erection down.

"Give me your phone," he said softly. She handed it to him, eyes narrowed in suspicion that did not mask her desire. He entered his number and returned it.

"Text me when you get home, Roxanne"

A faint smirk curved her mouth. "You think you're smooth."

"I know I am."

She shook her head lightly. "And why did you call me Roxanne?"

He smiled slowly. "From A Goofy Movie. You remind me of her. Always have because you have the same color hair and beauty mark."

Her face lit up despite herself. "I used to love Roxanne. I think I snuck and dressed up as her for Halloween one year in high school." He could tell Aniyah's mind drifted to the memory.

"I remember. It was Junior year. I saw you that morning at the lockers. I never wanted to be Max so badly in my life." he said, and he meant it.

Color rose to her cheeks, he loved her like this.

"Trevor! You are lying."

"I'm not, but we can talk more about that on our date," he said with a smug smile backing away from her.

Aniyah playfully rolled her eyes in response.

"Goodnight, Trevor."

"Goodnight."

He waited until she pulled away before turning back to his car. Trevor drove home slower than usual. Zara slept the entire way, her small snores barely audible over the hum of the engine. At a red light he glanced in the rearview mirror, watching the rise and fall of her chest, the way her curls framed her face without worry. Therapy had not fixed everything in an hour, but it had loosened something inside them.

When they made it home, he carried her inside without waking her fully. He changed her into her pajamas, easing her into bed and tucking the blanket around her shoulders with a care that bordered on ritual.

"I floated good," she murmured again, half in dream. Trevor had a feeling floating was going to stick with Zara for a while.

"You did," he whispered back, brushing his lips against her forehead.

When he stepped into the hallway, the house felt different than it had a month ago. It no longer echoed. It breathed.

He moved through the kitchen, poured himself a glass of water, and leaned against the counter for a moment, replaying the evening in quiet fragments. The red sweater. The way she waited beside her car. The look in her eyes when he called her Roxanne.

His phone buzzed against the counter with a text from an unsaved number.

Made it home.

He knew exactly who it was without her giving a name. The

fact that she deliberately sent that plain text amused Trevor. A slow smile spread across his face. He opened the message to save her number, typed her name in, then paused.Instead of Aniyah Henderson, he saved it as: *Roxanne.* He stared at her text message for a second longer than necessary before typing back.

Thank you for following directions. I appreciate a woman who listens.

He hit send and waited. Three dots appeared almost immediately. Then a single response came through.

He laughed out loud, the sound filling the kitchen in a way it had not in weeks.

*Yeah, we're going to get along just fine***,** he typed but didn't send it. He decided to let her have the last word tonight.

He set his phone down and walked toward his bedroom.

The mattress had been replaced the week after the divorce was finalized. He had not realized how much history could cling to something as ordinary as a bed until he removed it from the house entirely. The new one felt firmer. Neutral. Untouched by memory.

He stood at the edge of it for a moment, remembering how many nights he had chosen the couch instead, convincing himself he preferred it there. Tonight he did not hesitate. He pulled back the covers and lay down, staring at the ceiling for a few seconds before turning onto his side. The sheets were cool. The room was quiet. For the first time since Katelyn walked out of his life, the bed did not feel like a reminder of failure.

It felt like space.

His phone lit up once more on the nightstand. He reached for it, already smiling expecting it to be Aniyah. But it was only a weather alert. He set the phone back down on his nightstand, amused at himself.

When he closed his eyes, he did not see flashes of old memories. He did not hear regret. He did not replay what had been lost. He saw a red sweater in soft stage lighting clinging to the most delectable body. He heard a little girl declaring herself the Ghost of Christmas Past. He felt warmth where fear had been. That night Trevor fell asleep in his own bed without running from anything.

CHAPTER EIGHT

A CRAVING THAT STARTS AS A SPARK

"When did you first fall in love with hip hop?" - *Syd, Brown Sugar (2002)*

"I'm going on a date with Trevor Porter. Nothing to freak out about... Bitch, you're going on a date with Trevor Porter!?" Aniyah was sure she had gone crazy because here she was, talking to herself in front of the mirror as if it would help calm her nerves. How did they even end up here? She had no idea. If you would have told her months ago after she laid eyes on him for the first time in years that she would end up not only kissing him but going on a date as well? She would have laughed and slammed the door in your face. But here she was looking carefully over the outfit she had on, once again.

Aniyah stood in front of the mirror longer than she cared to admit.

The soft yellow light from the bathroom fixture caught the edges of her wand curls as she adjusted them for the third time, pulling a few loose strands forward before letting them fall again. Her reflection stared back at her with the same skeptical expression she had been wearing for the last fifteen minutes. This was a date.

A real one.

The kind where a man actually picked you up and took you somewhere instead of sending a vague text asking if you were "free tonight" with no follow through.

She stepped back from the mirror and smoothed her hands over the front of her dress.

The sweater knit was thick enough for the cold but soft against her skin, a deep cinnamon brown that hugged her curves before falling just above her knees. The fabric was thick enough to hide her puckered scars. Even though she wouldn't have given a damn if they did show. Over it she wore a cream wool coat that cinched neatly at the waist, the belt tied into a careful knot she had retied at least five times already.

Her boots were black leather, sleek and tall enough to reach the curve of her knees.

Warm.

Simple.

Intentional.

Definitely *not* trying to impress that man (this was a lie).

Aniyah grabbed the gold hoops from the edge of the sink and slipped them into her ears. If she kept fretting she would talk herself out of this date entirely.

"You are doing entirely too much," she muttered under her breath, forcing herself to leave the bathroom.

Aniyah walked into the living room and paused by the window, watching the dark waves roll toward shore. The lights from the boardwalk lamps scattered faint gold across the sand. It was actually a gorgeous day outside, one that was perfect for a date. Yes, it was still cold but the sun was shining bright. The kind of brightness that seeps into your pores and cheers you up, which is exactly what she needed. She looked at her watch. It was 1:25pm which meant Trevor would be to her within the next five minutes.

Her stomach tightened again. It didn't make any sense how badly she wanted this man. The thought had been sitting in the back of her mind all week, showing up in the quiet moments between lesson planning and rehearsals for the Christmas play. Every time Zara mentioned her dad, every time she saw him at school drop-off, the memory of him asking her out had returned like a small pulse beneath her skin. Replaying on a loop, the soft kiss he gave her. The look of admiration in the dark pools of his eyes, the-

"Okay Aniyah, it's Trevor, not Michael B. Jordan. Get it toget —" The sound of her doorbell cut off her thoughts. How did he get past the concierge?! She began to walk nervously towards the door and then remembered Megan Thee Stallion would not approve, so she held her head high, squared her shoulders and walked the rest of the way like the Goddess she was.

She looked through the peep hole and saw Trevor standing in her hallway holding a very audacious bouquet of lilies and roses. A slow smile spread across her face.

He wore a dark charcoal overcoat that fell nearly to his knees, the wool heavy and structured across his broad shoulders. Beneath it she caught a glimpse of a black turtleneck and dark denim that fit him comfortably without looking careless. His beard was trimmed neatly, the shadow along his jaw catching the light from the hallway. She carefully opened the door and Trevor's eyes met hers immediately before taking the rest of her body in. The smile that followed was slow and genuine.

"Well damn," he said quietly. Aniyah blinked.

"What."

"You look..." He paused, studying her for a moment before finishing the sentence. "You look good, damn good.." There t was again, that rush of heat. How was she supposed to make it around this man when the simplest things he did drove her crazy? This could not be normal.

"You clean up nice yourself. Are these for me?" She said referencing the flowers in his hand.

"Oh! Yes. I saw them and their beauty and instantly thought of you." He handed the vase over. Aniyah couldn't lie, the bouquet was gorgeous, and heavy.

"Come in while I place them. Thank you so much, Trevor, these are gorgeous."

"Just like you," he responded smoothly before closing the door behind him. He turned to take in her place and let out a low whistle.

"This place is gorgeous. I can tell you took your time with it," he said while walking over to the window and observing the ocean.

"This has to be beautiful during storms." He said. Aniyah turned in her kitchen to look at him in her space. There were certain people that entered a room and threw off the energy with their aura. That wasn't Trevor though. He seemed to add to the calmness in her space, briefly wondering what it would be like to have him over more often. She deaded that thought as quickly as it came because this was only a first date. No need to rush.

"Yeah, when I first did the walk through, I knew I had to buy it. I'm a woman that craves sunlight. This gave me that and the space always feels like a warm hug when I walk inside. What I desperately need after-" She cut herself off before she talked about her family.

"Hey," Trevor started while walking towards her in the kitchen, "whatever just made that dark cloud settle over your face, I want you to forget it today, aight? We have some fun stuff planned and my goal is to ensure that a smile stays on your face."

How was a girl supposed to keep her sense when a fine ass man was talking like this? Aniyah thought to herself.

"Okay," She responded simply looking up at Trevor. He nodded and then hooked his arm around her waist bringing her body flush against his, where she could feel every plane of muscle he had. His mouth connected with hers with every bit of heat she was feeling. It didn't take long for it to deepen, their tongues colliding in a feverish exchange.

Aniyah couldn't pinpoint the exact moment she ended up on her counter with her legs wrapped around Trevor's waist and his hands gripping her ass tightly pulling her closer to him. All she knew is, she didn't want it to stop. Reluctantly, Trevor pulled away.

"Damn girl...if we don't leave now, we won't be." His voice grumbled out heavily with desire. "I just had to get that out of the way because I felt like we both needed it." With that he placed a quick kiss on her lips headed out the kitchen towards the front door.

"You ready?" He asked, pulling open the door.

Aniyah put on her coat and grabbed her mini Coach purse. "I think so."

Trevor watched her lock up and then grabbed her hand to hold as they walked out her building. Aniyah was absolutely buzzing. The two of them walked down the short path toward the street together, their footsteps echoing faintly against the quiet winter pavement.

Trevor reached into his coat pocket and pressed a button on

his key fob. A pair of headlights flashed to life and Aniyah stopped walking almost immediately. Her eyes moved from the sleek black SUV parked at the curb to Trevor, then back again.

"Trevor."

He glanced down at her, already knowing from her tone that she had something to say. "Yeah?"

She pointed toward the truck. "That's your car?"

Trevor followed her gaze and gave a light shrug like it wasn't anything special, which only made her look at him harder. "It's just a car."

Aniyah let out a short laugh. "That is not just a car. And this is not the Jeep you drive to school everyday. "

Of course, this man drove an Aston Martin. Of course he did. She didn't know why she was surprised. Trevor Porter looked like money without trying to. Not in a flashy, look-at-me kind of way. More like the kind of man who had grown into himself so fully that nice things just settled around him naturally. It was annoying. And attractive. *Extremely* attractive.

Trevor stepped ahead of her and opened the passenger door. "It's good to know that you pay attention to me," He chuckled. "I don't bring this baby out unless it's important...It gets us where we need to go."

Aniyah narrowed her eyes at him, but she climbed in anyway, carefully gathering her coat beneath her as she settled into the seat. Warmth greeted her almost instantly, the heated leather seeping through the layers of her dress and coat, and she had to stop herself from making a sound. The inside of the truck smelled expensive too, cedar and leather and something clean that felt distinctly him.

Trevor closed her door gently before walking around the front, and Aniyah found herself watching him through the windshield like she didn't have any home training. There was something about the way he moved. Nothing rushed. Nothing forced. Just easy, sure steps like he belonged wherever he stood. Like he had already decided this night was going to go well and the rest of the world needed to catch up.

She looked away before he got in and caught her staring.

When Trevor slid into the driver's seat, the truck came alive with a low hum so smooth it barely sounded like anything at all. He pulled his seatbelt across his chest, one hand resting easy on the wheel, and Aniyah turned just enough to study him without making it too obvious.

"So," she said, buckling herself in. "Where are we going?"

Trevor pulled away from the curb with that same irritating calm. "You'll see."

Aniyah sucked her teeth softly, "You know women hate that answer."

The corner of his mouth lifted in amusement at her pouting, "Good thing you're patient."

She turned her head slowly. "Who told you that lie?"

His laugh was quiet, but it did something ridiculous to her stomach.

The city unfolded around them little by little as they drove away from Long Beach, the boardwalk disappearing behind them while streetlights stretched gold across the damp pavement. The earlier drizzle had left a soft sheen on the road, making everything outside look just a little shinier than it probably was. Inside the truck, though, it was warm and low-lit and far too intimate for a first date. A soft jazz track played through the speakers, horns floating gently through the car like they were there to mind their business and set a mood.

Aniyah rested her elbow near the door and watched the lights pass outside her window. The silence between them wasn't awkward. That was the part that surprised her. She was used to men filling every spare second with noise, trying too hard to impress, talking just to hear themselves talk. Trevor didn't seem to need that. He let the quiet breathe. Let it settle. And somehow that made her even more aware of him.

After a few minutes, she looked over at him. "Can I ask you something?"

Trevor glanced at her briefly before turning back to the road. "You can ask me anything."

She studied his profile for a second, gathering her thoughts. "How did you and Katelyn actually happen?"

The question sat between them for a beat. Trevor didn't answer right away, and Aniyah almost thought maybe she'd overstepped, but then he slowed at a red light and exhaled through his nose like he was reaching back further than he usually liked to.

"We got together sophomore year," he said. "Back when the biggest decision in my life was whether I wanted to play basketball after school or go home and eat whatever my mom had cooking."

Aniyah smiled despite herself. "That sounds like a nice problem to have."

"It was." He glanced at the light, then eased forward when it changed. "I wasn't trying to be serious about anybody back then. I was sixteen. Commitment wasn't exactly at the top of my list."

"I would hope not."

That pulled another small smile from him before he kept going. "One afternoon I was outside with Chris and Andrew. We were about to head to the court when I saw somebody running down the block." His jaw tightened slightly at the memory. "It was Katelyn. She looked frantic. Lip busted, blood on her shirt, hair all over her head."

Aniyah's brows pulled together. "Damn."

"Yeah." His voice dropped a little. "I asked her what happened and she told me her parents had been fighting. She tried to get in the middle of it and her father swung."

Aniyah turned in her seat, her chest tightening. "And hit her."

Trevor nodded once. "She got caught in it."

There was a heaviness to the story already, one that made perfect sense with the man sitting beside her. Trevor carried himself like somebody who had been taking care of people for a very long time. Like being needed had shaped him early.

"I took her back to my house," he continued. "My mom saw her face and didn't even ask a bunch of questions at first. She cleaned her up, got some ice for her lip, sat her down at the kitchen table. Told her she could stay the night if she didn't feel safe going home."

His voice softened when he spoke about his mother, and Aniyah caught that immediately. It was in the way he said it. Like that memory, even with all its mess, still held something warm because Della was in it.

"She looked so small sitting there," he said after a moment. "Like somebody had knocked the wind out of her life."

Aniyah looked at him quietly, then out through the windshield. "And you decided you were going to save her."

Trevor glanced over, a little surprised, then gave a faint smile. "Yeah. Pretty much."

Of course he did, she thought. Because that was who he was. Because some people saw broken things and wanted no parts of them, while others stepped closer like their hands had been built to carry weight. Trevor had clearly always been the second kind.

"From then on, I just felt like she needed somebody in her corner," he said. "And I wanted to be that person."

Aniyah nodded slowly,"You became her Superman."

Trevor huffed a quiet laugh. "That's exactly what it felt like."

They rode in silence for a moment after that, the city growing around them as the road stretched ahead. Then Trevor shook his head lightly, almost smiling to himself. "Once we started dating, that was it. I didn't play about Katelyn. Nobody could say anything sideways about her around me."

Aniyah bit back a grin. "The Puerto Rican princess."

Trevor frowned and looked over at her. "The what?"

This time she couldn't help it. She laughed, covering her mouth with her hand. "That's what I used to call her."

"You are joking."

"I'm not joking." She leaned back into the seat, smiling now. "The whole school called her that."

Trevor blinked. "I never heard that."

"Well, you weren't supposed to. You were too busy being her bodyguard." She shook her head, still amused. "You ever watch Love and Hip Hop?"

The look he gave her made her laugh all over again.

"I did not expect that question from you."

"Why? Because I'm cute and wholesome?" she asked.

Trevor's smile deepened. "Something like that."

Aniyah rolled her eyes. "Please. My parents would've grounded me until I turned forty if they knew I used to sneak and watch it at night."

Trevor laughed, full and warm this time, and she hated how much she liked being the reason for it.

"I'm learning new things about you."

"You're not learning that much," she said quickly. "Stay focused."

"Yes, ma'am."

His tone was smooth enough to make heat creep up her neck, so she turned toward the window and prayed he couldn't see it.

"Senior year she got pregnant with Zara," Trevor said after a moment, his voice settling again.

Aniyah looked back at him, her smile fading into something softer. "That had to be scary."

"It was." He nodded slowly. "It happened two months before graduation. I remember staring at that test thinking, we're kids. We don't know what the hell we're doing."

"But you loved her."

He looked over at Aniyah then, and something about his expression made her chest ache. "Yeah," he said quietly. "And that baby was made from love."

There it was. The thing about Trevor that made him dangerous. Not just that he was fine, though Lord knew that wasn't helping anything. It was that he was sincere. Even now, talking about another woman, another life, his voice carried no bitterness.

"We decided to keep her," he continued. "For a long time... things worked. Marriage, parenthood, building a life. We made it work."

Aniyah heard the shift before he even said the next part.

"Then Katelyn got that job in Manhattan."

She didn't say anything, but she understood immediately. Some stories only needed one sentence to tell you where they were headed.

"And she got the taste of a new life," she said softly.

"Yes, that came with new money and new expectations." Trevor gave a humorless little smile. "She got to experience a different life. Somewhere along the way, she started looking at the one we built like it was too small for her. Like it was holding her back."

The words settled between them and Aniyah stared out at the passing lights, thinking about all the ways people outgrew each other. Or maybe never really fit in the first place.

"Sometimes I wonder if we were ever really in love," Trevor admitted after a while. "Or if we were just two kids trying to save each other from the worlds we came from."

Aniyah looked at him then, really looked at him. At the quiet set of his mouth. The way his fingers tightened on the steering wheel just a little before easing again. It took a lot for a man to say something like that out loud. To admit that maybe the foundation of his whole adult life had been built on survival instead of love.

"I know a thing or two about someone thinking you're not enough," she said.

Trevor glanced over. "Oh yeah?"

Aniyah nodded, "My father, he's very..." She paused, searching for the kindest word. "Structured."

Trevor smirked. "That sounds diplomatic."

"It's the nicest word I have."

He chuckled, and Aniyah let herself smile a little before continuing. "My father wanted me to be a doctor. It wasn't a hope. It was a demand. I had no say in my own damn life. For a while I went along with his demands and then..."

"You said no. And he lost his shit, right?"

Aniyah laughed softly. "Yes, and you would've thought I had stolen from him."

Trevor's smile widened. "How bad was it?"

"There were rules for everything," she said, shaking her head at the memory. "No hanging out. No late nights. No distractions. Everything was about image and discipline and doing what made him look good and made sense. I had no room to be myself and figure out what kind of life I wanted. You know I was banned from going to prom?"

"You've never been the type to just do what made sense." It was the way Trevor said it that gave her pause. His voice was open, honest. The moment was vulnerable.

"No," she admitted. "I haven't."

Trevor adjusted his grip on the wheel. "What saved you? Because I vividly remember you in a silk lilac dress at prom."

Aniyah smiled before she could stop herself, "Your memories of me never cease to amaze me. My grandpa Earl saved me."

Trevor's brows lifted, "I told you I was serious about noticing you back then. How did Grandpa Earl do that?"

"He threatened to write my father out of the will if he didn't let me go."

Trevor let out a loud laugh, the sound filling the truck. "I like him already."

"Everybody liked Grandpa Earl." Her voice softened. "By senior year I was living with him full-time. That's when life finally started to feel... breathable."

The word sat with her for a moment because that was exactly what it had been. Breath after years of holding it.

"The only things I really had before that were my morning runs and my poetry."

Trevor looked over at her. "You write poetry?"

She nodded. "That's how I kept my sanity."

He was quiet for a second and when she glanced back at him she caught the genuine interest on his face. She hadn't expected that.

"That's funny timing," he said.

"Why?"

"I'm directing a docuseries right now about Black creatives." He glanced over at her again. "Painters, photographers, sculptors, poets. We are trying to capture the love behind their art and everything that goes into it."

Aniyah blinked, she decided to play it cool instead of letting it be known that she had googled him and knew about the series. "A docuseries?"

"*Making Love: The Art of Us.*"

She stared at him for a second longer than she meant to. Lord, this man was really out here building things.

"Trevor Porter," she said, shaking her head. "That's a huge fucking deal."

His laugh was quieter this time, but pleased. "I'm glad you think so."

"I know so."

He looked forward again, but the smile stayed on his mouth. "Maybe one day you'll let me hear some of that poetry."

Aniyah turned toward him, letting a little mischief slide back into her expression. "Keep being a good date and maybe you will."

Trevor grinned then, slow and easy, and something inside her gave a dangerous little flutter in response.

Yeah.

This was already feeling like trouble. The kind of trouble that came dressed in a black turtleneck, drove an Aston Martin, and looked at her like he had all the time in the world to figure her out.

"You really have us out in Queens?" Aniyah asked, looking around.

Trevor eased his car into a parking space near the museum and cut the engine.

For a moment neither of them moved.

Aniyah looked across the street, her eyes settling on the large building ahead of them. The modern glass façade reflected the streetlights in soft streaks of gold.

"The Museum of the Moving Image," she said slowly.

Trevor leaned back slightly in his seat, watching her instead of the building.

"You've heard of it."

Aniyah pushed open her door and stepped out into the winter air. "Of course I've heard of it." She wrapped her coat tighter around herself before glancing back at him. "I've just never been."

Trevor stepped out and rounded the front of the car, the wind lifting the collar of his coat slightly as he joined her on the sidewalk.

"Well," he said, nodding toward the entrance as they started across the street, "now you have."

Inside, warmth wrapped around them almost immediately.

The museum carried the quiet reverence of a place where people came to study the things they loved. Soft lighting glowed over glass displays and wide gallery spaces stretched ahead of them. Somewhere deeper inside the building, visitors spoke in low voices that blended into a gentle hum.

Aniyah slowed almost immediately.

The exhibits stretched out in careful rows. Vintage film cameras sat beside editing equipment, costumes, and wall screens looping scenes from decades of cinema.

"This is incredible," she murmured.

Trevor didn't answer right away.

Instead, he watched her.

The way her eyes moved across the room, taking everything in, made something in his chest settle quietly into place. She looked entranced and excited.

"Come on," he said after a moment, nodding toward the first gallery.

They moved through the space slowly, their steps echoing softly against the polished floor.

Trevor stopped beside a vintage film camera encased in glass. The metal body looked heavy, mechanical in a way modern equipment rarely did anymore. The plaque beside it detailed its use in several films from the seventies.

He leaned slightly closer to the case.

"The Arriflex 35BL changed everything for a while," he said.

Aniyah stepped beside him, folding her arms loosely as she studied the lens. "How so?"

Trevor gestured toward the camera.

"In the 1970s, color film stock was notoriously calibrated for lighter skin tones, using 'Shirley cards' making it difficult to capture detail in darker skin tones without intense lighting." He shook his head slightly. "A lot of Black actors ended up looking washed out or overly shiny on screen because the equipment just wasn't built with them in mind."

Aniyah leaned a little closer to the glass, looking at the camera again like it held some kind of quiet apology inside it.

"What changed?"

Trevor's voice warmed as he answered, the shift almost immediate. "People started experimenting. Different film stocks, different lighting setups. They realized if you adjusted the exposure and bounced warmer light, darker skin actually reflected light beautifully."

He glanced down at her.

"But it required filmmakers who actually cared enough to figure that out."

Aniyah nodded slowly. "That sounds about right."

Trevor's mouth lifted slightly.

They moved to the next exhibit where a row of modern digital cameras lined the wall, each one smaller and sleeker than the last.

Trevor pointed toward one of them.

"You remember when *Sinners* came out a few years ago?"

Aniyah's head snapped toward him. "The Ryan Coogler movie?"

"Yeah." Trevor nodded toward the camera. "He used 65mm Kodak Ektachrome film stock that let him shoot wide format while still preserving the depth of darker skin tones."

Aniyah stared at the camera like it had suddenly grown more important than the others around it.

"That kind of technical choice changes how people see the entire story," Trevor continued.

She shook her head softly. "I never thought about it like that."

Trevor smiled faintly. "Most people don't. They just feel it when they watch."

They continued through the gallery, stopping here and there as Trevor pointed out different pieces of equipment. Editing consoles. Lighting rigs. Early sound recording devices that looked almost prehistoric compared to what filmmakers used now.

As he talked, his hands moved naturally, sketching invisible shapes in the air. His excitement to pull her into his world warmed something in Aniyah.

At first, she paid attention to the exhibits. But somewhere along the way she realized she was mostly watching him.

There was something about the way Trevor spoke about film. The quiet confidence in his voice had nothing to do with ego. It came from knowing something deeply. Loving it deeply. When he talked about lighting or composition his entire posture shifted slightly forward, like someone leaning toward a conversation they'd been waiting to have.

The warmth of it was... magnetic. She could tell he took pride in his craft and that did something for her.

Trevor paused mid-sentence and glanced over.

"What," he asked looking into her starry eyes.

Aniyah blinked quickly, "Nothing."

He lifted one brow. "You've been staring at me for the last two minutes with your mouth slightly open."

She shrugged, pretending to study the display again. "I'm admiring your passion for this."

Trevor huffed out a quiet laugh but Aniyah caught the blooming red gliding across his face, "That's a new one."

"Don't get used to it," She retorted, walking off to a different direction.

They drifted toward a large wall screen where a montage of iconic film scenes played silently. Light from the screen flickered across the gallery, painting soft shadows across the floor.

Aniyah glanced at him again.

"So this docuseries you mentioned," she said. "*Making Love: The Art of Us.*"

Trevor nodded, "What about it?"

"You're really traveling all over filming artists?"

"Yeah." He slipped his hands into his coat pockets. "We're filming in a few different places. My overseas time is limited though. Two weeks in March and two weeks in April."

Aniyah looked at him again, disbelief written all over her face.

"Trevor, that's huge."

He gave a small shrug, "I'm glad somebody thinks so."

She nudged his arm lightly, "Don't do that. I won't let you down talk your success in front of me. You know it is."

They continued walking through the exhibit together, the quiet warmth of the museum settling around them like a soft blanket.

Somewhere between the glow of the displays and the steady rhythm of Trevor's voice explaining the art he loved, Aniyah realized something she hadn't expected when the evening began.

She was enjoying herself.

More than enjoying herself. She was starting to understand why people fell for Trevor Porter in the first place.

That realization felt just a little bit dangerous.

When they stepped out of the museum, the sky had begun its slow surrender to evening.

The winter sun hung low, stretching long shadows across the sidewalks as they walked back toward the car. The temperature had dropped while they were inside, the kind of cold that crept under coats and curled around your ankles if you stood still too long. Aniyah slid her hands deeper into the pockets of her coat as Trevor unlocked the car.

"You still haven't told me where we're going next," she said, slipping into the passenger seat.

Trevor started the engine, the heater rumbling gently to life, "You ask a lot of questions."

Aniyah settled into the warmth of the seat and smirked, "I'm a teacher."

"That is no excuse outside of school hours."

She rolled her eyes, but the smile stayed on her mouth as he pulled away from the curb.

The drive into Brooklyn unfolded slowly beneath the fading daylight. Traffic thickened as they moved through neighborhoods buzzing with weekend energy. Restaurants glowed along the sidewalks. People clustered near doorways with their shoulders hunched against the cold. Somewhere a group laughed too loudly as they hurried across the street, scarves flying behind them.

Eventually Trevor turned onto a quieter road that curved along the edge of Prospect Park.

Aniyah glanced toward the stretch of dark trees rising behind the stone wall. "Prospect Park?"

Trevor nodded once. "Trust me."

He parked near one of the entrances and stepped out, the last threads of sunlight were slipping through the bare branches.

Aniyah followed him through the park entrance, her boots crunching softly along the gravel path. Winter had changed the park's personality. The crowds were gone, replaced by quiet pockets of space where the wind moved freely through the trees.

They walked for a few minutes before Trevor slowed near a small clearing.

Aniyah noticed the setup before he even said anything.

Two low wooden chairs sat beneath a small canvas dining tent, the sides rolled down and zipped tight against the cold. A small portable heater hummed gently inside, casting a warm golden glow across a low table set between them. The whole space looked like a tiny pocket of warmth tucked into the middle of the winter park.

Aniyah stopped walking.

"You did not."

Trevor's mouth curved slightly as he stepped forward and unzipped the entrance flap, "I might've."

She looked at the tent again, then at him, "Trevor Porter..."

He held the flap open, gesturing for her to step inside, "Come on before all the heat escapes."

Aniyah ducked inside and the difference in temperature wrapped around her almost instantly. The heater warmed the small space comfortably, the canvas walls blocking the wind while soft lights strung along the frame gave everything a quiet glow.

"Oh my God," she breathed.

Trevor zipped the entrance closed behind them.

Inside the tent sat a thick wool rug layered beneath the chairs, with blankets folded along the backs like someone had thought through every detail and wanted them to be cozy.

Aniyah slipped off her coat almost immediately followed by her shoes since the tent had a floor and the rug was on top of it, "Okay, this is actually genius."

Trevor shrugged as he set the picnic basket onto the small table, "I wanted us to have a good dinner, but I'm also selfish and wanted you to myself. This is a good medium."

She laughed softly, flexing her toes against the rug with a sigh, "This is the first time my feet have been warm all day."

Trevor watched her settle into the chair across from him, the glow of the heater warming the cinnamon tone of her dress. For a second he said nothing at all.

Aniyah noticed the look almost immediately, "What?"

Trevor leaned back slightly, "Nothing."

She narrowed her eyes in suspicion, "That was not a nothing look."

His smile deepened but he reached into the basket instead of answering, pulling out wrapped sandwiches.

The smell hit her before she even saw what they were.

Aniyah's eyes widened, "No way."

Trevor peeled the paper back slowly, "Yes way. I got Philly cheesesteaks."

She stared at him like he had just performed a magic trick, "How in the hell did you get authentic Philly cheesesteaks and we're in Brooklyn?"

Trevor handed her one and leaned back in his chair, "It pays to have a brother that's famous."

Aniyah laughed as she took the sandwich. "You used Jackson Porter's connections for a sandwich."

Trevor lifted his shoulders. "I used grandpa's connections for *you*."

"Your brother know you out here calling him grandpa?" Aniyah asked while laughing. Trevor looked at his watch.

"It's seven PM, that geriatric is probably in the bed, the title is fitting." They laughed in response. Aniyah finished opening her sandwich. The warmth of the bread and melted cheese hit her tongue and she closed her eyes for a second.

"Oh my God," She moaned. Immediately she noticed Trevor shift and fix his jeans in his seat. Heat thrummed through her core at the thought of him getting hard just from the sound of her satisfaction.

Trevor chuckled quietly, "Still your favorite?"

She opened one eye at him,"You remember that?"

"You used to eat them every Friday after track practice."

Aniyah paused mid-bite, Trevor would be around but she never knew he paid any attention to her. The realization of what that meant moved slowly across her face.

"You remember what I ate in high school?"

Trevor shrugged lightly trying to play off his eagerness, "I remember a lot about you from back then."

Something about the way he said it made her look down at her sandwich for a second longer than necessary.

Lord, this man was going to be her undoing.

"You keep surprising me, Porter. I like it. For the record, I remember you from back then too."

They ate slowly, conversation drifting between easy laughter and comfortable pauses. They talked about her best friends and his life as the youngest.

"Man, it was rough as hell. Having a brother that's twelve years older than me was damn near like having a second father. And don't factor in Lou who is ten years older than me. He used to say mom and dad found me on the sidewalk and decided to bring me home...asshole." That made Aniyah cackle.

Trevor pulled strawberries and wine from the basket after a while, pouring two small cups while the heater hummed steadily beside them.

Aniyah leaned back in her chair, stretching her legs out beneath the small table, she took in her surroundings again, "You really did all this."

Trevor handed her a cup of wine, "You're more than worth the effort."

The sincerity in his voice landed somewhere deep in her chest.

"Can I ask you something?"

Aniyah glanced up from her wine, "You've been answering my questions all night. Go ahead."

Trevor rested his elbows on his knees, studying her with quiet curiosity. "Why teaching?"

The question caught her off guard. She sat there for a moment, the answer forming slowly in her chest.

"I love kids," she said finally.

Trevor waited for more. Aniyah smiled softly, looking down at the cup in her hands before continuing, “But it’s more than that.”

Her voice grew quieter, more thoughtful.

“When I was growing up, my house wasn’t exactly... easy.” She shrugged lightly. “Everything was so strict, as we talked about in the car earlier. I hated coming home. That was not a place I felt at peace in.”

Trevor watched her carefully taking in the way her hands nervously moved together.

“School was the only place that felt different,” she continued. “There were teachers who saw me for who I truly was, a human being.”

She lifted her eyes to his.

“I remember this one teacher in fifth grade who used to keep her classroom open during lunch for kids who didn’t want to sit in the cafeteria. Some days there’d be five of us in there just sitting on the floor reading while she graded papers.”

Aniyah smiled faintly at the memory.

“She never made it a big thing. Never asked questions we didn’t want to answer. She just... made space.”

Trevor felt something tighten quietly in his chest.

“That stayed with me,” she said. “The idea that a classroom could be a safe place for somebody. That a kid could walk in and breathe for a few hours before going back to whatever was waiting for them at home.”

She lifted one shoulder gently.

“That’s what I try to be. A safe space. A soft place to land if they need it.”

The warmth in her voice made something shift behind Trevor’s ribs. He studied her for a long moment.

“That makes a lot of sense,” he said quietly.

Aniyah tilted her head, “Why?’

Trevor's mouth curved slightly, "Because Zara talks about you like you hung the moon."

Aniyah blinked, clearly not expecting that, "She does not."

"She absolutely does."

Her cheeks warmed instantly and she looked down at the table, "Zara is a very special little girl. You definitely hit the jackpot having her as a daughter."

Trevor beamed at the mention of his baby girl, "I did. I tell myself that every morning. That little girl is my world. You saying that means a lot."

Trevor watched the way the soft light caught the curve of her face, the way she tucked a loose curl behind her ear when she got shy. Something about that small movement made the air between them shift. The easy flow of things was now charged.

He reached for another strawberry and held it out to her.

Aniyah raised an eyebrow, "You feeding me now?"

Trevor's voice dropped just slightly, "Depends."

"On what."

"Whether you're going to behave."

She took the strawberry anyway, her fingers brushing his as she did. The contact lasted less than a second. Still, heat shot up her arm like a spark finding dry wood. Aniyah chewed slowly, pretending she hadn't noticed.

Trevor leaned back in his chair, watching her in that quiet way he had that made her feel like he was memorizing something.

The tent suddenly felt smaller.

Warmer.

Too warm.

Aniyah shifted in her seat and stretched her legs toward the heater, trying to ignore the way Trevor's gaze followed the movement.

"So," she said lightly, clearing her throat. "You take all your dates to heated tents in the park?"

Trevor's eyes lifted to hers, they were darkened, "No, just you."

The answer came too quickly to be casual. The laughter from earlier had softened into something heavier now. Something slower. The space between them seemed to thicken, the quiet inside the tent pressing gently against her pulse.

Trevor leaned forward slightly, resting his forearms on his knees. Taking in Aniyah's shallow breaths.

"You nervous?"

Aniyah met his eyes. "Should I be?"

His mouth curved slowly, "If you knew what just went through my mind...Probably."

Her breath caught before she could stop it.

Lord have mercy.

Aniyah suddenly became aware of everything. The way his voice had dropped. The way his shoulders filled the space of the chair. The way his eyes had settled on her mouth for half a second too long.

It was sexy and *very* tempting.

She leaned back in her chair, pretending she had more control over the moment than she actually did. "You're very smooth tonight, Mr. Porter."

"I've had a good day with you today."

"So have I," she admitted softly.

The words hung between them, heavier than they should have been. For a moment neither of them moved. The tent glowed warmly around them while the night settled deeper into the park outside.

Sitting there across from Trevor Porter, Aniyah realized something that made her heart beat just a little faster.

If he leaned forward right now...

She wasn't entirely sure she'd stop him. Because she wanted to be devoured by him.

The drive back to Aniyah's house was quieter than the rest of the evening had been.

It wasn't an uncomfortable quiet. Just the kind that came after two people had said enough for one night and were now sitting inside everything they had learned about each other. Settling into feelings of desire that they couldn't stop. Aniyah looked down and saw how Trevor's hands gripped the dear shift...she never had been jealous of a car part before today. She had to get a grip!

When Trevor parked the car in front of her building neither of them moved.

Aniyah stared through the windshield at the entrance; her fingers loosely wrapped around the strap of her purse resting in her lap. The warmth from the heater still lingered in the car, but the quiet between them had grown thicker somehow.

Trevor exhaled slowly beside her.

"Well," he said softly.

Aniyah turned toward him, a small smile touching her mouth, "Well."

That was the cue to get out, however, neither of them reached for the door.

Aniyah could feel it sitting there between them. That pull. That dangerous little spark that had been building all evening. The kind that made her want to invite him upstairs just to see what would happen next.

Trevor was feeling it too.

She could see it in the way his jaw flexed slightly when he looked at her, the way his eyes lingered on her mouth before lifting back to her eyes again.

"You had a good time tonight?" He asked.

Aniyah let out a quiet laugh. "You took me to a museum, fed me Philly cheesesteaks, and built a heated tent in Prospect Park." She tilted her head slightly, "What do you think?"

Trevor smiled, but there was something softer behind it now.

"I think I want to come upstairs," he admitted.

The honesty of it made heat bloom low in her core.

Welp, there goes my panties. Get a grip!

Aniyah held his gaze for a second longer than she probably should have. The answer sat right there on the tip of her tongue.

She wanted him to. But something about the way Trevor had moved through the night— patient, thoughtful, and intentional with everything he had planned— made her pause. Like rushing this would somehow cheapen what had grown between them over the past few hours.

Trevor seemed to reach the same conclusion at the exact same time.

He shook his head slightly and leaned back in his seat.

"But I'm not going to," he said.

Aniyah blinked.

"Why not."

Trevor looked at her again, his voice lower now. "Because I want to do this the right way."

Her chest tightened unexpectedly.

Because the truth was... she did too.

Aniyah opened the door before she could talk herself into changing her mind. The cold air rushed in immediately, biting at the warmth of the car as she stepped out onto the sidewalk.

Trevor followed her, meeting her near the front of the car.

For a moment they just stood there beneath the glow of the streetlamp, the ocean wind tugging softly at the edges of her coat.

Aniyah tucked a loose curl behind her ear.

"So," she said quietly.

Trevor stepped closer.

"Yeah."

The space between them closed naturally, like neither of them had to think about it.

Trevor lifted his hand and rested it lightly along her waist, his thumb brushing the fabric of her coat as he studied her face one more time.

"You sure you don't want me to come up?"

Aniyah smiled faintly.

"You sure you're strong enough not to?"

Trevor huffed a quiet laugh, "Barely."

She leaned up then, pressing a soft kiss to his lips before either of them could second guess it. The kiss was gentle at first. Sweet even. But the moment Trevor's hand slid slightly deeper against her waist, something warmer sparked between them. The kind of heat that made the kiss linger just a little longer than it should have. Aniyah pulled back first, her breath catching slightly as she stepped away.

"Text me when you get home," she said.

Trevor nodded once, "I will."

She studied him for a second longer before turning toward the building.

The lobby doors closed behind her with a soft click.

Upstairs, Aniyah slipped off her boots and coat slowly, the quiet of her apartment wrapping around her like a familiar blanket. She walked over to the window and leaned lightly against the glass. Today had been...different from what she expected. Trevor Porter had always been handsome. She'd known that since high school. But tonight she had seen the other pieces too. The patience. The thoughtfulness. The way his voice softened when he talked about the things he loved. The way he looked at her like she was something worth paying attention to.

Aniyah stepped away from the window and decided to go

shower to settle her mind. However, her thoughts were still filled with him when she laid down for the night. She was in trouble. Because somewhere between the museum and the heated tent and that kiss outside her building... She was starting to fall for him. Her phone buzzed softly in her hand.

Zara's Daddy: Home.

Aniyah smiled to herself before typing back.

I love a man that listens.

Three dots appeared almost immediately.

Zara's Daddy: Baby I'd listen to anything you say.

Aniyah shook her head, laughing softly as she leaned against the kitchen counter.

Flattery will get you everywhere.

His reply came a second later.

Zara's Daddy: I hope so Roxanne. Sleep well.

Aniyah stared at the message for a moment and decided not to respond. Instead, she reached over to the small notebook resting on her nightstand and flipped it open to the page where the familiar words waited.

Her *What I'm Not* haikus. The pen moved across the page slowly.

What I'm Not
is…
Afraid of the fall
Love feels less like danger now
More like open sky

CHAPTER NINE

LET IT SNOW

"So, technically, you slept with Santa?" - *Mel, This Christmas (2007)*

The night of the Christmas play arrived faster than Aniyah expected.

Two weeks earlier the production had been little more than scattered scripts, misplaced props, and a classroom full of second graders who could not remember whether they were supposed to enter stage left or stage right. Somewhere between rehearsals, costume fittings, and the quiet rhythm of nightly phone calls with Trevor, everything had slowly come together.

Those phone calls had become... their thing.

Every night after Zara went to sleep and Aniyah finished grading papers, her phone would buzz. Sometimes they talked for twenty minutes. Sometimes it stretched past midnight. They talked about everything and nothing. Movies. Poetry. Zara's latest observations about the world. Which student had forgotten their lines that day and which one had suddenly remembered them.

The conversations had settled into a comfortable habit so easily it almost scared her.

And now here they were.

Aniyah stood near the side curtain with her clipboard pressed lightly against her chest, watching the controlled chaos unfold with the kind of quiet pride only teachers understood.

Tonight the stage looked like a real set.

The cardboard fireplace had been reinforced and repainted so the bricks looked almost convincing. Cotton batting draped along the back curtain to resemble snowbanks beneath a sky of construction paper stars. The borrowed spotlight from the high school theater department cast a warm glow over the center of the stage where the student playing Scrooge would soon sit in exaggerated misery.

Parents filled the folding chairs in the audience, bundled in coats and scarves.

Aniyah scanned the cast one more time.

"Remember," she called softly from the wings, her voice calm but firm. "Project your voices so the audience can hear you. And if someone forgets a line, you help them find their way back."

A small hand shot up from the row of ghost costumes.

"Ms. Henderson," Christopher whispered loudly beneath his gauzy sheet. "If I float too fast, will I still be a ghost or will I turn into a superhero?"

A ripple of laughter traveled through the children backstage.

Aniyah crouched down and adjusted the paper chain draped around his shoulders. "You will remain a ghost, Chris," she assured him gently. "But a very enthusiastic one."

The curtain rustled softly as parents settled into their seats.

Across the stage Trevor stood near the lighting controls,

sleeves pushed up to his forearms while he checked the brightness levels one last time. Even surrounded by the bustle of volunteers and parents, his presence carried a steady focus that somehow calmed the room rather than adding to the noise.

Their eyes met briefly across the stage.

The moment was quick enough to look accidental.

It wasn't.

There had been too many quiet conversations between them lately for that.

Zara appeared beside him wearing her ghost costume, the translucent fabric tied neatly at her shoulders so it floated around her small frame. She lifted both arms dramatically.

"Daddy, I practiced floating at TT Mac's house and Uncle Jackson said I looked professional."

Trevor crouched down so he was eye level with her. "That's because you are a professional."

Zara beamed and spun in a slow circle causing the fabric to flutter around her ankles.

Aniyah watched them for a moment longer than she should have.

It had become impossible not to notice how naturally Trevor moved through fatherhood. The way his attention always settled on Zara even when a dozen other things demanded it. The way he listened to her explanations about ghosts and stage cues like they mattered just as much as any film premiere he had ever attended.

Her chest tightened with something she didn't bother naming.

The house lights dimmed.

Parents quieted.

Aniyah straightened and lifted her hand toward the curtain.

"Places, everyone."

The play unfolded with the uneven magic only children could create.

Tiny Tim delivered his line about blessings with such dramatic sincerity that the audience burst into laughter before the scene was even finished. One of the boys playing a townsperson forgot his cue entirely and wandered across the stage holding a lantern while whispering loudly to another student, which only made the parents laugh harder.

When Zara's moment arrived she stepped forward with absolute commitment, lifting her arms as if the entire future of theater depended on her.

"I am the Ghost of Christmas Past," she declared proudly. "And I remember when you were mean, but you can be nicer now."

The audience applauded.

Aniyah pressed her lips together to keep from laughing and clapped softly along with them.

When the curtain closed, the children were buzzing with adrenaline and parents were already standing to take photographs.

The room filled with congratulations, coats rustling, and the excited chatter of students explaining the plot to adults who had literally just watched it happen.

Aniyah stepped out from the wings to help gather props when she noticed Trevor walking toward the audience.

Only now she saw how many people were waiting for Zara.

Mackenzie and Jackson stood near the front row, Mackenzie clapping proudly while Jackson held up his phone to record Zara bowing dramatically with the other children. Beside them stood a man she recognized as an older Angelou with a toddler balanced on his hip while another little girl clung to a woman she recognized as Mackenzie's business partner, Nina.

Nina leaned down to whisper something to them that made both girls giggle, their tiny braids bouncing as they laughed. Behind them stood Leon, Zara's grandfather, his chest puffed out with pride as if his granddaughter had just won an Oscar instead of reciting a ghost speech in a second-grade play. She only knew this because of her Google search.

Aniyah noticed two older couples standing nearby as well, just as excited as the rest of the group.

The group looked less like separate families and more like one big, joyful village that had gathered to celebrate a seven-year-old girl pretending to haunt Ebenezer Scrooge.

Aniyah stood there for a second longer than necessary. Zara had an entire room of people who loved her. Parents. Grandparents. Aunties. Uncles. Cousins. A whole support system orbited around her like she was the center of the sun. Aniyah felt something quiet and aching move through her chest. She wished her family had ever looked like that. She was even happier that Zara was not losing out on love just because her mother abandoned her.

Trevor eventually found her near the prop table where she was folding the makeshift curtain.

"That was impressive," he said, his voice carrying genuine admiration.

Aniyah glanced up at him; the exhaustion in her shoulders softened by pride. "They did the work. I just made sure they stayed pointed in the right direction."

"They adore you," he said.

Her gaze drifted back toward the stage where Zara was now explaining to the twins how ghosts floated with intention.

"They're good kids," she murmured.

Behind Trevor, Mackenzie approached with Jackson beside her and Zara skipping happily between them.

"Miss Henderson," Mackenzie said warmly, extending her hand. "I've been hearing about you for weeks."

Aniyah froze for half a second.

She had seen Mackenzie Levi Smith's work in galleries and

magazines. She had even assigned one of Mackenzie's photo essays to a writing prompt earlier in the semester.

Now the woman stood in front of her wearing a cream wool coat and smiling like they had known each other for years.

Aniyah shook her hand carefully. "It's nice to meet you."

Jackson nodded beside his wife with an easy grin. "Zara has been rehearsing her ghost speech at dinner every other night."

Zara puffed up proudly at that.

"We're stealing her tonight," Mackenzie continued gently. "Sleepover at our place. That way Trevor can relax after all this production work."

Zara pumped both fists in the air, "Sleepover!"

Trevor laughed quietly, "Okay, I will see you tomorrow , Superstar. You did an amazing job tonight." He leaned over and kissed Zara's forehead before she turned to leave, bouncing happily on her toes between her aunt and uncle.

When Mackenzie, Jackson, and the rest of the family began gathering coats and shepherding the kids toward the exit, the room slowly emptied around them.

Aniyah watched Zara disappear into that big, laughing group of people who loved her.

Trevor noticed where her attention had drifted.

"She's lucky," Aniyah said softly.

Trevor glanced toward the door where his family had just walked out.

"Yeah," he agreed.

Aniyah looked back at him.

Trevor studied her for a moment before speaking again.

"Dinner?" he asked.

"Tonight," he clarified. "Now that the star of the show has abandoned me."

She hesitated just long enough to feel that familiar flutter in her chest.

Then she smiled, "Okay."

"I've been teaching here for years but never stopped to eat here," Aniyah admitted as they were seated at their table.

The restaurant Trevor chose was small and warm, tucked between two narrow storefronts downtown where Christmas lights wrapped around every lamppost outside. Inside, amber light reflected softly against dark wood tables, and the low hum of conversation drifted through the room like background music.

Aniyah wrapped her hands around the glass of water the server had placed in front of her, letting the cool condensation steady the flutter in her chest. It was ridiculous that she felt nervous. They had just navigated a room full of second graders, wrangled ghosts made of bedsheets and survived the chaos of a school play. Still, sitting across from Trevor now, with nothing to distract her from the way his attention settled on her, made her aware of everything.

Trevor leaned back slightly in his chair, watching her with a quiet smile. "You didn't look nervous directing a room full of second graders."

"That's because I know them," she replied, glancing up from her glass. "Adults are unpredictable."

His laugh was low and easy, the kind that warmed the space between them. The server arrived with their food, and conversation slipped forward naturally after that. They talked about the play first, replaying the moments that had made them both laugh —Christopher nearly flying across the stage in his ghost costume, Zara bowing like she'd just finished a Broadway run.

Trevor shook his head, smiling into his drink. "She's going to be talking about that performance all week."

"She should," Aniyah said, cutting into her food. "She carried that scene."

"She commits to everything with so much passion...it's inspiring," he replied, pride threading through his voice.

Aniyah noticed the softness there, the way his expression changed whenever Zara came up. It was the same look she'd seen earlier when he crouched beside her backstage, listening to her explain ghost logistics like it was the most important conversation in the room. The man loved that little girl with his whole chest.

For a moment the conversation quieted while they ate. The restaurant hummed around them, glasses clinking and low laughter drifting from nearby tables, but their corner of the room felt oddly still.

Aniyah set her fork down and tilted her head slightly. "Can I ask you something?"

Trevor didn't hesitate. "You can ask me anything."

She studied him for a moment before speaking. "What would it actually look like... if we were together?"

The question hung between them for a second. Trevor leaned back slightly, considering it, his fingers tracing the rim of his glass while he thought.

"I think it would look like showing up," he said finally.

Aniyah lifted a brow. "That's vague."

He smiled faintly. "Not really. I could see us showing up and being there for each other in all aspects whether work or personal. We'd be there for each other in every season. It looks like being at peace, finally."

She watched him carefully, the sincerity in his voice settling somewhere warm in her chest.

"And arguments about movies," he added.

Aniyah laughed softly, "You started that." Mentioning the night they went back and forth about which *Sister Act* movie was the best. Trevor thought the first one and Aniyah heavily disagreed.

"I was right."

"You were not."

Trevor chuckled, but the humor faded into something softer as he met her eyes again. "I think it will be steady," he said after a moment. "Talking to you has given me a sense of peace that I didn't know I was capable of experiencing"

His shoulders lifted in a small shrug like what he was saying wasn't swoon worthy and continued, "we're two people building something as they go."

Aniyah leaned back slightly in her chair, absorbing that. The way he said it made the idea feel less like some distant possibility and more like something quietly unfolding already.

"What about Zara? When she spent the afternoon with me, we talked about getting manicures. I would like to take her, if that's okay?" she asked.

"I would love that, and I know she would too. Tell me when and I will bring her to meet you."

"Thank you. She is an amazing little girl that means a lot to me."

Trevor didn't hesitate in his response, "You already matter to her."

The answer surprised her enough that she blinked.

"She talks about you," he continued. "More than you probably realize."

Aniyah glanced down at the table for a second, warmth creeping up the back of her neck.

"And I trust you with her," he added gently.

Trevor exhaled slowly and rubbed the back of his neck like he was working through something out loud. "The truth is... I didn't expect to feel like this again so soon."

Her gaze lifted from her wine. Trevor met it without flinching.

"I'm falling for you, Aniyah."

The words landed quietly, but their weight settled deep in her chest.

For a moment she just looked at him. Trevor gave a small, almost self-conscious smile. "I know it's early. I know we're still figuring this out."

He lifted one shoulder slightly.

"But pretending it's not happening feels dishonest."

Aniyah let out a slow breath she hadn't realized she'd been holding. "I'm not pretending either," she admitted softly. "I tried so hard to. I enjoy my solitude and the peace it's brought me to shut everyone out. Now? I find myself day dreaming about you more often, wondering when we will spend time together again. I'm falling for you too, Trevor."

Something in Trevor's expression softened then, the tension easing out of his shoulders like he'd been bracing for something else entirely. Aniyah was happy their feelings were finally out in the open.

Dinner drifted forward after that in an easier rhythm, the kind that came when two people had said something important and were now letting it settle between them.

"You want some ice cream for dessert?" Trevor asked. Aniyah knew she shouldn't have it, dairy was one of her triggers. But the night was beautiful and she hadn't had ice cream in months. Her face lit up as she nodded.

When they finally stepped back outside, the night air felt colder than before. Trevor walked her to her car, the glow of Christmas lights reflecting off the pavement beneath their feet.

They stopped beside the driver's door.

"You had fun tonight?" he asked.

Aniyah leaned lightly against the car and looked up at him, "I did."

Trevor stepped closer, not enough to crowd her but enough that the space between them disappeared.

His hand brushed her waist as he leaned down.

The kiss started soft, almost careful. But when Aniyah's hands slid up the front of his coat, Trevor pulled her a little closer and the warmth between them deepened quickly, the kind of kiss that blurred the street around them and made the cold air feel distant.

When they finally separated, they were smiling.

Trevor rested his forehead briefly against hers. "Come to Christmas dinner with my family."

Aniyah blinked, surprised.

"My dad's hosting this year," he said quietly. "You should be there."

The invitation carried more weight than the kiss.

She nodded slowly ignoring the voice at the back of her head telling her *hell no*, "Okay."

Later that night, Aniyah stepped back into her condo and leaned against the door for a moment while the quiet wrapped around her again. Today had been amazing and that dinner with Trevor...everything she needed and more. She sent him a quick text to let him know she was inside.

Her phone buzzed in her hand.

> Zara's Daddy: Thank you for following directions.

Aniyah laughed softly and sent back a middle finger emoji before kicking off her boots. This was their routine if they weren't talking on the phone.

A second later his reply appeared.

> Zara's Daddy: Goodnight, Roxanne.

Her cheeks warmed instantly.

She stared at the message for a moment longer than necessary before setting the phone down on the counter, shaking her head to herself.

She was falling for him too

"Girl, what is all this shit in your hand?!" Aniyah asked.

The next evening, her condo looked less like the carefully curated sanctuary she usually kept and more like what it became every year once Christmas break started. A place for her girls. A place where the three of them could slip back into the easy rhythm of being known.

Aniyah winced as she placed an ornament on her small Christmas tree. She knew she should've said no to ice cream the night prior, now she was dealing with a flare under her arm like she was a teenager again.

"I'll get through this like I've gotten through everything else," she thought to herself.

Mya arrived first, balancing two overnight bags on one shoulder while clutching a bottle of tequila in one hand and an alarming amount of snacks in the other. Her faux locs were twisted into a high bun tonight, and she wore a long wool coat over the matching plaid pajamas she had bullied them into buying weeks ago.

"You preparing for the apocalypse?" Aniyah asked, stepping aside to let her in.

Mya dropped the bags onto the couch and kicked the door shut with her foot. "Please. If we get snowed in, you'll thank me.

Also, I refuse to experience emotional conversations without snacks."

Aniyah laughed, taking the tequila from her and setting it on the counter.

Stephanie arrived twenty minutes later, hair already in a bonnet and carrying a paper bag high over her head like a victory flag. "If either one of y'all says you already ate," she warned from the doorway, "I'm turning around and leaving with these tacos."

Aniyah took the bag quickly. "Come inside before the sour cream gets soggy."

"How are you feeling today boo?" Mya asked, setting all of her snacks out on the counter, "I know you had a flare. It's been a minute since the last one right?"

Aniyah nodded, feeling a sense of comfort with the care displayed in Mya's eyes.

"This one is not as bad as others I've had in the past. But it's still painful. I think it had something to do with the ice cream I shared with Trevor last night, because waking up with a flare the size of a quarter under my arm was not on my bingo card for Christmas."

Stephanie and Mya continued to listen closely, they had seen firsthand how Hidradenitis Suppurativa had wrecked Aniyah's life throughout the years. They had been there through her embarrassment, her pain, her uncertainty. They knew she preferred being alone because she feared rejection when someone saw her scars or learned of her illness.

"Ice cream with Trevor huh? We'll put a pin in that," Mya noted, "continue."

"I've been taking my ibuprofen 800s, doing the hot compresses, drinking my turmeric tea and rubbing my salve on it. You know I'm a pro at this now. I just have to get through it. I will say, I'm glad this waited until the school season was over for the semester. Trying to run with kids while not being able to raise your arm is a bitch."

"I understand honey. So sit your ass down and put that compress back on. We got everything else," Stephanie commanded.

"Okay okay, I'm sitting."

Within an hour the condo smelled like seasoned meat, cocoa powder, cinnamon, and the candle Mya had lit despite Aniyah insisting she didn't need one. They changed into their matching pajamas, thick socks sliding softly across the hardwood floors as they built their usual nest in the living room with blankets, oversized floor pillows, and the good throw that still made Aniyah think of Grandpa Earl every time she unfolded it.

Almost Christmas played first, followed by This Christmas not long after, the television casting a soft glow across their faces while they ate tacos straight from foil wrappers and argued over which movie had the better family fight scene.

As the cocoa was poured into oversized mugs and marshmallows began dissolving into the surface, the room had settled into the kind of warmth only years of friendship could create.

Mya tucked her legs beneath her and held out her left hand dramatically. "Before we get into what's been going on with Mr. Director and our golden girl. I have something to say. Will proposed!"

Stephanie grabbed her hand and squinted at the ring like a jeweler inspecting merchandise. "Girl what?! When?! How are we just now finding out about it?!"

Mya giggled, "It literally happened last night. Y'all know I thought he had been sneaking around, turns out he was trying to plan when to pop the question."

Aniyah leaned forward to look too, the Christmas lights from the tree catching the stone as it sparkled. "That's amazing Mya. I'm really happy for you," she said softly.

Mya's expression softened immediately. "I know. And thank you. I still look down sometimes and get surprised all over again."

Stephanie lifted her cocoa and sighed dramatically. Then looked at them with a sly smile on her face "Meanwhile I'm over here becoming somebody's mama..."

Aniyah's head snapped up so fast she almost spilled her drink. "What."

Mya nearly choked, "Bitch, what."

Stephanie burst out laughing at their faces and held up both hands. "Relax. I just found out this week. And before either of y'all starts hollering, I wanted to tell y'all tonight. Deshawn is excited. He's already fixing up the nursery, crazy ass." They all laughed at that. "And... I also got promoted."

She took a long sip of cocoa like she hadn't just dropped three major life updates at once, "Life apparently decided I needed all my blessings at the same damn time."

The room exploded.

Aniyah and Mya lunged forward at the same time, nearly knocking the coffee table over as they wrapped Stephanie in a hug. Stephanie laughed into their shoulders, muttering something about regretting telling them before midnight while they squeezed her tight.

When they finally fell back into the mountain of blankets again, Mya turned her attention slowly toward Aniyah.

"All right," she said calmly. "Your turn."

Aniyah blinked into her mug. "My turn for what."

Stephanie pointed at her immediately. "For whatever has you over there smiling at cocoa like somebody wrote a love letter in it."

Aniyah drew her knees up beneath the blanket and pretended to think harder than necessary.

"It's nothing huge compared to the information that was just shared," she said carefully.

Both women stared at her in perfect silence until she sighed.

"Trevor invited me to Christmas dinner with his family."

That landed exactly the way she expected it would.

Mya sat up straighter. "First ice cream, now Christmas dinner. Y'all basically go steady at this point. Where is dinner?"

"At his dad's house," Aniyah answered.

Stephanie leaned back against the couch and let out a long whistle. "Oh that man is serious enough to be dangerous."

Aniyah looked down at her mug. "I don't know if dangerous is the word I'd use anymore after the time we've been spending together."

"It is," Mya said calmly. "Because that is not just casual friendly behavior. Men do not bring just anybody to Christmas dinner. Especially not men with families like the Porters."

Stephanie nodded emphatically. "Tight tight families like theirs? You get folded into something like that and suddenly everybody knows your business and feeds you at the same time."

Aniyah traced her thumb along the handle of her mug, "I almost said no."

"But you didn't," Mya said.

"No."

Stephanie grinned. "Good. Because both of us are out of town this year and I refuse to imagine you sitting here by yourself eating leftovers while that man and his fine ass family are somewhere passing greens and arguing over who burned the mac and cheese."

Aniyah laughed despite herself. "You only care because you want information."

Stephanie leaned forward shamelessly. "Listen! I had the biggest crush on Angelou when we were kids."

Mya groaned immediately. "Oh brother, here we go again like we didn't have to live through that obsession."

"No because I'm serious," Stephanie continued, fanning

herself with a pillow. “Remember when he had them braids? That boy used to walk through the hallway when he came to pick up Trevor like rent was due and he owned the building.”

Aniyah laughed so hard she had to set her mug down.

“You are ridiculous.”

“I’m honest,” Stephanie corrected. “There’s a difference.”

Mya shook her head, but her smile stayed. Then her tone shifted slightly, not harsh but careful.

“All jokes aside,” she said, looking directly at Aniyah now. “I think you should go. I really do. You deserve to be around some warmth.”

Aniyah felt the sincerity in that.

But Mya wasn’t finished, “I just need you to keep your eyes open,” she added gently. “Trevor is newly single. I’m not saying he’s not a good man. Everything you’ve told us says he is. I just don’t want you getting pulled into something tender while he’s still figuring out what’s left of him. Other than that, have a good time with his family.”

Aniyah nodded slowly, “I will.”

Stephanie reached across the blanket pile and squeezed her ankle. “You can know that you need to be careful and still enjoy yourself. They’re not opposites. There is room for both.”

Mya nodded. “Exactly. Go. Eat good food. Let that family love on you like we know they are going to.”

Aniyah thought for a moment, then a picture popped in her head of all those friendly faces she met the night before standing around the Christmas tree filled with warmth and love she hadn’t experienced since her grandpa’s passing.”

“I’m going.”

Both of her friends answered at the same time, loud enough to drown out the movie.

“Good.”

Aniyah's kitchen smelled like brown sugar, butter, and cinnamon when the sweet potato soufflé came out of the oven, the top puffed golden and delicate the way her grandfather used to like it. She stood there a moment longer than necessary, oven mitt still on one hand, watching the steam curl into the air like it carried pieces of memory with it. Of course she had chosen this dish. Papa Earl used to say no Christmas table was respectable without it, and the thought steadied her nerves in a way nothing else had all afternoon.

Thankfully her flare had gone down in the last few days which helped lift her spirits tremendously today.

Her phone buzzed against the counter.

Patrice.

Aniyah stared at the name long enough for the call to roll itself to voicemail, the familiar heaviness settling briefly in her chest before she reached over and tapped the screen again. Block caller. The quiet that followed felt immediate and clean, like opening a window after a storm.

Nothing good ever came from those conversations. And she didn't need that. Not on a day that felt fragile in a way she wanted to protect.

She wiped her hands on a towel and leaned her hip against the counter, letting her mind drift the way it always did around Christmas.

Her last holiday with Papa Earl rose easily.

The brownstone glowing like a lighthouse on the block, every window strung with lights because he said decorations should be seen from the street. The smell of food drifting down the hallway while he hummed along to old Christmas records. Them singing badly together in the kitchen, laughing when the notes slipped away from them. Movies playing back to back while snow gathered along the window ledges and neither of them bothered to check the time.

She smiled softly.

That Christmas had been perfect in a way that never asked for anything more.

And because they had that time, because she had filled that house with love while he was still there to enjoy it, the ache of his absence never swallowed the holiday the way people always warned it would.

It simply sat beside it.

A quiet companion instead of a wound.

By the time she slid the covered dish into her car and began the short drive toward Leon Porter's house, the neighborhood had already fallen into its evening glow. Lights hung from every railing and porch, wreaths fastened to doors, children's laughter drifting faintly through the cold air whenever someone opened a window.

When she turned onto the familiar street, her chest tightened in a way she hadn't expected.

Papa Earl's brownstone sat only a few blocks away.

She slowed instinctively as she passed it, her eyes drifting toward the stoop she used to climb every day after school. Tonight the house was lit from top to bottom, the windows glowing with the kind of warmth that meant people were inside laughing, eating, living.

Her smile came easily.

Good.

The house deserved that.

A few doors down, a bay window revealed a family gathered around their Christmas tree, all of them wearing matching pajamas while music spilled into the street. The parents were dancing badly, their children spinning between them in loose, happy circles while someone tried to clap along with the beat.

Aniyah watched for a second longer than she meant to.

Then she pulled away, warmth settling quietly in her chest.

The Porter house appeared at the end of the block in a soft blaze of light and evergreen garlands; the front porch wrapped in gold ribbon and red bows. Through the windows she could see silhouettes moving inside, hear laughter rising and falling over the music playing somewhere deeper in the house.

A home full of people.

A home full of ease.

She stood outside Leon Porter's front door with the covered dish in her hands and her heart behaving like it had somewhere urgent to be.

She had spent enough holidays in silence to know the difference between entering a house and entering a family.

Before she could knock twice, the door swung open.

Trevor stood there in a cream cable-knit sweater and dark jeans, and for a second the winter air between them disappeared entirely.

He stilled when he saw her. Just enough that Aniyah noticed the way his shoulders settled, the way his gaze softened like he had been looking forward to this exact moment longer than he intended to admit.

Yearning lived there.

Quiet but unmistakable.

Aniyah suddenly became aware of the soft curl of her hair against her shoulders, the careful sweater she had chosen, the way her fingers tightened slightly around the dish.

Trevor stepped forward and pressed a brief kiss against her cheek before taking the soufflé from her hands, his fingers brushing hers as he did.

"You came," he said.

The words were simple, but the relief in them loosened something in her chest.

"I said I would."

His smile deepened, dimples appearing like they had no business being that effective on a grown woman. "I know. I just... I'm glad you did."

"I'm glad I did too," Aniyah beamed. "Let's get inside, it's freezing out here."

The warmth from inside wrapped around her the moment she crossed the threshold. The house smelled like roasted meat, brown sugar, spices, and something savory that reminded her immediately of Sunday dinners from another life. Music floated through the rooms, laughter bursting from somewhere deeper in the house with the confidence of people who had loved each other a long time.

Trevor leaned closer as he closed the door behind her, his voice dropping just enough to brush against her ear. "You nervous?"

Aniyah glanced up at him. "A little."

He smiled gently. "Don't be. They've already decided they like you."

"Already?"

"You should hear the phone calls I've been getting."

Before she could ask what that meant, Zara's voice rang out from the living room.

"Ms. Henderson!"

The little girl barreled toward her in velvet red tights and gold hair clips, all delight and momentum. Aniyah barely had time to bend before Zara wrapped her arms around her waist.

"You came for real," Zara said, pulling back just enough to beam up at her. "I told Daddy you would."

Aniyah laughed softly and touched one of the gold clips in her curls. "Well, I couldn't miss Christmas with the star of the play."

Zara puffed up proudly before darting away again toward the chaos of children somewhere near the tree.

Trevor chuckled beside her.

Then the welcoming truly began.

Mackenzie and Nina approached first, Mackenzie glowing in deep emerald and Nina wrapped in burgundy knit that somehow looked both elegant and comfortable.

"Ms. Henderson, so lovely to see you again." Nina said with a knowing smile.

Aniyah laughed softly, glancing between them. "Please, call me Aniyah. It's so nice to see you again... Nina?" She stated her name slowly to ensure accuracy.

Nina pulled her into a hug immediately. "You got it right. I see Trevor has been running that mouth."

Behind them Trevor groaned. "Nina."

"What?" she said calmly. "It's Christmas."

Mackenzie stepped in next, her smile warm and curious. "We're really glad you came. Trevor has been smiling suspiciously hard these past few weeks."

"Mac," Trevor muttered again.

Aniyah laughed before she could stop herself, the nervousness already easing.

The house folded her in quickly after that.

Leon Porter greeted her with both hands wrapped warmly around hers, welcoming her like she had always belonged there before introducing her to Ms. Teri, a graceful woman whose presence seemed to soften the room around Leon in a way that didn't go unnoticed.

Trevor leaned toward her shoulder as they moved toward the kitchen.

"My brothers haven't figured it out yet," he whispered.

Aniyah tilted her head slightly, “Figured what out?”

“That my dad is sweet on Ms. Teri.”

Aniyah glanced across the room just in time to see Leon smile at the woman in question.

“Oh,” she murmured amused.

Trevor grinned, buzzing at the secret that the two of them now shared.

The introductions continued.

Jackson appeared carrying glasses, locs pulled back neatly, while Angelou followed behind him looking every bit as devastating as Stephanie had once described. Nina and Mackenzie’s parents were introduced soon after, both greeting her warmly like Trevor had mentioned her more than once before.

Somehow none of it felt overwhelming.

Aniyah barely had time to finish greeting Leon before the house seemed to sweep her along with it.

Someone took her coat, someone else guided her toward the kitchen where the counter had already become a crowded landscape of casseroles, pies, and serving dishes, and before she could catch her bearings she was being introduced again.

“This is Aniyah,” Trevor said for what had to be the fourth time, though his voice carried a quiet pride that made the repetition feel intentional.

Cousins appeared, babies balanced on hips, family friends who greeted her with warm familiarity of someone they’ve known for a long time. Someone pressed a glass of cider into her hand while another asked if she needed somewhere to put the sweet potato soufflé she brought. The movement from room to room should have been overwhelming, but somehow it wasn’t.

She found herself ushered from the kitchen into the living room, then into the den where a group of older relatives were deep in conversation about something that sounded like church politics, every greeting layered with warmth.

At one point Mackenzie reappeared at her side, gently steering her toward two older couples seated near the fireplace.

"Mom, Dad, Ms. Juanita and Mr. Richard, I'd like to introduce you to Trevor's special guest Aniyah."

"My daughter Nina has told me about you. Trevor speaks highly of you," Juanita said with a knowing look that made Aniyah glance instinctively toward where Trevor stood across the room.

He caught her eye at that exact moment. The small smile he gave her held something softer than pride. If she didn't know any better she'd think it was a look of love.

Aniyah should have felt nervous about it, but she didn't. Somehow, it all felt natural.

As everyone finally gathered around the dining table, the room glowed with candlelight and warmth. Candles burned low at the center of the table, their reflections dancing across polished glass and serving dishes crowded with food. Plates moved from hand to hand while conversations overlapped in easy waves.

"Angelou, stop stealing rolls before the children get their share," Nina said without even looking up from her plate.

"I'm tasting for quality control," he replied calmly.

Jackson quietly slid a slice of ham onto Mackenzie's plate without her asking while she continued talking, and Nina wiped one of the twins' mouths with a napkin mid-sentence like it required no effort at all.

Aniyah found herself laughing more than she had in weeks.

At one point Mackenzie leaned toward her, curiosity dancing in her eyes. "Tell me something. Was my brother-in-law as ridiculous in high school as I imagined?"

Aniyah nearly choked on her drink.

Trevor looked up sharply from two seats down. "You don't have to answer that."

"Oh, she absolutely does," Nina said immediately.

Aniyah wiped her mouth, laughter already threatening again as she looked between them before surrendering. "I only really knew Trevor like that because we were in the same grade," She stopped pointing her fork at Trevor and his brothers, "but you and your brothers definitely had reputations."

Angelou leaned back in his chair with dramatic offense, placing a hand over his chest, "Reputations for what?"

Aniyah lifted a brow slowly, "You really want me to describe the Porter brothers as young bulls? Please don't make me say that at Christmas dinner."

Angelou turned a shade of red that made Jackson laugh instantly.

Mackenzie dropped her head against Jackson's shoulder, already losing it while Nina grinned wickedly across the table.

"Say it anyway."

Angelou pointed at Aniyah like she had personally betrayed him. "You really don't have to."

Aniyah took a slow sip of water, pretending to gather courage before placing her glass down again. "Fine. They were all very fine. Very well known. And very committed to not settling down."

The table erupted.

Angelou exhaled dramatically. "I was a young man exploring my options."

"Exploring," Mackenzie repeated through laughter.

Aniyah shook her head, smiling as she looked directly at him. "Exploring? More like ho'in, Santa."

Jackson nearly knocked his glass over laughing while Nina slapped the table.

Aniyah pointed at Angelou again. "Don't remember the motto you had Trevor walking around school saying?"

Both Trevor and Angelou turned red immediately.

"Babe," Trevor said quickly, leaning forward like he might

physically stop her. "Please do not repeat that. That was such a long time ago."

The word hung in the air.

Babe.

Aniyah's eyes widened slightly as the table went quiet for half a second before the teasing started immediately.

"Now why am I in it?" Angelou demanded, his voice slipping into a perfect imitation of 50 Cent.

Trevor shook his head, smiling despite himself. "You walked right into that one."

Laughter rolled around the table again, louder this time, folding Aniyah deeper into the warmth of the room.

The dessert appeared and the children had begun sliding under the table with sugar buzzing through their systems, Aniyah leaned back in her chair and looked around the room.

At Trevor laughing beside his brother.

At Leon shaking his head at something Nina said.

At Mackenzie and Jackson sharing quiet smiles between bites.

Spades came out later, Aniyah found herself sitting beside Nina with absolute confidence while Trevor and Angelou watched the cards like their reputations depended on it.

"We just ran a Boston on your asses, get up from my table," Nina announced loudly.

Angelou stared at the table like betrayal had just occurred. When really it was him underbidding and reneging on 3 of his hands. Trevor leaned back in his chair groaning while Jackson laughed loud enough to rattle the glasses.

"They will never let us forget this," Trevor muttered.

Aniyah smiled sweetly, "Correct sweetie, now move along."

Later the twins climbed all over her lap calling her "TT," and she found herself laughing with Leon over vinyl records, proudly informing him she owned a few Coltrane pressings he was still missing.

Then *Gee Whiz, It's Christmas* began to play.

All the Porter men rose like it had been choreographed.

Aniyah blinked in surprise as Trevor, Jackson, and Angelou began singing loudly and unapologetically off-key while Mackenzie leaned toward her with a grin.

"It was their mom's favorite song," she explained. "They sing it every year to honor her memory."

Aniyah watched them, warmth filling her chest as the room erupted in laughter and clapping.

They looked happy.

Really happy.

She loved that moment more than she expected to.

When Let It Snow by Boyz II Men floated through the speakers next, Trevor appeared beside her again, his hand extended.

"May I have this dance?" He asked smoothly. Aniyah slipped her hand into his without any hesitation.

Across the room Leon danced slowly with Ms. Teri while Angelou swayed Nina around the floor and Jackson pulled Mackenzie close with quiet ease.

Trevor's arms wrapped around her gently, guiding her into a slow rhythm beneath the soft glow of Christmas lights.

"This is perfect," he murmured near her ear. "I love everything about this moment. Thank you for coming."

Aniyah rested lightly against him, her voice soft with truth. "Thank you for inviting me. This will go down as the best Christmas I've had since my grandpa died."

At that moment Aniyah wanted Trevor to kiss her so badly, but she restrained herself. They would have their time alone soon, she hoped. For now, she was happy slow dancing to music with him lost in the feels of Christmas.

"We could have this every Christmas, if you want," Trevor

stated casually as if he didn't just insinuate something serious. Aniyah allowed herself to be in the moment. Not letting her past traumas cloud what was on her heart.

"I'd like that," she replied softly. Trevor kissed her forehead in response, held her tighter and continued to sway to the music.

When coats were pulled from closets and leftovers packed into containers nobody needed but everybody took, Aniyah knew she would carry the feeling of that house home with her.

Trevor walked her to the door, then out onto the stoop, the night air biting just enough to make the warmth they had left behind feel more vivid. For a moment they stood side by side under the porch light, breath clouding faintly in front of them.

"So," he said, glancing at her. "Still think adults are more unpredictable than children?"

Aniyah smiled, "Your family might be the exception."

He shifted closer, hands tucked into the pockets of his coat, his eyes lingering on her face in a way that made the cold irrelevant.

"They liked you," he said softly.

She looked toward the door behind them where laughter still leaked through the walls, "I liked them too. It's nice to see a big family that genuinely loves each other. I...I only experienced that with my friend's family."

His mouth curved, "They are a good bunch although they get on my nerves. The smile on your face lets me know I was right in my decision to invite you."

Aniyah laughed under her breath, "You're very pleased with yourself tonight."

"I'm pleased you came. More than you know..."

The honesty in that settled between them.

When he stepped closer, she did not move back. When his hand lifted to touch the side of her face, she leaned into it before she could stop herself.

The kiss started warm and deepened quickly, months of tension and curiosity answering one another in the cold. Her back met the door with a soft thud, his body close enough to steal the rest of the winter from her skin. His hands moved from her waist to her thighs, then up again with the kind of care that made the heat more dangerous, not less.

Aniyah slid her hands beneath his coat, fingers clutching the sweater at his back as he kissed her harder. The porch light burned above them. The cold night wrapped around them. Neither of them cared.

His hand slipped beneath the hem of her dress, palm pressing against the sensitive peak between her thighs. Her breath broke in a soft sound against his mouth, and his forehead dropped briefly to hers. They were fighting hard against their desire to make love on this stoop.

"Trevor," she whispered, though it was not a warning. It sounded too much like surrender.

His fingers moved higher, his mouth finding the line of her jaw, then her throat, and the world narrowed to touch and breath and the hard line of him against her. Trevor's hands rubbed against her warmth. She was absolutely drenched. Was she gonna let him finger her to completion on his father's stoop? Right now, it didn't matter what was going on in the outside world. All she cared about was the feelings of his hand moving back-and-forth across her clit, his lips on her and the moans that were escaping her. She wanted this man as much as she wanted to breathe.

A throat cleared behind them.

The sound sliced through the moment with surgical precision.

They sprang apart just enough to turn.

Katelyn stood at the foot of the stoop in a camel coat, her expression carved from something colder than the weather. Her gaze stayed on Trevor first.

"You don't waste any time moving on, do you, Trevor?" Then she looked at Aniyah, and the air changed.

"And you," she said, voice low and sharp with recognition and fury. "Didn't I tell you to stay the fuck away from my family?"

CHAPTER TEN

FAMILIAR, BUT NOT THE SAME

"Frankly, my dear, I don't give a damn." - *Rhett Butler, Gone With The Wind (1939)*

Trevor froze.

For a split second his brain refused to process what his eyes were telling him. The cold December air pressed against his skin, the porch light spilling warm gold across the steps, and standing at the bottom of the stoop like something dragged out of a past he had already buried was Katelyn.

His first instinct was disbelief, "Katelyn?"

Her posture straightened slightly when she heard her name, chin lifting the way it always had when she wanted to reclaim control of a room. She wore a long winter coat that looked expensive but thin, the kind of coat someone bought for appearance rather than warmth. Her now blonde hair framed her face in soft waves, makeup flawless enough to suggest she had expected to be seen tonight.

Trevor stepped forward instinctively, placing himself between her and Aniyah without even thinking about it.

"What are you doing here?" The question left his mouth low and controlled, but the shock in it was obvious. Before Katelyn could answer, Aniyah's voice cut through the air like glass snapping.

"Actually," she said sharply, stepping closer to Trevor's shoulder, "who the fuck do you think you're talking to?" Trevor blinked. For half a heartbeat he forgot the tension sitting in front of them and glanced sideways at Aniyah. There it was. That fire. He had not seen it since high school, back when Aniyah Henderson had been the quiet girl who rarely spoke but could dismantle somebody with a single sentence when she did. The sight of it now sent a strange warmth through him even in the middle of chaos.

Katelyn's eyes narrowed, "Excuse me?"

Trevor's attention returned to her quickly.

"Answer the question," he said, voice firm. "Why are you here?"

Katelyn's expression shifted then. The hardness softened around the edges, her shoulders lowering just enough to suggest vulnerability.

"This is the first Christmas without Zara," she said quietly. "Do you have any idea how hard that is for me? I miss my daughter, Trevor. I miss her more than you know." The silence that followed lasted only a moment.

Aniyah laughed. It was not a cruel laugh. It was the kind of laugh someone made when a lie was so obvious it almost insulted their intelligence. Katelyn's head snapped toward her.

"What exactly is funny?" Aniyah folded her arms slowly.

"Oh nothing," she replied calmly. "It's just interesting that you suddenly miss your daughter tonight of all nights."

Katelyn's lips pressed into a thin line. Trevor glanced between them, sensing the tension shift in a way he did not fully understand yet. Aniyah tilted her head slightly.

"Especially after the article that ran this morning."

Katelyn's eyes flickered to Aniyah with a hint of surprise.

"Excuse me?"

Aniyah reached into the pocket of her coat and pulled out her phone. The screen lit up as she tapped once before turning it outward.

"Mya sent this to me earlier today," she said casually to Katelyn because she was tired of the song and dance. "Apparently your boyfriend has been busy."

Trevor frowned in confusion not understanding what Aniyah was talking about.

"What article?"

Aniyah held the phone up where Katelyn could see it clearly.

The headline sat beneath a polished photo of a square-jawed man whose physique looked like he had been carved out of granite.

FINANCE HEIR VICTOR STRAUSS ANNOUNCES ENGAGEMENT TO SOCIALITE LILLIAN ASHBURY

Trevor let out a low breath. The name rang a bell immediately. The Ashbury family was old money. The kind that appeared on museum boards and gala invitations. They were the sort of family people compared to the Kennedys when they wanted to imply legacy and power in the same sentence.

Katelyn's jaw tightened at seeing that stupid article again. It came as a total surprise to her this morning when her code no longer worked to get into the penthouse. There had been no warning and Victor hadn't said a word to her. Aniyah slid the phone back into her pocket.

"So forgive me if I'm not buying the sudden motherly nostalgia."

Katelyn's eyes flashed with irritation.

"And why exactly are you here anyway?" she snapped. "This is a family gathering."

Aniyah's brow lifted in indignation, "Yes," she replied evenly. "I was invited, unlike you."

The words landed across Katelyn's face like a slap.

Katelyn stepped closer to the stairs, anger replacing the fragile vulnerability she had tried to perform moments earlier.

"You're trying to insert yourself into a family that isn't yours," she said sharply. "I understand that you don't have one, but that doesn't mean you get to play house with mine."

Trevor felt Aniyah stiffen behind him as Katelyn continued.

"Newsflash Aniyah, Trevor and Zara will always belong to me. Enjoy pretending to be step mommy while you can."

"Girl, fuck you and that delusional horse you rode here on in that cheap ass coat," Aniyah spit out.

The front door opened behind them. Warm light spilled onto the porch as Nina stepped outside, one hand holding the door open as she scanned the scene with mild curiosity. She had come outside expecting something entirely different. Inside the house, she and Leon had been laughing quietly over a bet they had made earlier in the evening about how long it would take Trevor and Aniyah to make their first real move. Nina had confidently said it would happen tonight. Leon insisted Trevor would overthink it until after Christmas. Two hundred dollars was currently riding on the outcome. Naturally, Nina had stepped outside to check. What she found instead was Katelyn standing at the bottom of the steps in a cheap looking winter coat glaring like a Disney villain.

Nina blinked once.

"Is everything alright out here?" she asked lightly.

Nina's gaze moved slowly across the scene in front of her, taking in every detail with the calm scrutiny of someone who missed very little. The porch light cast a warm halo behind Trevor and Aniyah on the stoop, but her attention slid past them toward the figure standing at the bottom of the steps.

Katelyn.

For a brief second Nina said nothing. She simply looked at her, eyes traveling from the glossy waves of blonde hair to the thin winter coat that looked more expensive than warm. The woman stood there like she had every right to occupy the space, chin tipped upward with that familiar air of entitlement Nina had always disliked.

Then Nina's gaze returned to Trevor.

Her voice was light, almost conversational.

"I didn't realize trash collection ran on holidays." The words settled into the cold air with surgical precision.

Katelyn's head snapped toward her so quickly the ends of her hair swung across her cheek.

Trevor let out a slow breath through his nose. Up until that moment he had been holding himself together with sheer restraint, but the sight of Katelyn standing on his father's property like she had any claim to it made something inside him shift.

"Katelyn," he said, his voice losing the last thin thread of patience it had been clinging to. "Why are you really here?"

For a moment she looked like she might try to hold onto the fragile vulnerability she had been performing earlier, but Trevor didn't give her time to answer.

"You haven't given a shit about us this entire time," he continued, the words coming slower now, heavier. "The divorce was finalized over a month ago. Our marriage was dead a year and a half before that and Zara hasn't seen you in damn near four months."

The porch had gone completely quiet. Trevor's voice sharpened with the weight of everything he had swallowed for too long.

"So tell me what exactly it is you think you miss," he said. "Because it wasn't us. You made it very clear you didn't want this life. Remember that conversation? I was just the guy you picked because everybody wanted me." His eyes held hers. "Isn't that what you said?"

Behind him, Aniyah felt the tension radiating off his body like heat from asphalt in July. His shoulders had gone rigid beneath his coat and the muscles in his jaw flexed. It looked like he was trying to swallow the anger that was threatening to spew itself everywhere in that moment. Without thinking, she lifted her hand and placed it gently against the center of his back. The contact was light but deliberate. Trevor stilled under her touch, drawing in a breath that filled his lungs before he released it slowly through his nose. Katelyn started up the steps. Nina's voice cut through the movement immediately.

"Not too close." There was no raise in volume, but the authority in it carried just as clearly. "You're trespassing."

Katelyn stopped two steps below them. For the first time since she arrived, the composure she had been clinging to cracked. Her shoulders sagged slightly and when she spoke again her voice sounded thinner.

"I made a mistake," she said quietly.

Trevor watched her without moving.

"I thought I was suffocating," she continued, her gaze dropping briefly to the steps between them. "I felt like I didn't have an identity outside of you and Zara. Every day felt like I was disappearing into someone else's life."

Her throat bobbed as she swallowed.

"I thought my life didn't have meaning." The words trembled now, breaking apart as tears began sliding down her cheeks. "I should have never done what I did," she whispered. "Trevor, I'm so sorry. You didn't deserve that. None of it."

She looked up at him then, eyes glassy. "I love you. I always have. I will spend the rest of my life earning your forgiveness if that's what it takes." Another tear slipped free. "Please."

Trevor didn't move. Behind him, Aniyah watched the rise and fall of his shoulders as he breathed. The porch light caught the edge of his profile, highlighting the tension that had settled across his face.

And for one fleeting second something cold slipped into her chest.

This was his wife.

The woman he had married.

The woman who had given him Zara.

A history she could never compete with no matter how strong the connection between them felt.

Aniyah stepped back quietly. "I should go," she murmured.

Trevor's head turned slightly.

"Aniyah, wait—" But she was already moving down the walkway toward the street, her coat pulled tighter around her as she disappeared beyond the reach of the porch light. Trevor watched the darkness swallow her figure. He would call her the moment he got home. He turned back to Katelyn slowly.

Whatever softness had flickered across his face moments earlier was gone.

"You really thought you could walk your ass back up here and claim your family like we were on fucking layaway?"

The tears stopped falling from Katelyn's face almost instantly. Go figure. Katelyn blinked, the fragile expression dissolving so quickly it was almost impressive.

"You've lost your mind." Trevor shook his head once. "I don't want anything to do with you. Let me guess. Your boy got engaged and suddenly you remembered you had a husband."

Katelyn rolled her eyes in response feeling like a fool.

"Why did I even bother?" she muttered. "Clearly you've downgraded." Her gaze flicked toward the dark street where Aniyah had disappeared.

"What is it, Trevor? Couldn't get another bad bitch so you settled for the scarred up mute?"

"Enough." Nina stepped forward. Her voice carried the unmistakable weight of someone who had been patient long enough.

"Katelyn, you need to leave," she said calmly. "Nobody here wants you around and you're not about to stand out here arguing with my brother on the street." The front door opened again behind them. Angelou stepped onto the porch, tall and imposing as he glanced between them.

"Babe, is everything—"

Nina lifted a hand without turning around.

"Give me a minute."

Angelou closed his mouth immediately. Nina descended one step, stopping just high enough above Katelyn that the power dynamic remained exactly where she wanted it.

"You wanted to run around New York acting like you were single instead of being there for your family," she said evenly. "That was your choice." Her voice hardened. "You made your bed. Lay in it."

Katelyn scoffed under her breath. Nina leaned slightly closer.

"And before you fix your mouth to say anything about Aniyah again, understand something very clearly." Her eyes darkened. "She is one of the most beautiful women I have ever seen in my life. Inside and out."

Katelyn opened her mouth to protest. Nina cut her off without hesitation.

"So a woman who likes to cosplay Blackness when it's convenient should probably think very carefully before criticizing someone who actually lives it." The silence that followed crackled like static in the winter air. "Now get the fuck off my father-in-law's porch before Zara comes looking for her father." She stepped back, turning to look at Trevor. "Trevor, go back in the house. Angelou and I will handle the trash."

Trevor looked at Katelyn one last time.

"Don't you ever speak on Aniyah again. You're dead to this family." Trevor said before stepping fully into the house, closing the door behind him was symbolic for his chapter with Katelyn that was done forever.

Inside, warmth wrapped around him immediately. The scent of cinnamon, roasted meat, and hot chocolate lingered in the air, and somewhere in the living room the television hummed softly beneath the chorus of children laughing. The shift from confrontation to comfort was almost disorienting. For a moment Trevor simply stood there in the entryway, letting the quiet settle in his chest. Just minutes ago, Katelyn had been standing on that stoop crying and begging for forgiveness. Now the house felt exactly the way it always had. Full. Alive. Safe.

His gaze drifted toward the living room where Zara sat cross-legged on the floor with Imani, Matthew, and Kennedy. The three-year-olds had built some sort of chaotic toy fortress out of blocks and plastic animals, and Zara was laughing so hard she could barely explain whatever rule they had just invented. The sound filled his chest in a way that surprised him. He had thought seeing Katelyn tonight might reopen something in him. Something old. Something tender. The way thinking about his mother sometimes still did. But there was nothing.

No ache.

No longing.

No pull toward the past. Instead, his mind wandered somewhere entirely different. Aniyah's laugh. The warmth of her body pressed against his on the porch minutes earlier. The way her voice had softened last night when they stayed on the phone until three in the morning talking about everything from childhood memories to whether pineapple belonged on pizza. The way she had gone quiet and blushed when he called her beautiful.

Trevor washed his hands at the kitchen sink, the warm water running over his fingers as he stared at the tile for a moment.

Then he stepped into the living room.

"Superstar," he called gently. Zara looked up instantly.

"Daddy!"

Her curls bounced as she ran over to him, wrapping her arms around his waist with all the momentum of a seven-year-old who had not yet learned to approach anyone slowly.

Trevor scooped her up, kissing her forehead.

"We're heading home," he told her softly. Her face scrunched in disagreement.

"But Papa said I could stay tonight." Right on cue, Leon appeared from the hallway with the quiet confidence of a grandfather who had already made up his mind.

"That's correct," Leon said warmly. "We're watching Frosty the Snowman and making another round of hot chocolate." Trevor laughed under his breath.

"Well, I guess I lost that vote." Zara grinned triumphantly. He kissed her forehead again.

"I love you, Superstar. I'll see you tomorrow."

"I love you too."

Trevor set her down and grabbed his coat from the chair near the door. Angelou and Jackson stood near the hallway talking quietly, looking up as he approached. Angelou leaned against the wall, arms folded across his chest.

"You good?" he asked. Trevor nodded slowly.

"Better than I thought I would be."

Jackson studied his face carefully, the same way he had when Trevor was younger and tried to pretend something hadn't bothered him.

"You know you don't have to front with us," Jackson said calmly.

Trevor chuckled.

"I'm not frontin'. Last year I probably would've been hurt. Today, it felt like I had to get rid of a rodent." He shrugged lightly. "Katelyn is dead to me now."

Angelou tilted his head slightly.

"And the teacher?"

Trevor's smile crept in despite himself.

"She's not the teacher," he said. "She's Aniyah." Jackson exchanged a glance with Angelou.

"You sure about this?" Jackson asked. Trevor met his brother's eyes.

"Yeah."

Angelou pushed off the wall slowly. "You know what I'm about to say," he said.

Trevor raised an eyebrow in question. He was used to getting lectures from his brothers and it looked like tonight wouldn't be any different.

"If you're not sure," Angelou continued, "leave that woman exactly where she is. Don't drag her into something you haven't sorted out yet." Trevor didn't hesitate to respond.

"I'm sure."

Jackson nodded once.

"Well then," he said, stepping aside. "Go get your girl."

Angelou grinned with pride because he hadn't seen his brother look this light in a long time and that was the best Christmas gift he could receive.

"That's my little brother."

Trevor laughed under his breath and headed for the door. The cold night air greeted him again the moment he stepped outside again. Katelyn was long gone and he hoped, for her sake, that it stayed that way.

The porch light cast long shadows across the walkway as he moved toward his car, his breath fogging faintly in front of him.

Trevor stepped out onto the sidewalk and pulled his coat tighter against the cold, the quiet of the street settling around him now that the house behind him had gone muffled with walls and warmth. A few porch lights glowed along the block, wreaths swaying gently in the winter wind, but the space where Aniyah had disappeared only minutes earlier felt strangely empty.

He slid into his car and sat there for a moment, hands resting on the steering wheel while the engine idled low beneath him.

His mind replayed the porch in pieces.

Aniyah's laughter from dinner.

Her hand against the center of his back when Katelyn started talking, anchoring him in the moment with her support..

The warmth of her body against his when they kissed.

Then the way she had stepped back when she thought there was more to the moment.

The way she had quietly said she should go and quickly disappeared into the night.

He exhaled slowly.

Forty-five minutes later he was still sitting in the driver's seat, parked outside his own house, staring at the phone in his hand like it held a decision he didn't want to make wrong.

He dialed before he could think himself out of it.

It rang once.

Twice.

Then her voice came through.

"Hello." It was quieter now and he could tell she was on guard.

Trevor leaned back in the seat, eyes lifting briefly toward the dark sky above the windshield.

"What's wrong?" he asked gently.

There was a pause long enough that he could picture her

standing somewhere inside that condo, pacing slowly across the hardwood floors with her arms folded tight across her chest.

"Maybe we're moving too fast," Aniyah said softly. "Maybe we should slow down. You have a lot on your plate and I don't want to jeopardize that."

Trevor closed his eyes briefly.

Of course she would think about it like this.

Of course she would try to protect him from something he hadn't asked for protection from.

"I think I should go," she added quietly.

He stayed silent just long enough for her to shift on the other end of the line. Then he spoke.

"I'm about to pull up."

There was a beat.

"What?"

"You heard me."

The sound of his car shifting into gear filled the space between them as he eased away from the curb.

"Trevor—"

"What I need to say to you isn't something I'm doing over the phone," he continued calmly. "I need to say it where I can see your face, so you don't go making up theories and acting like a brat."

Her tone sharpened immediately.

"Who exactly do you think you're talking to?"

Trevor smiled slowly at the sound of her attitude, "You."

Silence stretched between them, thick with the tension that had been simmering between them since that porch.

"You've got a lot of nerve tonight," she said finally.

"I do."

"Trevor—"

"I'm pulling up," he repeated. "You can either come downstairs like the grown woman I know you are..."

He let the rest hang there for a second.

"...or I can come up there and knock on your door until you do."

Her breath came out through the phone in a sharp huff.

"You are unbelievable."

"I've been called worse."

Another quiet beat followed.

"You're ridiculous," she muttered.

"And yet you're still on the phone with me."

That earned him another exhale.

"Say whatever you need to say and go," she replied finally.

The line went dead.

Trevor stared at the screen for a second before letting out a low laugh. Aniyah Henderson had just hung up on him. The adrenaline buzzing through his chest had nothing to do with irritation.

It was her.

That woman had the nerve to challenge him, push him, snap back without hesitation like she wasn't the least bit intimidated by him at all.

The truth sitting squarely in his chest was that he loved that shit. He pulled onto the road, city lights sliding past the windshield as he headed toward the shoreline. Because if Aniyah thought she could dismiss him that easily tonight, she was about to learn something very important.

Trevor Porter wasn't the kind of man who walked away from something that felt this right.

Not now.

Not *ever*.

ACT III

The Becoming

CHAPTER ELEVEN

THE SHAPE OF SOMETHING NEW

"You know, maybe if I had the luxury of getting my ass whooped, I could be calm right now. But I have been drinking tequila shots, my hormones are raging out of control, I'm emotional, I'm horny, and I don't wanna hear about no goddamn peas! Fuck you! Good night!" - *Jordan Armstrong, The Best Man (1999)*

What I'm Not

I am not the woman
who mistakes proximity for destiny.
I am not the girl
who confuses a kind smile
with permanence.
I am not so lonely

that a man standing in my doorway
becomes the center of my gravity.
I am not naive enough
to believe that a heart
fresh from breaking
knows how to love again this quickly.
And yet here I am
thirty minutes after hanging up the phone
with my pulse racing
and the ocean outside my window
asking me questions
I do not have answers for.
I am not reckless.
I am not foolish.
I am not already falling for Trevor Porter.
At least that is what I keep telling myself.

Aniyah had cleaned her condo three times.

The place had never been messy to begin with. Her space rarely was. Living alone had trained her into a kind of quiet order that made everything feel intentional. Books were stacked neatly beside the couch. The throw blanket folded just so along the armrest. The kitchen counter wiped until it shined beneath the warm pendant lights.

Still, she wiped it again. The cloth moved in slow circles across the granite countertop. She kept cleaning as if that would help her nerves.

Thirty minutes.

Thirty minutes had passed since she hung up on Trevor. Thirty minutes since she hung up on him like she had lost every ounce of sense she possessed. Aniyah dropped the cloth beside the sink and glanced toward the living room window. She wasn't going to meet him downstairs so he had no choice but to come up to her place.

She checked the front door.

Then she checked the time...Again. Trevor Porter was coming to her house. The thought alone made her stomach twist itself into knots.

Outside the wide stretch of glass that framed her living room, the Atlantic rolled quietly beneath the winter sky. The ocean looked like a sheet of black glass tonight, the moonlight scattering silver across the surface every time the tide shifted. The December wind came in long steady breaths that rattled faintly against the balcony railing.

Normally that quiet soothed her. Tonight it did absolutely nothing to slow the thoughts racing through her head.

This was ridiculous.

Completely ridiculous.

Trevor Porter had finalized his divorce at the beginning of November. It was the end of December.

That was barely enough time to move on from a bad haircut, let alone a marriage that had lasted years and produced a child.

And yet here she was.

Standing in the middle of her living room waiting for him like she had lost every ounce of good sense she possessed. Aniyah dragged a hand down her face.

"You are delusional," she muttered to herself. Her voice

sounded small in the quiet room. Because what exactly did she think this was? A love story? The thought almost made her laugh. Trevor had been married for years. He had a daughter. A life. A history that stretched long before she ever reappeared in it.

And somehow in the span of a few weeks, she had allowed herself to start imagining what it might feel like to exist inside that world. That alone should have been enough to send her running in the opposite direction. But instead, she gave him the okay to come over. She walked toward the window again, wrapping her arms around herself as she stared out.

Thirty minutes.

What if he didn't come? Her stomach twisted again at the thought. Not because she expected him to prove her wrong. But because some foolish hopeful part of her had already decided that he would.

The doorbell rang. Aniyah's heart nearly jumped out of her chest. For two full seconds she froze where she stood, her body suddenly unsure whether to move forward or run in the opposite direction. Her pulse hammered in her ears. She exhaled slowly. Then forced her feet to move.

When she reached the door she had managed to gather just enough composure to pretend she wasn't spiraling internally.

Aniyah opened it.

And there he was.

Trevor stood on the other side of the threshold, tall and broad shouldered in the soft glow of the hallway light, the winter air curling faintly around him like it had followed him all the way from the street.

For a moment neither of them spoke. But the way his eyes settled on her made it feel like something had already been said. Something neither of them was quite ready to name yet.

Trevor did not move immediately.

For a moment he simply stood there in the doorway, taking in the quiet of her space.

His eyes moved slowly across the room. The stack of books beside the couch. A candle burning low on the coffee table. A pair of thick socks abandoned near the rug made the space look cozy. Trevor stepped inside and closed the door behind him.

Aniyah had already moved back toward the center of the living room, her arms crossed loosely across her chest. She looked composed on the surface, but he could see the tension in the way she held herself. The slight tilt of her chin. The careful distance she kept between them. She was bracing for this conversation that she knew would leave her gutted. Her gaze flicked toward him, sharp and impatient.

"Well," she said, lifting one brow. "You made it." Trevor slipped his hands into the pockets of his coat.

"Of course...I told you I would."

"That doesn't mean you had to show up."

A corner of his mouth lifted, he'd never seen this side of Aniyah before, but he was loving it.

"This entire time we have been talking, have I ever given you a reason to believe I'm not a man of my word?" He let those words hang in the air, Aniyah knew he was right. "You hung up on me," he followed up calmly.

"You were being bossy."

"You liked it." Aniyah scoffed softly.

"You came here to say something," she replied, her tone deliberately cool. "So say it. Then you can go."

The words were firm, but there was something else underneath them. Something restless. Trevor watched her for a long moment before he began to walk toward her slowly. Each step closed the space between them until the distance she had carefully placed between them no longer existed. Aniyah's shoulders straightened. Her chin lifted slightly.

But she didn't step back. She would not give him the satisfaction of seeing how he affected her.

"Still giving orders," he said quietly.

"I'm setting boundaries."

"That's not what this is." Her eyes flashed.

"And what exactly do you think this is?" Trevor stopped directly in front of her.

Close enough now that the faint citrus scent of her body wash reached him. Close enough that he could see the slight rise and fall of her chest.

"You're scared," he said softly. Aniyah laughed once under her breath. "Katelyn showing up at the brownstone this evening shook your sense of security in this. You thought I would go running back. But you should know–"

"You're freshly divorced," she shot back, cutting him off. "You have a child. Your ex-wife just showed up at Christmas crying about loving you. And somehow you think the logical next step is showing up at your daughter's teacher's house at night. What? You think we are in an insta-love romance novel?!"

Trevor did not interrupt her.

"So forgive me," she continued, voice tightening, "if I'm trying to be the one person in this situation with a little bit of sense. We are on a dangerous line, because we have reached the point where if you decide you want your family back I will be the one heartbroken."

Her words hung between them. Trevor studied her face. Then he lifted his hand slowly. Aniyah's breath caught when his fingers reached her throat wrapping around it softly. This had to be a kink of hers because this was the second time Trevor had done it and her body instantly was set aflame. His palm rested lightly along the side of her neck, his thumb settling just beneath her jaw on her pulse point . The touch was firm but careful, grounding rather than restraining. Trevor tilted his head slightly so she had no choice but to meet his eyes.

"Look at me," he said quietly. Aniyah already was looking deep into those darkened pools that barely restrained his desire. Aniyah knew she was in trouble, but she wouldn't run. Those issues could wait until the morning. The way he said it though, it wasn't just her looking at him but seeing him. The man that looked like he was seconds from ripping her clothes off any having his way with her.

"You're right," he continued. "My divorce was finalized in November on paper." His thumb brushed lightly along the curve of her neck as he spoke, sending a shutter down her body.

"But that marriage was over long before a judge signed anything. You want honesty, Aniyah? I'll give it to you..."

Trevor held her gaze for a long moment after saying it, the quiet confidence in his voice settling into the room like gravity.

"The first day I really noticed you was freshman year of high school. You were trying to get your locker open and Coach Summers had to come help you. You were so beautiful, but I knew you didn't take any shit so I kept it moving."

Aniyah should have stepped away. The shock of his confession rooted her in place.

"We had run-ins through the years of school and every time I would be stuck just admiring you before I snapped back to reality," He continued. "When I realized it was you who was going to be Zara's teacher, my heart skipped a beat. I didn't know what it meant at the time, but I know now."

She should have reclaimed the space she had been guarding all night, the careful distance she had insisted she needed to keep her heart intact. Instead, she stayed exactly where she was. Her hand still resting against his chest. Her palm feeling the steady rise and fall beneath his sweater. His hand still wrapped around her neck.

"What do you know," she questioned.

"That we were meant to run into each other again."

"You're very sure of yourself," she said softly, though the edge she tried to put into the words didn't quite land the way she intended.

Trevor watched her for a second longer, the corner of his mouth lifting slightly, "Not about everything."

The admission caught her off guard.His hand slid from the front of her neck to the back, fingers threading gently into the base of her hair. The touch wasn't forceful. It anchored her there in the moment.

"I'm sure about you," he said quietly.

Her eyes searched his face as if she might find hesitation hidden somewhere behind the certainty in his voice. She wanted to believe him, wanted to lean fully into the warmth of the moment unfolding between them, but the image of Katelyn standing on that porch earlier lingered in the back of her mind like a warning she couldn't quite silence.

"You say that now," she murmured.

Trevor's brow furrowed slightly, "What does that mean?"

Aniyah exhaled slowly, her fingers tightening against the front of his sweater, "It means tonight feels good," she said, her voice quieter now. "It means you're here and you're saying all the right things and it's very easy to get swept up in that."

"But tomorrow," she continued, meeting his eyes again, "you might wake up and remember the life you had with her. The family you built. I'll just be the woman who was convenient at the moment."

Trevor stilled. His hand that was on her waist moved gently to her chin, lifting it just enough that she couldn't look away from him.

"Aniyah," The way he said her name carried both patience and authority, the kind that made her spine straighten instinctively.

"I didn't come here tonight because I was lonely," he said.

His thumb brushed slowly across the curve of her jaw as he spoke, the touch steady.

"I didn't come here because my marriage ended and I needed something to fill the space it left behind." His voice dropped slightly, "I came here because when you walked away from that porch tonight, the thought of you sitting in this apartment believing you were just a distraction didn't sit right with me."

Trevor leaned closer, the warmth of him closing around her again.

"You're not a rebound," he said quietly.

His hand that was on the back of her neck slid down her arm, fingers tracing the length of it until they found her wrist. He lifted her hand slowly and placed it flat against the center of his chest.

"You feel that?"

His heartbeat moved steady and strong beneath her palm.

"That's not confusion."

Aniyah swallowed, her pulse racing in response.

Trevor watched her carefully, the small shifts in her breathing, the way her lips parted slightly like she was standing on the edge of a decision she hadn't fully admitted to herself yet.

"I feel it, Trevor. I do, but I'm still cautious. What we are doing...it's messy."

"You're scared," he said softly.

"I'm careful," she corrected.

A faint smile touched his mouth, "That too. But I know you're also scared."

The room held them there for a moment longer, the quiet between them thick with everything neither of them had said yet.

"Aniyah," he murmured near her ear, his voice warm and steady, "look at me."

Her eyes lifted to his again, dark and uncertain and full of want she was trying very hard not to show.

"You don't have to figure out the rest of your life tonight," he said.

His thumb brushed lightly along her cheek.

"You just have to decide whether you want me right now. But just know I will still want you tomorrow and the day after."

Her breath hitched. Because the answer to that question had been sitting in her chest from the moment she opened the door. Her hand moved slowly from his chest to the back of his neck, fingers sliding into the short curls there as she held his gaze.

"I want you," she admitted quietly.

The honesty of it shifted something in Trevor's expression. His hand tightened slightly at her waist, pulling her flush against him as his mouth found hers again.

This kiss carried a different kind of heat now. Slower at first, deliberate in the way his lips moved against hers, but beneath it was a rising urgency neither of them bothered pretending wasn't there.

Aniyah's fingers tightened at the back of his neck as the warmth between them deepened, her body leaning instinctively into his as if it had already decided what her mind had been trying to resist all night.

Trevor's hand moved gently along her back, the touch firm and steady, guiding her closer as the kiss continued. When he finally pulled back, his forehead rested against hers again.

"You're still thinking," he murmured.

Aniyah let out a soft breath that might have been a laugh or a moan. "I'm always thinking."

"Tonight," he said quietly, "I want you to feel instead."

Aniyah's heart hammered against her ribs as she searched his face one more time.

"You're sure?" she asked softly.

Trevor's answer came without hesitation, "I've never been more sure of anything."

This time, when Trevor kissed her again, Aniyah didn't hold back. For a moment, neither of them moved. Aniyah could feel the warmth of his hand still resting at the back of her neck, the steady weight of it grounding and dangerous all at once. Her pulse fluttered beneath his thumb, and she had the fleeting thought that he could probably feel exactly how fast her heart was beating.

Her fingers slipped beneath the hem of his sweater again, brushing warm skin this time feeling his abs beneath her fingertips.

Trevor caught her wrist gently, stilling the motion before it could go any further. "Easy," he murmured, his voice low and steady.

"I'm not in a hurry," he said. "I've been wanting you for weeks, shit years. I'm not about to rush the first time I get to touch you."

His hand slid back into her hair, guiding her gently as his mouth returned to hers. The kiss deepened again, the quiet rhythm of it matching the slow pull building between them.

Trevor moved with quiet intention, guiding her backward a few steps until the living room couch brushed lightly against the back of her legs.

The shift in space made her breath catch. He noticed immediately.

"You alright?" he asked softly.

Aniyah nodded, though the warmth in her chest had spread everywhere now causing a delicious ache between her legs. The nervousness she had been clinging to earlier had softened into something else entirely—she wanted this man something serious.

"Yes, I just need..." Her voice trailed off because Aniyah was shocked with how needy she sounded.

"Don't worry, I'm going to take care of you tonight," then he leaned down and kissed her again. When he leaned back up his face turned serious.

"I want to take your clothes off."

Aniyah's breath caught and her center began to drip, "Then take my clothes off." Trevor started with her top gently pulling it over her head. Her breasts in the pink lace bra made his mouth water. He couldn't wait until his mouth was on her. He noticed discolored marks of raised skin across her chest.

"They're keloids," she said softly. She wasn't afraid of her scars. They had been with her since she was a little girl. She had been in remission for years, but the scars of her past decorated her body reminding her of how far she'd come. They were all in spots that she could cover up, so no one ever knew unless they got to this point...She saw Trevor taking her in. She felt his fingers undo her bra and her breast fall slightly in freedom.

"You are so fucking beautiful," He groaned out before kissing her chest, kissing those hidden scars. Aniyah moaned out. The feeling of his lips on her was heavenly. Then he took a hardened nipple into his mouth and Aniyah could've sworn her legs buckled. Trevor held her up, not stopping his fest. He hands gripped her ass as hers held on to his head wishing he would never move and that he could kiss her all over.

'Trevor, please."

"Please what, Pout?" Trevor asked briefly, breaking his contact with her body to switch over to the other breast.

"Pout," Aniyah questioned as a moan. Trevor stood back up to his full height. His hands worked the button of her jeans before pulling them down her legs. His hand went to cup her center and felt her wetness. Feeling how turned on she was for him made him groan. He reached inside her panties and began to slowly message her clit.

"Yes, Pout. 'Cause you tend to get an attitude when you don't get your way. It showed itself tonight, I'll make sure to handle it going forward." Trevor began to move his hand faster. Aniyah cried out feeling her orgasm building. Just when she felt herself about to crash over the edge, Trevor pulled his hands away.

"What–why did you stop?" Aniyah asked in a voice she didn't recognize. Trevor ignored her and pulled her panties off.

"I love to touch, but I rather taste." He answered before kissing her lips softly.

"Now, are you gonna open up for me? Or are you gonna keep whining?"

"Trevor, don't start your shi–" Trevor promptly picked Aniyah up causing her to yelp out. He placed her on the couch, opening her legs and looking at the most beautiful pussy he had ever seen in his life. Trevor saw more scars littered across her upper thighs and lower stomach. He kissed every one before diving in for his most anticipated meal. The taste of Aniyah was perfection on his tongue. He could drink her nectar all night long if she let him.

Aniyah's back arched off the couch, the way Trevor was eating her was absolutely insane. She had gotten head before because of course she had, but this? This was something different. From the gentle licks, to Trevor sucking on her clit, Aniyah felt herself spill onto her couch without a care in the world. The praise of his name continued to fall from her lips. Just when she thought she had enough, he inserted two fingers into her heat and began to move them with professional precision.

"Oh shit, Trevor. You're going to make me cum again."

"You look so fucking beautiful, baby. Cum for me." Aniyah felt the crescendo build like the waves outside her window, and she crashed just as violently. The euphoric sensation rolled throughout her body and instantly shot up again because Trevor was still eating her like a man starved. Fingering, slurping, spitting—he would not stop. Her cries filled the space so beautifully.

Aniyah wasn't sure what was happening but she began to crash again and again. Until her body was absolutely on fire from the repeated orgasms. She pushed Trevor's head away causing him to laugh.

"You," she started chest heaving, "are an absolute demon."

Trevor's face, glistening with her juices, broke out in a handsome smile.

"You are fucking delicious. I could stay between them thighs all night." He pulled his shirt over his head and pulled his pants down. Aniyah's eyes zeroed in on his dick through his briefs.

"Damn, where do you hide that thing?" She exclaimed as he pulled his briefs off and his dick sprung free. A shade darker than his butterscotch skin. Thick and veiny, she couldn't wait for the time when she could return the favor and taste it. Right now, she just needed to feel it. Trevor climbed between her legs and gave her the sweetest kiss.

"You are so beautiful, Aniyah." He said while staring in her eyes, "Every scar I would kiss for the rest of my life," he began to sink into her. "If you let me."

"Trevor, you can do any-fucking-thing you want. Oh my God, you're stretching me out." She whined from the delicious burn of being filled after such a long time. His rhythm was slow at first. Letting her get accustomed to his size. His head dropped into her shoulder as he pumped his hips faster into her. She had perfect access to his neck. She began to suck and bite on the spot just below his ear. Her hips met his thrusts. This wasn't just fucking, this was making love. Their bodies were in sync and Aniyah wanted to keep this feeling forever.

"Damn girl, you gripping me tight." Trevor stated while lifting up on his arms, pumping deep and slow into her.

"I don't want to let go."

"Then don't, keep gripping my shit like that and you can have it forever."

"Yes, give it to me. Oh! I feel it, Trev. I feel it."

"Give me that shit, so I can cum with you. Fuck, I'm about to cum deep in this muthafucka. Is that where you want it, baby?"

"Yes! Please! Fuck, I'm cumming." Aniyah's body locked up as her orgasm hit, the same time she felt Trevor flood her insides, the warmth of his release made her spasm again. It was like her body was trying to keep it all.

Aniyah felt the warmth of Trevor's hands, the steadiness of his presence anchoring her even as her pulse raced.

When the moment slowed again, Trevor brushed a kiss along her temple, his breath warm against her skin.

"You with me?" he asked quietly.

Aniyah nodded, her fingers still resting against his chest as she looked up at him.

"I'm with you."

Trevor studied her face for a second longer before leaning down to kiss her again, slower this time, the kind of kiss that carried both reassurance and promise.

"Can I ask you a question?" Trevor asked a little while later. They were still on the couch, covered by her thick throw blanket.

"Where did I get my scars?" Aniyah answered knowingly. Trevor nodded into her neck before placing a quick kiss there. His hands rubbing her hip slowly.

"I have a chronic illness called Hidradenitis Suppurativa. I know, it's a mouthful, which is why I call it HS. It's really a chronic inflammatory disease. I get these boils under my arms, breasts, between my thighs and on my ass. It started when I was 13. Imagine becoming a teenager and then immediately having to deal with this," She took a breath for a moment caught up in the memory, "You know my parents are perfectionists. This was not in their plans. It felt like my father had me in front of every specialist in the country. But no solutions. That pissed him off even more. Somehow, this was my fault."

Aniyah saw Trevor's sympathetic expression turn into one of anger.

"Just putting it out there, never let me meet your dad because from everything I learned, he needs his ass whooped and I will gladly handle it. "

"You won't ever have to worry about seeing him because of me. I've been dead to him for years now."

"Don't worry, you have a family who adores you now. Fuck them." Trevor said as if it was the most natural thing in the world. Aniyah sat up a bit to turn and look at him.

"I do?"

"Yes. You didn't see the way my family loved on you tonight? Welcome to Death Row. You need me to get you a chain?" Trevor asked, pulling Aniyah back against his chest.

"Yes, I want the diamonds to glisten too," Aniyah responded, causing them to laugh. When the moment got quiet again Trevor kissed her shoulder.

"What do you need from me if your HS is bothering you? Is there medicine you take? A special ointment I need to keep stocked? What?" Aniyah once again sat up. This time in disbelief. No one she's dated before has asked her that, now here this man is looking at her with quiet strength ready to be her anchor. Tears came to her eyes.

"Umm, well. I just recently healed from a flare, but they are mostly dormant now. I take a weekly shot for it, and it helps me. If I do get a flare, I wash with Dial soap or Hibiclens, use the *My Magic Healer* ointment and let it do its thing. I have ibuprofen 800s to take when the pain gets bad. Thankfully, right now I'm okay. The only thing to see are my scars."

"They are beautiful and so are you inside and out." Aniyah moved in to press a sweet kiss to Trevor's lips.

"I think we should go to my bedroom." She said in between kisses.

"Oh yeah?"

"Yeah," Aniyah stood up, letting the throw blanket fall from her naked body. She started to walk towards her bedroom. She stopped at the door to turn around and see if Trevor was still following her.

What she saw was him standing up looking at her with unbridled admiration. That made her cheeks flush. He slowly followed her in the room, ready for his next fill.

"I want you on your stomach," Trevor stated as he came up behind Aniyah. His hands wrapped around her waist, hard dick pushed against her plush ass. It did not make any sense how turned on he felt in the moment.

"Oh, you think you can tell me what to do now?" Aniyah sassed back. Trevor pulled back from her frame and then slapped her on the ass. Aniyah yelped in response, her body flooding again at the sensation.

"I know I can, now lay down...please."

"Just because you asked like a good boy," Aniyah responded as she laid down on her stomach. Trevor glanced around her room and spotted Aniyah's body oil on her dresser. He grabbed it before pouring a small amount in his hand and warming it between his palms. He started messaging her on her shoulders. A quiet moan released from Aniyah's lips.

This was heaven. Trevor's hands on her were laced with gold. Every scar he passed over, he kissed. When he finally reached Aniyah's feet, she was absolutely feral for him. It was the only reason to explain why she turned over, stood up, turned him towards the bed and pushed him down on it.

"Baby, you o—shit!" He moaned out as Aniyah placed his dick in her mouth and began to hollow her jaws out. The residual taste of them on him only turned her on more. A moan vibrated against him, causing his dick to grow even harder in her mouth.

Aniyah loved every part of this. Having him fully in her control as she took him deep within her throat. Her head began to bob up and down on him.

"Fuck, girl. That's how you feel?" Trevor moaned. Aniyah's response was to moan around him which made Trevor's toes curl. She kept up at it, letting saliva pool and drip down her chin. She didn't care about breathing, just giving Trevor the same pleasure he had been giving her.

When her pussy was absolutely crying, she popped him out her mouth before climbing over him and sinking down onto his length.

"Shit, you feel so perfect." She cried as she began bouncing up and down. She had years of repressed horniness that she was going to take out on Trevor that night.

Trevor's hands found her waist to guide her rhythm. He looked up at her, face strained, biting his lip. This was the sexiest she had ever seen him look.

"Gahdamn girl, you riding the fuck outta me. That's how you feel?"

Aniyah's head fell back as she hissed, "Yesss."

"Good, because I don't want you to stop. This my shit now. You hear me?" Trevor gritted out as his hips met Aniyah's with each bounce.

"If I'm yours then you are mine, this dick is mine," Aniyah cried out feeling her orgasm building.

"It's yours...shit...should've been yours from the moment we saw each other. We could've been married with our own kids by now."

"Boy what?!" Aniyah paused her movement, perplexed by Trevor's confession. In response he lifted her from his lap, flipped them over and dove back into her. He lifted both her legs to the point that they were damn near touching her ears.

"You heard what the fuck I said, Roxanne." His voice deepened as he began to slowly drive in and out of her deeply.

"Tre-Trev-baby, that's crazy. Oh fuck, I still don't believe you noticed me." Aniyah responded, tears coming to her eyes because his dick was constantly tapping on her spot in this position.

"Freshman year," He started, making sure to keep his strokes consistent. "The first day you had your hair in a high ponytail, and you were wearing a jean skirt. I knew then I wanted you."

They locked eyes as Trevor kept talking.

"I should've made you mine then. How could I waste time when it's obvious you were meant for me?" His hips sped up.

"So what you saying is, you owe me for our lost time?" Aniyah said as she grabbed the sides of his face bringing him close and kissing him, sliding her tongue in his mouth. Through it all, he never slowed down. Those strokes...those fucking strokes would be her undoing. She felt the crescendo of her release building.

"I will make it up for the rest of my life."

"Trevor, I'm about to—I'm 'bout to—"

"That's it baby, let go for me." Trevor's movements became more erratic as they both crashed over the edge together. He let her legs go but stayed on top of her for a moment longer. He pressed a kiss to her lips before attempting to get up. Aniyah wanted no part in that. She wrapped her legs around his hips keeping him locked in place.

"It's like that?" Trevor asked.

"Yes, it's like that." They stayed together trading soft kisses for what seemed like an eternity. For Aniyah it wasn't long enough.

Trevor got up to get a washcloth and clean them both up. Once he was back in bed he made sure to pull Aniyah into his arms.

"Can I just say that it's wild your ass has a California king bed when you're as small as you are?" He said while laughing.

"Oh, I see I have a hater in the room. I like the space, plus we will need space for the nights you can sleep over here. I'm not an all-night cuddle typa girl. I mean—"

"Before you overthink it, you're right. I do. Plus, you probably snore anyway. I definitely need my own side of the bed."

"Boy hush, I do not snore," Aniyah bit back.

"Sure, that's what they all say, then forty minutes later it sounds like Jason is standing in the corner of the room." Aniyah cackled so loud that she ended up snorting which made Trevor laugh aloud. This was the perfect ending to the perfect Christmas. Once they settled down, she looked out her window and saw snowflakes falling. She snuggled closer to his body and let her eyes close. She wasn't as scared for their future anymore and that brought peace she didn't know she needed.

CHAPTER TWELVE

BEAUTY BETWEEN THESE PAGES

"The real reason why I love you is because, when I was in the county jail— you sent me all them nice poems." - *Markell, Poetic Justice (1993)*

January settled over Long Island with a quieter kind of cold than December. The holiday lights had disappeared from most of the houses along the block, and the neighborhood had returned to its usual rhythm of early sunsets and the faint smell of fireplaces drifting through the air. Trevor didn't mind the stillness. After the chaos of the past year, the quiet felt earned.

His mind drifted back to New Year's Eve before he could stop it.

The Porter house had been full in the way it always was when his family gathered. Music in the kitchen. Angelou arguing with Jackson about something stupid while Nina laughed loud enough to drown them both out. Zara running between rooms with the cousins on a mean sugar high. And Aniyah had been there in the middle of it, barefoot on the living room rug helping Zara stack blocks while Mackenzie watched her with that knowing smile she got whenever she decided someone belonged with their family.

Trevor had caught that look.

He had ignored it.

Mostly.

A few minutes before midnight he'd leaned down beside Aniyah and murmured something in her ear, watching the way her eyes narrowed before she rolled them and stood anyway. She followed him up the stairs while the house counted down in the background, voices echoing through the hallway as they slipped into his childhood bedroom like two teenagers sneaking away from a party.

Ten.

Nine.

Eight.

Trevor had pushed the door shut behind them, his hands already finding her waist.

Seven.

Six.

Five.

"You're ridiculous your entire family is downstairs," she had whispered, though her hands had slid beneath his shirt like she'd already decided she wasn't leaving. She pulled it over his head.

Four.

Three.

Two.

He'd sank into her right as the house shouted *Happy New Year* downstairs, the sound of laughter and champagne corks rising through the floorboards while he murmured the same words against her mouth.

That was how they started the year.

Together—having a quickie trying not to get caught.

The memory still warmed his chest days later.

Life had been surprisingly steady since then. Zara's therapy with Dr. Sanders was helping, little by little smoothing out the tight sadness that had taken root after Katelyn walked away. She still had questions sometimes, still woke from the occasional nightmare, but the laughter had returned to her voice and that alone felt like a victory. Trevor saw it when she ran toward Leon's truck after school or when she called Angelou just to tell him about a spelling test she aced.

His family had closed ranks around her without discussion. The Porters didn't wait for invitations when one of their own needed something. They showed up. Always had.

A new development he loved? Zara and Aniyah getting manicures together every Saturday, his treat. Zara absolutely glowed when Aniyah dropped her off after their lunch. He could also tell how happy it made Aniyah. She always had the brightest smile when he opened the door. He would pull her in and convince her to spend the rest of the day with them. Those were the best days, his home was filled with love and laughter. The way it was always meant to be.

And Katelyn...

He hadn't heard from her.

Not really.

Every door she once used to reach him had been shut. Phone blocked. Social media gone. The only thing that slipped through was a short email two weeks earlier that sat unopened in a quiet corner of his inbox until curiosity got the better of him.

I'm sorry.

Trevor had stared at the screen for a long moment before closing it again. Some apologies arrived long after the damage had been done.

Tonight Zara was with her Papa. Trevor had dropped her off earlier, watching the way she launched herself into her grandfather's arms while Leon pretended the impact nearly knocked him over. That had been the entire point of the night. Zara got time with Leon, and Trevor got the first real break he'd taken in weeks.

Which meant he got to take Aniyah out.

The restaurant had been her choice. A small place tucked along the water where the windows looked out over the dark Atlantic and the lights were low enough to make the room feel intimate. Trevor watched her across the table while she talked about something one of her students had said earlier that day, her hands moving gently through the air as she explained it.

"You should've seen his face," she said, shaking her head with a soft laugh. "He was so serious when he asked if sharks get cavities."

Trevor leaned back in his chair, studying her the way he had started doing more often than he probably should. "And what did Miss Henderson say?"

"I told him sharks don't brush their teeth, so cavities probably aren't the biggest concern."

He chuckled under his breath.

Aniyah tilted her head. "Why are you looking at me like that?"

"Like what?"

"Like you're about to say something ridiculous."

Trevor lifted his glass.,"I'm behaving."

"For now."

"You don't want me to tell you that you taste better than anything on my plate right now. Or that I'm ready to eat?" He saw her breath catch. The way she adjusted in her seat.

"Trevor," came from her lips so softly.

The warmth in her voice settled somewhere deep in his chest. He ended his teasing there, knowing that she would be just as turned on as him for the rest of dinner was satisfying enough.

As Aniyah talked about her last girls' dinner, Trevor thought about how easy it had been for them to be together.

They kept things careful during the day, especially with Zara still in her class. Trevor never lingered too long during pickup, never crossed the invisible line between parent and boyfriend while they were on school grounds. But moments like this—quiet dinners, shared laughter, the soft brush of her knee against his beneath the table—reminded him how real this thing between them had become.

When they returned to her condo Trevor barely closed the door before pulling her into his arms, his mouth finding hers like he'd been waiting all evening.

"You're impatient," she murmured against his lips.

"Very."

She laughed softly before kissing him again, and the sound followed them down the hallway. That night, they made love on her kitchen counter. Trevor made a home inside of Aniyah and he wasn't leaving anytime soon.

Later, much later, the bedroom had fallen quiet. Aniyah slept curled beneath the blankets, one arm stretched across the empty space where Trevor had been moments earlier. He'd slipped out of bed carefully, pulling on a pair of sweats before wandering back into the living room, his mind already drifting toward the long list of production details waiting for him tomorrow.

The lamp beside the couch cast a soft golden light across the room.

That was when he noticed the notebook.

It sat on the coffee table like it had always been there, its worn cover softened by time and use. Trevor picked it up absentmindedly, expecting lesson notes or grocery lists.

The first page stopped him cold.

A poem.

He read it softly, the quiet of the apartment wrapping around the words.

When I Was Eight
My grandfather says
words are seeds.
He hands me a notebook
like it is a garden.
"Plant what hurts," he says.
So I do.
The page fills
with things I cannot say
out loud.

Trevor flipped the page slowly.

Another poem waited.

This one was written in the uneven handwriting of a teenager trying to make sense of a house that no longer felt like home.

Daughter
My father says
greatness has a uniform.
White coat.
Stethoscope.
Prestige.
I try it on.
It fits his dreams
perfectly.
But my lungs collapse

inside it.

Trevor leaned back slightly, the weight of her words settling in his chest. He kept turning the pages. Another poem caught his eye. This one was quieter, more fragile.

Scars
There are places on my body
that bloom pain
like flowers no one asked for.
I learned early
to hide the garden.
I learned early
to apologize
for the soil.

Trevor exhaled slowly. He turned the page again. The handwriting had grown steadier now, stronger.

Mirror
I stood naked
in front of the truth
one night.
Not the kind
the world tells you.
The quiet one.
The one that says
a scar is still skin
that survived.

Trevor shook his head softly, "Damn..." He kept reading. Grief appeared next.

Earl

My grandfather laughs
like thunder.
The kind that rolls
through your chest
before the rain comes.
When he leaves this earth
the sky will not change.
But my weather will.

Trevor swallowed hard.
Another page.
Another life.
Bad dates.
Broken expectations.
A woman slowly learning herself.
Then he reached the more recent poems.
The title repeated again and again.

What I'm Not

He read this one aloud.

What I'm Not

I am not the woman
who mistakes attention

for affection.

I am not the girl
who builds a home
inside potential.

I am not lonely enough
to confuse
temporary warmth
with fire.

What I'm Not 2

I am not the woman
who loses herself
in gravity.

But Trevor Porter
walked into my life
with the patience
of sunrise.

Now I am learning
how light
feels on my skin.

Trevor leaned back against the couch.

"Jesus..." Her words had broken something open in his chest. When Aniyah told him she wrote poetry on their first date, he didn't know it would be like this. Her art was...gut-wrenching in all the right ways. Her words landed exactly where they were supposed to, his heart. This type of work should be shared. The idea struck him like lightning.

"You weren't supposed to find that."

Her voice floated from the hallway.

He looked up to see Aniyah standing there in one of his t-shirts that fell halfway down her thighs, her curls loose around her shoulders and sleep still softening her expression.

Trevor held up the notebook. "How long have you been writing?"

She crossed her arms like she'd been caught doing something illegal. "Since I was a kid."

"This is more than a notebook."

"It's a habit."

He flipped another page. "Aniyah, there's three hundred pages in here."

"That just means I've had a lot to say."

Trevor met her eyes, the weight of what he'd just read still sitting heavy in his chest. "You should be part of my docuseries."

She blinked like the suggestion had physically hit her. "Trevor, absolutely not."

"Why not?"

"Because this," she said, tapping the notebook as she walked closer, "was never meant to be public. I don't even know what I would say."

He studied her a moment before leaning forward slightly.

"Your art is too good to stay hidden."

Aniyah huffed softly, "Boy please."

"I'm serious."

Her gaze softened just enough to tell him she knew he meant it.

"You ever thought about publishing this?" he asked.

She stared at him. "Publishing poems about you?"

"You could change my name."

She lifted her chin with mock offense, "I would never change my muse."

Trevor laughed then, the sound filling the room as he handed the notebook back to her. When she reached for it, he pulled her down by his side on the couch and wrapped his arms around her.

"You're doing the docuseries," he said gently.

Aniyah studied the worn pages in her hands, her thumb brushing over the edge like she was deciding whether the world deserved to see them.

Finally, she sighed.

"One poem."

Trevor leaned back against the couch, a slow smile spreading across his face.

"One poem."

CHAPTER THIRTEEN

AND YET, WE STRAY

"Derice, a gold medal is a wonderful thing. But if you're not enough without one, you'll never be enough with one." - *Irv, Cool Runnings (1993)*

"Today must have crack in it," Trevor said to himself.

By midmorning, he already knew the day had teeth. Sharp ones too, like Eddie Murphy in *Vampire in Brooklyn*, because what the actual fuck was going on?

It started with the email.

He stood near the monitor in the Lower East Side studio while the sculptor shaped a slab of wet clay into the slow curve of a woman's shoulder. The room smelled like damp earth and plaster, and the air carried that particular hush artists made when they were deep in it, when their hands were doing the thinking and everybody else knew better than to interrupt. Behind him,

Marcus adjusted a lens with quiet precision while the camera hummed low and steady. Trevor's phone buzzed in his palm with the ordinary impatience of production, another message in a long line of messages that usually needed solving, shifting, approving, fixing.

He glanced down without thinking much of it.

Then he saw the subject line.

The artist in London had pulled out.

Just like that.

Trevor read the email once. Then again, slower the second time, his jaw tightening the longer the words sat on the screen. Months of coordination. Flights. Holds. Interviews arranged through too many people in too many time zones. All of it gone because the artist suddenly had a "scheduling conflict," which was clean professional language for *this is not your problem to unpack, but it absolutely just became your problem to fix.*

Hassan—his new assistant—noticed the shift in him first, "Something wrong?"

Trevor lowered the phone and exhaled through his nose, trying to keep his irritation from spreading all over a set that had nothing to do with London. Across the room, metal scraped gently against clay. Somebody near the lighting rig whispered a question. "Our UK segment just died."

Hassan blinked, "You're serious?"

"Completely."

For a moment Trevor just stood there listening to the studio breathe. The scrape of tools, the low motor of the camera, the soft foot traffic over concrete. It should have calmed him. Normally it would have. Instead it made the frustration inside him louder, because that segment mattered. It had been one of the first things he wrote down when *Making Love: The Art of Us* was still just a title in his notebook and a risk in his chest. A conversation about art and intimacy stretching beyond boroughs and borders. Love translated through process, through distance, through Black hands making beauty anyway.

Now it was gone.

Trevor dragged a hand down his face and texted production before he could think too hard about it.

Cut it.

There wasn't time to rebuild overseas this late in the game. He knew that. Logically, it made sense. Emotionally, it felt like somebody had pulled a thread loose from the center seam and expected him to act like the whole thing wouldn't eventually come apart.

His phone buzzed again. It was Aniyah.

> Roxanne 😚: Should I move the chair closer to the window or is the couch better for lighting?

A second message came through immediately after.

> Roxanne 😚: Also I'm nervous.

Trevor rubbed the back of his neck.

Of course she was nervous. Tonight was the night they were filming her segment at the condo, the poetry piece he had been fighting all week to keep from getting cut every time the network started talking about "momentum" and "episode shape" like intimacy was somehow dead weight. Her part was the heartbeat of that episode. The soft center. The truth of it. He refused to lose it.

He started typing back, wanting to tell her the chair was fine, the window light would be beautiful on her skin and that she would be amazing once she started talking because she always was. Then another call came through from the office halting all of those thoughts.

Trevor answered with a clipped, "Yeah."

"Trevor," the coordinator said quickly, already sounding like she wanted no parts of whatever she was about to hand off, "we've got someone here asking for you."

He frowned, "Who?"

"A Katelyn Porter."

Trevor closed his eyes.

Of-fucking-course.

As he stepped out of the elevator, Katelyn was pacing the reception area like she could wear a hole through the floor before he made it downstairs. The first thing he noticed was how different she looked. The careful polish she used to keep on like armor had cracked somewhere along the way.

Her hair was twisted into a loose bun that was halfway to giving up, strands falling around her face, and the makeup under her eyes had smudged enough to make it obvious she either hadn't slept or had cried until nothing held.

When she saw him, she rushed forward like she'd been keeping herself upright out of spite alone, "Trevor."

His chest tightened on instinct, old habit and old history moving before thought, "What are you doing here?"

"I needed to talk to you."

"This isn't the place," his voice stayed even, but his body had already gone on alert taking in everyone around them. Receptionist behind the desk. Two assistants pretending not to look. Glass walls everywhere. Of all places this is where she wanted to show her ass.

"I didn't know where else to go," her voice cracked on the last word and for one ugly second that familiar reflex rose in him—that old urge to reach out, calm her down, fix it before it got worse. He hated how quickly it still lived in his bones.

"You could've called."

"You blocked me," she laughed, bitter and ragged. "Remember?"

Trevor rubbed his temple. "Katelyn—"

"My life is falling apart!" She shouted, and every head in the reception area found something suddenly fascinating to stare at except the scene right in front of them. She didn't care. "Do you hear me? It's falling apart and you're acting like none of this matters."

His jaw flexed, "Lower your voice."

"No," tears brimmed and spilled almost as quickly as the words came. "You were supposed to love me for life. That's what you promised me. You don't just walk away after one rough patch."

Trevor looked at her for a long time. *One rough patch.* The phrase sat so wrong in his chest it almost made him laugh.

"One rough patch?" He repeated quietly.

Her hands flew up, "I made mistakes. I know I did. I know that. But I've learned my lesson, Trevor. I have. We can fix this. We can go back to how things were."

For a second, the room blurred around the edges.

Because he remembered her.

Not this woman unraveling in his office lobby, but the girl. The one who used to wait for him after school. The one whose hand fit into his so easy back when life felt survivable because they were surviving it together. The one he spent years trying to protect from a world that had been too rough, too loud, too cruel too soon. He remembered all of that in one sharp rush, and before he could stop it, a tear slipped loose and tracked hot down his cheek.

Katelyn saw it and grabbed it like a lifeline, "See?" She whispered, stepping closer. "You still love me."

Trevor wiped his face slowly, "I do."

Her whole body sagged with relief.

But he kept talking.

"Just not the way you want anymore."

The words landed between them and stayed there. Heavy and final. Katelyn stared at him like she hadn't expected the truth to sound so plain.

"Trevor—"

"I spent half my life trying to save you," he said softly, and that was the part that hurt, the part he hadn't been able to name until now. "Since we were kids. I wore that cape so long I forgot I even had it on." Her expression cracked a little wider, but he didn't stop. He couldn't. "I would've given you anything. Everything your heart wanted. I would've bent myself into whatever shape made you feel safe and protected inside my world."

His chest tightened. He thought of all the years he confused love with rescue. Thought of how tired that kind of love left a man.

"I can't do that anymore."

Her face collapsed, "So that's it?"

"That's it for us."

Katelyn shook her head hard enough to send tears flying, "You're choosing someone else over me."

"This isn't about another woman."

"Then what is it about?"

Trevor held her gaze and gave her the only answer that mattered. "Zara."

That silenced her.

He took a breath and let his daughter anchor him all the way back into himself, "If you get yourself together—really together—we can talk about visitation. I want my daughter to know her mother. I do. But I'm not doing this with you like this. Not in lobbies. Not in chaos. Not while you're still making your mess everybody else's emergency."

Katelyn's lips trembled, "You'd really turn your back on me?"

Trevor's voice stayed calm, and maybe that was the part that made it final, "If you keep showing up like this, I'll file a protection order."

The words shattered whatever control she had left. She broke open right there, sobbing, cursing, saying his name like it could still pull him back toward her if she said it enough ways. Trevor turned toward the elevator before his body could betray him with one last instinct to comfort pain that was no longer his responsibility to carry.

When he passed the receptionist, she was looking at him with pity—he absolutely hated it.

"Call security and revoke her visitation access." Katelyn continued to cry in the lobby.

Her voice followed him down the hallway, ragged with grief and fury, bouncing off the glass walls while he kept walking.

He didn't turn back.

Some doors only closed once.

This one was closed for good.

Trevor reached Aniyah's condo that evening, the day had settled into his body like bad weather. The hallway outside her door smelled faintly of garlic and somebody's fabric softener, and beyond the insulated hush of the building, he could hear the ocean shifting against the shore. He stood there a second longer than necessary, hand braced at the back of his neck, trying to leave the rest of the day out in the corridor where it belonged.

When the door opened, Aniyah's face did that thing his chest had gotten entirely too used to. Softened first. Then sharpened when she really looked at him.

"Hey," she said, stepping back to let him in. Her voice was warm, but careful now, her eyes moving over his face with that quiet perception of hers that never missed much. "Everything okay?"

Trevor stepped inside and the first thing he noticed was the setup. She had done exactly what he'd texted her about earlier. The chair was angled near the window to catch the last of the natural light. The throw on the couch had been smoothed. Her notebook sat on the coffee table with two candles burning low beside it, and for one brief second the care in it hit him square in the chest. She had been nervous and still made this space ready. For him. For the work. For something she wasn't even sure she wanted strangers to see.

He should've said that. Should've told her it looked perfect. Instead, he dropped his bag by the couch harder than he meant to and watched her flinch almost imperceptibly at the sound.

"I'm fine," he said, even though they both knew that was bullshit.

Aniyah closed the door slowly, still watching him, "That answer doesn't match your face."

A tired laugh nearly escaped him, but it died before it could become anything real. She was wearing something soft, one of those cardigans she favored when she wanted comfort without looking like she was asking for it, and there was a pen tucked behind her ear. He noticed that too. Noticed everything, actually, which somehow made him feel worse. Because the more clearly he saw her, the more obvious it was that he needed to get his shit together before he said something stupid.

He bent to unzip his camera bag, buying himself a second. "It's been a long day."

"I can tell." She stepped closer to the window and glanced at the chair. "I moved everything around a little. The light was falling weird on the couch, so I thought maybe this would work better. If you want, I can move it back. Or we can try both and see what Hassan thinks."

Trevor looked up at the chair. Then looked at the notebook. He noticed the way her fingers kept rubbing together like she was trying not to let the nerves show. Guilt tugged at him, immediate and sharp. She had been texting him all day about this. She was clearly nervous. Wanting to get it right. And he'd shown up carrying Katelyn, London, the network, and every other piece of his frustration like he planned to dump it in her living room.

He straightened, forcing himself to inhale. "It looks good." His voice came out flatter than he intended. "Really good, actually."

Aniyah's shoulders eased a little, "Okay. Good." She gave him a small smile that felt more like relief than happiness. "I know this matters to you."

That made it worse.

Because it did matter. Her piece mattered more than half the people at the network understood. It was the soul of the damn episode. And after the day he'd had, the thought of anybody touching it, cutting it, reducing it to pacing notes and runtime concerns, made something ugly scrape against his ribs all over again.

Aniyah tilted her head, studying him, "Did something happen with the shoot?"

Trevor rubbed his jaw, "It's handled."

She paused, "That doesn't sound like handled."

He said nothing.

The condo had gone quiet in that way spaces do when two people are trying not to trip over the thing sitting between them. Trevor wanted to reach for her. Wanted to put his forehead to hers and breathe until his mind stopped feeling like a fist. Instead, he stood there feeling every inch of the distance he was creating in real time.

Aniyah glanced back toward the chair and tried again,

because of course she did. "Well, if the light's still good for another twenty minutes, we can probably get a clean first sit-down before the crew comes up. I can start with the grandfather story if you want, or the What I'm Not poems, or—"

"God dammit! Can we just start, Aniyah?!" The words came out sharper than he meant them to, edged with all the jaggedness he'd been trying and failing to keep buried. "Without you turning this into a whole thing? It's not that deep." He barked.

Silence hit the room so fast it damn near echoed.

Trevor felt it immediately. The shift in her face. The way surprise gave way to hurt, then to that stillness women got when they refused to let hurt be the only thing visible. Her arms came across her chest slowly, not defensive exactly, but contained.

"What did you just say to me?"

His stomach dropped. "Aniyah, I—"

"No." She stepped back, shaking her head once like she needed the movement to keep herself steady. "Actually, hold on." A humorless laugh slipped out of her. "Fuck this docuseries."

Trevor closed his eyes for half a second. Here it was.

"And fuck you if that's how you're going to talk to me."

The quiet after that felt deserved, heavy and humiliating. Trevor dragged a hand down his face and wished for a second he could take the last thirty seconds and burn them clean off the timeline.

"Yo," he said, voice lower now, stripped of the irritation because it had nowhere to hide anymore. "That was out of line."

Aniyah didn't move. "Completely."

"You're right."

"You don't get to come into my space carrying whatever happened out there and drop it on me." Her voice wasn't loud, which somehow made it cut deeper. "I'm not a punching bag for your frustrations. You either talk to me or hold it in, but you don't yell at me."

He nodded immediately, because there wasn't a single part of that he could argue with, "I know."

Her eyes flashed, "Do you?"

That question landed. Trevor leaned his hip against the kitchen counter like it was the only thing holding him upright, then looked at her fully for the first time since he walked in. "The artist in London pulled out this morning. The whole overseas segment is dead. The network spent half the day trying to convince me your piece should be cut because it's 'too intimate' and 'slows pacing.'" His mouth twisted on the last two words. "And right before I got here, Katelyn showed up at my office screaming in the lobby."

Aniyah blinked, "Wait. What?"

"She came up there crying, talking about I was supposed to love her for life, talking about fixing things, talking about one rough patch like she didn't blow up the whole fucking marriage and leave Zara in the smoke." He let out a breath through his nose, anger and exhaustion tangling together in a knot he was sick of carrying. "So by the time I got here, I was already not right. And instead of leaving that outside your door like I should've, I brought it in here and snapped at you."

The room went still again, but this time the stillness was different. Less like a break. More like a reckoning.

Aniyah looked down for a second, then back at him, and when she spoke her voice had softened without losing any of its shape. "I grew up with people talking to me like that. My parents did it my whole life. Sharp when they were angry. Dismissive when they were disappointed. Like I was supposed to absorb whatever they felt just because they felt it." She swallowed once, and Trevor saw the effort it took to keep the emotion from rising higher. "I will never accept that from a man I'm sharing a life with."

Shame moved through him slow and hot.

"You shouldn't," he said quietly.

Her arms loosened some, though she didn't uncross them completely. "I'm not saying we're done. But if we're going to keep doing this, you cannot bring that energy into my home...ever."

"I won't." He answered so fast it almost overlapped her. "I mean that."

Aniyah studied him for a long moment, measuring the apology, the man behind it, maybe the work she'd need to see before she fully trusted either. Then she sighed and glanced toward the equipment stacked by the door.

"Well," she said, exhaustion threading through the word, "we still have a docuseries to shoot."

Trevor frowned. "You still want to film?"

That earned him a small, tired smile. "I spent all day being nervous. I'm not wasting that anxiety."

Something in his chest loosened at that. Not enough to call it relief, but enough to breathe without feeling the room closing in. "Thank you."

"Don't thank me yet," she muttered, brushing past him to fix the angle of the chair one last time. "You still owe me for that little attitude."

Despite everything, the corner of his mouth twitched. "Noted."

A few minutes later Hassan and the crew arrived, carrying the usual hum of production in with them. Cables snaked along the baseboards. Light stands clicked into place. Someone tested audio twice. Trevor kept mostly to the wall, headset loose around his neck, watching Aniyah move through it all with quiet determination. She looked smaller in the chair once the camera was trained on her, hands folded in her lap, shoulders held a little too carefully, but she never once asked to back out.

"Whenever you're ready," Matthew—another crew member—said gently.

Aniyah took one breath. Then another.

"Tell us when writing first became important to you."

For a moment she said nothing. Trevor watched the nerves flicker across her face, there and gone like a match strike. Then her voice came, soft but steady.

"My grandfather gave me my first notebook when I was eight."

The whole room changed. You could feel it. Even Matthew seemed to shift behind the camera.

"He told me words were seeds," she said, a small smile pulling at her mouth. "If something hurts, I should plant it on the page instead of carrying it around in my chest."

Trevor felt his shoulders drop a fraction. Just hearing her settle into herself did something to him. The day had been scraping at his insides for hours, but watching her speak, watching the tremble leave her voice as memory took over, reminded him why he'd fought so hard for this piece to stay.

"I didn't understand what he meant back then. I just liked the way the notebook smelled." She laughed softly, and a few people in the crew smiled with her. "But eventually I realized writing gave me somewhere to put things that didn't make sense yet."

Her posture loosened as she kept going, like the truth itself was making room in her body. "My parents had very specific ideas about what my life should look like. Poetry wasn't one of them. I kept writing anyway. When things were hard. When I was grieving. When my body felt like something the world expected me to apologize for. When relationships didn't work out." She glanced toward the window where evening had gone soft and blue. "Poetry gave me a way to tell the truth without asking permission."

Trevor swallowed against the sudden tightness in his throat.

"And then recently...something changed."

Aniyah's eyes flickered toward Trevor before she could stop

them, and that one look landed harder than if she'd pointed him out by name.

"Falling in love changes the way you write," she said quietly. "You start noticing light in places you didn't even realize were dark."

That hit him like a hand to the center of his chest.

Matthew smiled behind the lens, "Cut."

Aniyah let out a groan and covered her face with both hands, "Well. That slipped out."

The crew laughed softly, the tension easing as equipment started coming down and conversation returned in low bursts. Trevor stayed where he was, not trusting himself to say anything yet. Because what was he supposed to do with that? She'd just cracked him open on camera, and he was standing there with an apology still drying on the walls.

When the last case was zipped and the last thank you exchanged, the condo had gone quiet again. Aniyah walked everyone to the door with her usual warmth, and Trevor waited near the entryway, bag in hand, feeling the shape of what he wanted to say and knowing none of it should be said tonight.

"Aniyah—"

She leaned her shoulder against the doorframe, arms folded loosely now, watching the elevator numbers change down the hall instead of looking at him, "I need some space tonight."

Her voice wasn't angry. If anything, that made it harder. Angry he could've fought through. Tired meant the damage had weight.

Trevor nodded, "Okay." He kissed her on the forehead before moving away.

He picked up his bag and stepped into the hallway. The door closed gently behind him, but her voice stayed with him all the way back to Brooklyn.

Falling in love changes the way you write.

Yeah. He thought, rubbing his hand over his mouth as he

headed for the elevator. *It also changed the way a man heard his own mistakes.*

Leon was sitting on the stoop when Trevor pulled up in front of the brownstone, the porch light casting a warm glow across the brick and the quiet stretch of sidewalk. The block had settled into its usual nighttime rhythm, laughter drifting from somewhere down the street, a car rolling slow past the corner, somebody's music muffled behind a closed window. The house itself felt steady, though. Familiar. The kind of calm that made a man realize how loud his own head had been all day.

Leon glanced up as Trevor stepped out of the car, and his eyes narrowed almost immediately, taking in the set of Trevor's shoulders, the way he shut the door a little harder than he meant to. "Evening, you look like shit."

Trevor climbed the steps and dropped into the chair beside him with a tired exhale, rubbing a hand over the back of his neck. "You ever have one of those days where the universe decides you're the main character in a disaster movie?"

Leon chuckled low, rocking once in his chair. "Son, you look like you wrestled a hurricane."

"Feels like it."

They sat in silence for a moment, the kind that didn't need help. The night air carried the faint scent of somebody grilling late, and the porch steps still held a little warmth from the day. Trevor leaned forward, elbows on his knees, staring down at the concrete like it might offer up a better version of the evening if he looked hard enough. "I messed up with Aniyah today."

Leon didn't ask what happened. He rarely needed to. Trevor

told him anyway, because the story had been sitting in his chest all night and he was tired of hearing it only in his own head. He told him about London falling through that morning, about the network trying to gut pieces of the project he cared about, about Katelyn showing up at the office like grief and bad decisions had learned how to wear lip gloss. When he got to Aniyah's condo, to the setup she had made for him, to the look on her face after he snapped—his voice had dropped lower and the shame in it was plain enough that he didn't need to dress it up.

Leon listened the way he always did, quiet and patient, gaze drifting down the block while Trevor talked himself all the way through it. When he finished, Leon leaned back and looked up at the sky like the answer might be written somewhere above the power lines.

"How you treat your woman in your angry moments shows a lot about how you value her in your relationship. Do you honor her enough to still speak with love even when you're upset? Today it looks like the answer was no to that, Bunny." Trevor's head hung low at his father's words. Shame engulfed him.

"You know," Leon said after a while, "you've always been the one who noticed things first."

Trevor frowned and glanced over. "What does that mean?"

A small smile touched Leon's mouth. "You figured out I had a crush on Miss Teri before anybody else."

That pulled the first real huff of laughter out of Trevor all night. "That wasn't hard."

"Probably not," Leon shifted in his chair, resting both hands on his stomach like he was deciding how much truth he felt like handing over. "Teri and I have been seeing each other."

Trevor blinked once, surprised even though maybe he shouldn't have been, "Seriously?"

Leon nodded, porch light catching the silver in his beard and at his temples. "For a little while now."

Trevor sat back and let that settle. He thought about all the little things he'd clocked and never pushed on. The way Teri lingered after dinner. The low conversations in the kitchen. The ease that had started creeping back into his father's face. Of course he'd noticed. That man had always looked at life like a puzzle he could solve if he sat with it long enough. Trevor learned half his own observation from him.

"She's good for you," Trevor said.

Leon smiled faintly, "She's good company. Makes the house feel less empty."

The words sat there for a second before Leon looked back out toward the street, and when he spoke again his voice had softened in a way Trevor only heard when his mother's memory was somewhere near. "Your mother was my soulmate, Trevor. Ain't no way around that. Della was the love of my life, and nothing in this world is ever going to replace what we had."

Trevor swallowed against the sudden tightness in his throat. Hearing his mother's name like that would do it every time.

Leon rubbed his jaw, thoughtful. "Teri and I talked about it before anything happened. We had a long talk too. We both had to sit with what it meant to feel something again after losing somebody who meant that much. It's sad, but I'm happy she knows exactly how I feel...it makes this easier"

"And?" Trevor asked quietly.

Leon let out a low chuckle, more reflection than humor. "Turns out love doesn't come back the same way."

He shifted, glancing over at Trevor now,"It's quieter."

Trevor raised an eyebrow.

Leon shrugged, "Feels like sitting down on a soft couch after standing all day. Peaceful. Like your shoulders finally remember how to relax."

Trevor laughed under his breath, "That is the most Dad description of love I've ever heard."

Leon grinned. "Doesn't make it less true."

The grin faded into something gentler as he looked away again, "I'll always love your mother. Always. But this here? This feels like a second chance at something good. At my age, you don't waste chances like that."

Trevor nodded slowly, thinking about Aniyah's face in the doorway tonight. Thinking about the way she'd looked tired more than angry. Tired enough to ask for distance. Tired enough not to argue when he left.

"You told Jackson and Lou yet?" he asked.

Leon snorted, "Not a chance."

That pulled a smile out of Trevor, "Yeah, they'd be insufferable."

"Exactly. I'll tell them when I feel like being annoyed on purpose." They sat in that for a minute, the kind of lightness that only really worked because something heavier was waiting underneath it. Sure enough, Leon turned his head and fixed Trevor with a look that let him know the soft part of the conversation was over.

"That girl hasn't left you."

Trevor exhaled slowly. "I know."

"But she saw a glimpse today of what loving you could look like if you don't get a handle on your hurt."

Trevor winced and looked down at his hands.

Leon didn't let him dodge it. "Anybody with eyes can see you care about her. Hell, you probably love her. But I can also see you're still bleeding from Katelyn, whether you want to admit that or not." His voice stayed calm, which somehow made it land harder. "That's not a crime. That's real. But if you try to build something new while all that is still leaking out of you, you'll stain it."

Trevor sat with that, jaw tight. Because it was true. He hated how true it was.

"I told her I was sorry."

"That's a start."

"It felt small."

"It was supposed to." Leon leaned forward, forearms on his knees. "Apologies are small. Change is what makes them mean something." He let that breathe before continuing. "Also, give this space. Space ain't always punishment. Sometimes it's mercy. Sometimes it's you realizing that if you stay in this moment—with her—you'll do more damage than you planned."

Trevor stared out at the street, hearing Aniyah's voice all over again. *I will never accept that from a man in my life.* She hadn't threatened him. Hadn't manipulated him. She'd drawn the line and stood there. He respected the hell out of that even while it burned.

Leon studied him for another beat. "If she slows this down, let her. Don't chase her because you're scared of losing the feeling. Sit with what's hurting. Mourn what needs mourning. Heal what needs healing. Then go to her when you have a handle on things. ."

Trevor huffed out a breath that held no humor. "That sounds easy when you say it."

Leon smiled faintly. "Didn't say it was easy. I said it was right."

Trevor nodded, slow and reluctant and certain all at once. "I'm not trying to use her to patch something up. I know that."

"I know you aren't," Leon said. "But knowing it and proving it are two different things."

That sat in Trevor's chest for a long time.

The porch had gone quiet again when his phone buzzed in his pocket. He pulled it out expecting Jackson, maybe Hassan with some stray production fire still burning, but it was Aniyah. His pulse jumped once, hard enough to annoy him.

He opened the message.

Roxanne 😘: I've been sitting with tonight. I need you to hear me all the way through before you respond.

Trevor straightened in his chair.

Roxanne 😘: What happened tonight does not make me want to walk away from you. But it does make me want to slow this down. We jumped into this fast, and I think we both know that.

His chest tightened, but he kept reading.

Roxanne 😘: You're still dealing with the fallout of Katelyn, Trevor. The marriage may be over, but you're still carrying it. I saw that tonight. I'm not judging you for it. I think it's human. But I need you to give yourself real space to mourn and heal, so when you choose me, it won't be because I fit inside the wound. It'll be because you're whole enough to know what you're choosing.

Trevor read that twice, slower the second time.

Roxanne 😘: This isn't me disappearing. I'm not asking you to leave my life. I'm asking us to take the pressure off. Breathe. Be intentional. Let this grow the right way. I will still be taking Zara on our Saturday dates.

Then one more message came through.

Roxanne 😘: I care about you too much to just be your bandage

Trevor stared at the screen until the words blurred at the

edges.

Leon didn't ask what she said. He just watched Trevor's face, took in the way something in him shifted, and nodded once like he already knew.

"She's right, ain't she?"

Trevor swallowed and looked back down at the message. "Yeah." His voice came out rough. "She is."

And that was the part that got him. Not just that she wanted space, but that she had given it shape. She wasn't pushing him away. She was trying to protect what this could become before they ruined it by rushing. Protecting herself too, sure, but him as well. That kind of love took vision. It took patience. It took more maturity than he had shown her tonight.

His thumbs hovered over the screen for a second before he typed back.

I hear you. And you're right. I'm sorry for how I spoke to you tonight, and I'm grateful you said this plainly. I care about you too much to make you carry hurt that isn't yours. We can slow it down. I'm not going anywhere.

He hit send before he could overthink it.

The response didn't come right away, and for once he didn't need it to. The act of saying it honestly, without trying to negotiate her boundary smaller, settled something in him.

Leon leaned back in his chair, looking annoyingly unsurprised. "That's the woman for you."

Trevor let out a tired laugh, "Yeah."

"She's got sense."

"She does."

"And she likes your hardheaded ass anyway." That made Trevor smile despite himself. Leon's expression was gentle again.

"You've always been the most in tune with people out of my boys. Blessing and curse of being the youngest."

Trevor rubbed his hands together and looked down the block. "Feels like the curse part tonight."

"Maybe." Leon shrugged. "But that same awareness is what'll help you do this right, if you let it."

Trevor nodded slowly, the resolve settling in not as fire this time, but as something steadier. Less urgent. More sure. He thought about work, Zara, the way grief still crept up on him wearing old faces. Thought about Aniyah refusing to be a wound dressing. Thought about what it would mean to show up for her healed enough to hold what she offered.

"I'm not losing her," he said quietly.

Leon glanced over at him, "Then don't rush to keep her. Become the man she doesn't have to question."

That hit deeper than Trevor wanted to admit.

He looked down at his phone one more time. Still no response from Aniyah. That was alright. She didn't owe him immediacy. Not tonight.

Trevor slid the phone back into his pocket and leaned forward, elbows on his knees, letting the night air cool the last of the heat in his face. He could still hear her voice from the condo. Could still hear her on camera talking about how falling in love changes the way you write. Maybe healing changed the way you loved too. Maybe it taught you not to grab too fast at what felt good. Maybe it taught you how to hold something carefully enough that it wanted to stay.

"I'm going to let this breathe and then show her I'm the man for her."

Leon rocked back in his chair, satisfied in that quiet dad way of his. "Good," he said after a while. "I know you can do it."

CHAPTER FOURTEEN

IT WAS ALWAYS YOU

"I don't want to sound foolish, but remember love is what brought you here. And if you've trusted love this far, don't panic now. Trust it all the way." – *Sharon Rivers, If Beale Street Could Talk (2018)*

Spring was always Aniyah's favorite time of the year, even when she was missing her man, that wasn't her man, that definitely was *her* man.

April had arrived without ceremony.

More time had passed since that night with Trevor than she realized.

At first the distance between them had been intentional. She needed space for the sting of his words to fade into something that didn't live so close to her skin anymore. Trevor had given her exactly what she asked for without protest, without hovering, without turning every conversation into a quiet request for forgiveness.

That alone told her more about the man he was trying to be than any apology ever could.

They still talked, of course they did.

Text messages in the mornings before school started, usually something simple. *Good morning. Hope the kids behave today.* He would send pictures of Zara holding up a drawing she did in the evening and insisted on showing Aniyah before she went to bed.

Aniyah still came to pick Zara up every Saturday for their nail dates and lunch. The little girl overflowed with joy every time her car pulled into Trevor's driveway. She hadn't come inside since their fall out. Trevor respected it and never pushed her—that made her heart ache more.

At night they spoke on the phone when their schedules allowed, exhaustion softening their voices into something easy and familiar. The conversations rarely lasted long, but they lingered afterward in ways Aniyah hadn't expected.

Trevor never pushed.

When he picked Zara up from school he stayed outside, leaning against the fence while the children spilled onto the sidewalk. Zara almost always threw her arms around Aniyah's waist before remembering she had a father waiting two steps away. Aniyah would lock eyes with Trevor and fight the urge to run to his arms.

Those moments were brief. Trevor kept the distance she asked for, even when the warmth in his eyes said he would have closed it in a heartbeat.

Still, the absence had weight.

Some nights Aniyah caught herself staring at her phone longer than she meant to, rereading one of his messages while a quiet ache spread behind her ribs.

The moments she saw something funny and reached for her

phone before remembering she shouldn't call him just because she wanted to hear his laugh. The way his voice sometimes lingered in her ears long after their nightly goodnight.

God, she missed that man.

The thought passed through her mind as she stood near the classroom window, watching Zara kneel beside another student on the reading rug. It was lunch time and just as Aniyah's teachers had done in the past, she opened her classroom for those who may not want to sit in the cafeteria. Only Zara and Jada choose to eat in the classroom. The girls were stacking bright plastic blocks into a tower that leaned dangerously to the left, their giggles filling the space every time the structure wobbled.

Zara had changed so much in the past few months that sometimes it caught Aniyah off guard.

She laughed easily now. Raised her hand when she knew an answer instead of shrinking into her seat. During story time she volunteered to read out loud, her small voice bright and confident in a way that made Aniyah's chest swell with quiet pride every time she heard it.

Dr. Sanders was doing good work.

Trevor was too.

Zara had done a complete one-eighty from the quiet, withdrawn child who walked into Aniyah's classroom at the start of the year carrying confusion she didn't yet have words for. Now she moved through the room like a child who understood she was safe, the kind of confidence that only grew when the adults in your life finally became steady ground.

Aniyah rested her hip against the edge of her desk, folding her arms loosely as she watched Zara carefully add another block to the tower.

The whole thing toppled immediately.

The girls burst into laughter, blocks scattering across the rug like confetti.

Aniyah smiled.

Her phone buzzed softly in the pocket of her cardigan.

She pulled it out without thinking, expecting Trevor's name to light up the screen the way it often did around this time of day. Instead the name staring back at her made her stomach tighten.

Dad.

Aniyah stared at the phone while it rang, the vibration humming faintly against her palm.

That man had always had impeccable timing when it came to reopening wounds.

The ringing continued.

Across the room Zara gathered blocks into a small pile, chatting happily with the other student beside her while they prepared to start again. Their voices drifted through the classroom like background music, light and unbothered.

Aniyah answered on the fourth ring, "Hello."

There was a pause before her father spoke, "Aniyah."

His voice sounded older than she remembered. The sharp edge that once lived in it had been worn down by time, though the familiarity of hearing him say her name still felt strange, like a sound from a life she had already stepped out of.

She leaned her shoulder against the wall, her gaze drifting back toward Zara and Jada across the room.

"What do you want?"

Another pause stretched across the line.

"I'd like to see you."

Aniyah watched Zara carefully rebuild the tower she and her classmate had just destroyed, the little girl's tongue poking out in concentration.

"For what?" she asked.

"I think we should talk."

The words hung between them. Years of unsaid things pressed quietly against the silence that followed. Dinner table arguments.

Expectations delivered like ultimatums. The moment she realized his approval had always come with conditions.

Aniyah exhaled slowly, her fingers tightening slightly around the phone. She was about to make a choice she knew she would regret in the future.

"Send me the address," she said.

On the other end of the line her father went quiet for a moment.

"All right."

Then the call ended.

Aniyah lowered the phone and slipped it back into her cardigan pocket as she pushed away from the wall. Across the room Zara finally managed to balance another block on top of the tower, her small face lighting up with triumph.

Aniyah walked over and crouched beside her, tapping the block gently with one finger.

"Well look at that," she said softly. "Engineering skills."

Zara beamed up at her. She wished she could feel that happiness that Zara felt in that moment.

What had she just gotten herself into?

"*It's just like Rodger to choose this swanky restaurant,*" Aniyah thought as she walked into the entrance of *La Petite Mort.* Her nerves over taking her. Trying to act like this is just a regular business meeting wasn't going to fly. Even with those nerves overflowing, she held her head high.

Aniyah paused just inside the doorway, letting her eyes adjust while she scanned the room. She found him near the back window exactly where she expected he'd be—upright posture, hands folded neatly on the table, the quiet authority that had defined most of her childhood still sitting comfortably in his shoulders. Time had softened the edges, though. Silver threaded through his auburn hair now, and the certainty that once lived in his expression had been replaced by something more careful.

When he saw her, he stood.

"Aniyah."

Her name landed softly between them, unfamiliar in a way that caught her off guard. For most of her life it had only been spoken when it was followed by instruction, correction, or expectation.

She walked over but didn't hug him. She slid into the chair across from him, smoothing her coat over her lap before resting her hands lightly on the table.

"You said you wanted to talk."

The waiter appeared at his elbow, already reaching for a wine list, but Aniyah shook her head politely, "I'm fine, thank you."

Her father dismissed the menu with a small nod before turning his attention back to her. He studied her quietly, his gaze moving over her face like he was trying to memorize the woman she had become without his permission.

"You look well," he said.

Aniyah felt the faintest curve touch her mouth, "I am."

He absorbed that, though his fingers tapped once against the table like the silence made him restless.

"I heard you're still teaching," he said after a moment.

"You heard right."

His gaze drifted briefly toward the window where evening traffic moved past in slow ribbons of light, "I always imagined you in a hospital, being an attendee."

Aniyah leaned back slightly, folding her arms loosely. The old script between them was so familiar she could almost hear the next line before he spoke it.

"I know, I've heard it for years. If this is what you wanted, I can go."

A quiet pause stretched between them.

"I realized now...that I may have been...too hard on you," he said finally.

Aniyah exhaled slowly, her gaze steady on his.

"You treated me like shit. No need to sugar coat it. I differed from the path you laid out for me, and I no longer was good enough to be your daughter," she said calmly.

His eyes lifted, he opened his mouth to rebut. Aniyah quickly cut him off.

"We are here because you never loved me without condition," The words were quiet, but they landed with weight. Her father flinched almost imperceptibly, the reaction small enough that anyone else in the restaurant might have missed it.

"Of course I loved you, Aniyah. I just wanted the best for you," he said, though the conviction in his voice sounded thinner than she remembered.

Aniyah tilted her head slightly.

"No," she replied gently. "You wanted the version of me that made you look good, which for the life of me I don't see how this one doesn't?! Is it the teaching? The scars I can't help or my 'wretched disease' as you called it in the past? Please, father, explain."

His gaze dropped to his hands. He looked much smaller than the man she remembered. His face wore the look of anguish, she almost felt sorry for him—almost.

"I spent years trying to come to terms with the fact that you didn't love me," she continued, her voice steady even as the memories behind it still carried teeth. "I isolated myself, dove into school and work without making genuine connections with the people around me. You did that."

His jaw tightened now in aggravation Aniyah was sure.

"I did love you, I just knew you were capable of more."

Aniyah let out a small breath that sounded halfway between disbelief and the other half in irritation.

"Do you hear yourself right now? Have you listened to anything I've said? More importantly, do you remember my sophomore year in high school?"

Her dad looked over at her in confusion. The fact that he didn't remember was yet another slice to the heart.

"That was the year I started realizing I didn't want to be a doctor," she said. "The year I told you I liked writing. That I wanted to be a teacher."

His expression stayed carefully neutral, but something in his shoulders stiffened.

"That was the year you stopped looking at me the same way, I wasn't your pride and joy anymore. I was a nuisance that dared to be different."

"Aniyah—"

"No," she said gently, cutting him off before he could steer the conversation somewhere safer. "Let's tell the truth tonight."

The restaurant hummed quietly around them, plates clinking somewhere behind her, a low conversation drifting past from another table.

"You remember the dinner table conversation," she continued. "The one where you told me I needed to stop thinking small."

His mouth opened slightly, but she kept going.

"You said I was wasting my potential. That if I insisted on throwing away the opportunities you worked so hard to give me, then maybe you'd made a mistake raising me to believe I could choose my own life."

Her father's gaze dropped to the table again. Aniyah felt the old ache brush against her ribs, but it didn't grip the way it used to. It passed through her instead of settling.

"Do you know what that sounded like to a sixteen-year-old girl?" she asked quietly.

He didn't answer.

"It sounded like I was a mistake, that my dreams were a *mistake*."

Her fingers tightened slightly against the edge of the table, though her voice remained calm.

"There are a lot of things I could forgive you for," she said. "Pressure. High expectations. Even the way you dismissed my career."

Her eyes held his.

"But making me feel like I was unwanted the moment I stopped being the daughter you planned for..." She paused, letting the weight of the truth sit between them. "That's not one of them."

Her father finally looked up again, regret flickering across his face.

"I never meant—"

"I know."

The answer came quickly.

"That's the thing about words, though. Intent doesn't erase impact."

He leaned back in his chair, rubbing a hand across his forehead like the conversation had pressed against something he'd spent years refusing to examine. This was not how this dinner was supposed to go.

"Your mother thought I was pushing you toward stability," he said quietly.

Aniyah nodded once, "I know she did. She reminds me every chance she gets."

"She still thinks you're wasting your education."

Aniyah released a soft breath.

"That's her choice, what she thinks is no longer my concern and let her know, I will no longer be answering her phone calls."

With that, she pushed her chair back and stood up.

"I'll make this easy for you, Rodger. You can live your life like I never existed," she said quietly. "That seems to be what you wanted anyway."

Rodger stood quickly attempting to stop her, "Aniyah—"

Aniyah was already starting to walk away. For a moment he looked like he might reach for her, then his voice called out, "I didn't ask you here so you could leave like this," he said.

Aniyah stopped to turn and meet his gaze, her voice held a finality that her father wasn't used to, "I came here so I could. For years I yearned for you to reach out and tell me these years were a nightmare, that I was still your little girl who you love more than anything. After Grandpa died, I got the reality check I needed. I was nothing more than a pawn in your chess game and your wife was complicit in your treatment of me. You're a sorry excuse for a man, and I want nothing to do with you. Give your wife my regards because after today, I don't want to hear from either one of you."

Aniyah turned, not giving Rodger the chance to interject again and walked out the restaurant with her head held high.

She stepped onto the sidewalk—the city air wrapped around her, cool and alive with the rhythm of Manhattan at night. Aniyah paused beneath a streetlight and drew in a slow breath. For years she had carried the weight of his disappointment like proof she had failed. Tonight she realized something else entirely.

It had never been hers to carry.

Her shoulders lifted as she exhaled, the tension leaving her body in a slow, steady release.

Free.

CHAPTER FIFTEEN

THIS IS MINE

"Let me tell you somthin'. This here, right now, at this very moment, is all that matters to me. I love you. That's urgent like a motherfucka." – *Darius Lovehall, Love Jones (1997)*

Two Months Ago (one month into Aniyah's break)

"I'm here because...I had a kid at 19, got married, tried to make that marriage work, it turned out my wife was fucking the entirety of NYC, divorced her, she terminated her rights to our daughter, I started seeing someone I've known for a long time... and she just put a pause on things because I have unresolved feelings of anger towards the dissolution of my marriage," Trevor felt like he was out of breath once he finished his introduction to Dr. Goodwin. She was an older Black woman. Strands of silver curved through her French roll. She had a welcoming aura that instantly relaxed Trevor when he walked in.

He made the decision to go to a therapist after his blow up with Aniyah. He had to be honest with himself, while he was 100% detached from his marriage with Katelyn the feelings of resentment and inadequacy still ran rampant throughout his mind. Talking to his family was nice, but he needed an unbiased opinion to be honest with.

"Wow, that is certainly an introduction, Mr. Porter," Dr. Goodwin began. "You said you got married at 19, what was that like?"

Trevor thought for a second before speaking, "At first? It was everything. We were young and naive. Our little girl was the center of our world. I was working and going to school then coming home and taking over the night shift with my daughter. I should've been exhausted, but I felt like the *Energizer Bunny*."

He laughed to himself at the thought.

"Then...things started to shift. Zara got older and Katelyn and I grew apart. I've tried to wrap my head around how I could've saved things. When I should've stepped in. But then that would mean admitting I was a side character in my own marriage."

Dr. Goodwin tilted her head slightly, studying him, "What would it mean to admit that?"

Trevor exhaled slowly, his hands clasping and unclasping in his lap. "That would mean that I missed it. That I was so focused on being a good father, a provider...that I didn't see my marriage falling apart in real time. Or maybe I did see it and just...kept choosing to believe it would fix itself."

He shifted in his seat, jaw tightening. "Now I'm stuck with those thoughts on a loop because it's like—how do I trust my judgment again? How do I know I won't miss something like that with Aniyah?"

There it was, the truth seeping through his lips that he had been afraid to admit.

"Tell me about her," Dr. Goodwin stated.

Trevor's expression softened despite himself, as it did whenever a thought of Aniyah popped into his mind. He had missed her something terrible this past month.

"She's...beautiful, inside and out. She has such a big heart and loves the children she teaches. She's a poet. She's built this life for herself that's so peaceful that I fear I may disrupt it. She took a break from me and I agreed without a fight." He swallowed. "I think that's what scares me."

"Why?"

"Because if I mess that up..." he trailed off, shaking his head. "It would be as if I didn't learn anything from my marriage and I don't want that to be the case."

Dr. Goodwin nodded, her voice calm, "So the anxiety you're carrying—it's not just about your ex-wife."

Trevor let out a quiet, humorless laugh. "Nah, if it was just about that it would be too easy."

"It sounds like some of your anxiety and anger is directed at yourself," she continued. "You didn't see your marriage's dissolution in time and didn't act quick enough. You also don't want to shake up Aniyah's life either."

Trevor leaned back, dragging a hand down his face. "Yeah... that sounds about right."

"Aniyah pausing things," Dr. Goodwin added gently, "Held that mirror back up to your face."

Trevor stared at the floor for a moment, then nodded once, slowly, "Yes, it did."

"So what do I do with that?" he asked, quieter now.

Dr. Goodwin offered a small, reassuring smile. "We start by separating what belongs to your past from what's actually happening in your present. And then," she paused, jotting down a note, "we figure out how to give yourself permission to move forward without carrying all of it with you."

He began seeing her once a week and it was the best thing he could've done because his shoulders didn't feel as heavy...If he wanted to be the father that Zara deserved, this was a necessary step.

Present Time

Trevor's plane touched down at JFK just as the sun was setting.

He stayed seated for a moment after the seatbelt sign blinked off, watching the cabin lights brighten while passengers reached for their bags and stretched stiff limbs. The familiar hum of the airport seeped through the walls of the plane—engines winding down, ground crew shouting faintly somewhere on the tarmac. Normally he would already be halfway up the aisle, moving with the practiced efficiency of someone who spent too much time in airports.

Tonight he stayed still.

Three months.

Three months since that night in Aniyah's condo when everything inside him cracked open and spilled through the wrong door.

Three months of dealing with he and Zara's new normal. To be honest, it was needed. That time alone with just he and Zara helped him reconnect to the pieces of himself that he lost when Katelyn left.

The docuseries had swallowed most of his daylight hours.

Editing sessions that bled past midnight. Producers who kept trying to shave the soul out of the project so it could fit neatly into a marketable box. The premiere was set for July now, which meant every decision carried weight. Every scene, every voice, every story he fought to keep intact had to survive the final cut.

Then there was Zara.

Trevor smiled faintly as he finally stood and pulled his bag from the overhead bin.

His daughter had been thriving, despite her world being shaken to its core with the loss of her mother.

Dr. Sanders helped her find her footing again, but Trevor knew the classroom had done something deeper. Watching Zara grow comfortable in that space—laughing more, raising her hand in class, running into the building each morning without hesitation—had become one of the quiet victories he carried through every long day.

Aniyah had been right there at the center of it.

Even when she wasn't.

The distance between them hadn't been full silence. If anything, they talked more now than they ever had before. Morning texts. Late-night calls when exhaustion softened both their voices. Random messages in the middle of the day about something Zara said or some ridiculous thing Marcus did in the editing room.

They just hadn't been together...in that way, since their first time. Trevor was in withdrawals. He missed the feeling of her body against his. The taste of her on his tongue. The smell of her vanilla body butter. Most importantly, he just missed *her*.

Every Saturday he saw her it took everything in him not to pull her body close to his.

All that would change tonight. While he was away, he mustered up the courage to ask her on a date. Aniyah responded yes without any hesitation and Trevor felt like singing.

Trevor stepped into the cool night air outside the terminal and pulled his phone from his pocket.

Her name sat right where it always did, in his favorites.

He hit call.

Aniyah answered on the second ring.

“Hey you,” she said, her voice warm enough to pull a quiet smile across his face.

“I just landed.”

“I figured you were close. Was the flight okay?”

“It was long,” he said, shifting his bag onto his shoulder as he moved toward the curb. “But worth it.”

She was quiet for a moment, and Trevor could almost hear the smile forming on the other end of the line.

“So... we still on for tonight?”

Trevor leaned against the side of the car he’d called, watching headlights drift past along the road.

“We’re absolutely on for tonight.”

Another pause followed, softer this time.

“Good,” Aniyah said quietly.

Trevor exhaled slowly, the tension that had lived in his chest for weeks loosening just a little.

“I’ll pick you up at seven.”

“I’ll be ready.”

The line clicked off, but Trevor stayed there for another moment before sliding into the car.

Tonight was the night.

Trevor knocked on Aniyah’s door, the sun had disappeared completely, leaving the quiet street outside her condo washed in the soft glow of porch lights and passing headlights. The evening air still held a hint of spring warmth, but Trevor barely noticed it. His mind had been rehearsing versions of this moment the entire drive over—what he would say, how he would say it, the careful balance between honesty and restraint he'd promised himself he would keep.

All of it vanished the second the door opened.

Aniyah stood there framed by the warm light spilling from inside the condo, and for a moment Trevor forgot how language worked.

She looked so fucking good...

Her hair fell softly around her shoulders, the loose waves catching the light in a way that made the deep brown of her skin glow. She wore something simple—nothing dramatic—but the sight of her after three months of distance hit him square in the chest anyway.

"Hey," she said.

Trevor stepped inside slowly, shaking his head like his brain needed a second to catch up with what his eyes were seeing.

"Hey."

The door clicked shut behind him, and suddenly the small entryway felt quieter than it should have. Three months of space sat between them in that hallway, invisible but undeniable. Trevor had imagined this moment more times than he could count, but standing here now with her only a few feet away felt different than any version he'd rehearsed.

Aniyah studied him for a second before a soft laugh slipped out of her.

"You gonna say something," she asked, tilting her head slightly, "or just stand there looking at me like that all night?"

Trevor stepped closer before he could overthink it. The scent of her perfume reached him then, familiar enough to stir something low and steady in his chest.

"I missed you."

The words left his mouth before he had time to measure them.

Aniyah's expression softened immediately, the teasing in her eyes giving way to longing.

"I missed you too."

The tension in Trevor's shoulders eased a fraction, the distance of the last three months shifting into something that no longer felt quite so wide.

He leaned down and kissed her, a moan immediately left Aniyah's mouth as her body sagged into his. Trevor knew at that moment that she needed this just as much as him. They made out against her door without a care in the world. That reconnection was exactly what he needed.

Finally, Trevor backed away from Aniyah, her eyes found him and the need he saw reflected there was his undoing.

"Baby," he began. "We have to go or we'll be late for our reservation." His eyes swept over her body taking in the black dress she was wearing that hugged her curves, something serious.

"You're right, let me get my things so we can head out." Aniyah responded, pushing away from the door. The movement brought her close to Trevor again. His hand reached out and grabbed her waist.

"We should have enough time for an appetizer." He said without thinking. The confusion that bloomed over Aniyah's face would've have made him laugh if he wasn't so fucking turned on right now.

"Appetizer? Trev, we have to go if you want that. Wait, what —" Aniyah stopped her question seeing Trevor drop down to his knees. His strong hands reached around to grip her ass bringing her body flush against his. From this angle her center was directly in front of his face.

"I have been dreaming about the way you taste for months. I know we still have a lot to talk about and we will tonight, I promise. But Roxanne, if I don't French kiss your pussy in the next 4.5 seconds, I fear I may lose my fucking mind." Trevor felt Aniyah's body shiver against him.

"Fuck yes, do what you gotta do, Trev. I want to make sure you're intellectually sound at dinner tonight."

Trevor laughed as he pushed Aniyah's dress over her hips and pulled her panties down.

"I thank you for your service." Aniyah's giggle quickly turned to a moan as Trevor swiped his tongue between his second favorite set of lips on her body. Her taste hit his tongue in an explosion of her personal ambrosia. He could die here, a happy man.

"Fuck, Trevor, don't tease me."

"I would never do that, baby. But I needed to get my quick taste in." As soon as he finished speaking, he immersed himself in her heat, doing exactly what he promised, French kissing her sweet entrance. Aniyah's hands shakily gripped his head as she ground against his face without a care in the world. All that mattered was the feeling of Trevor's lips on her and her clit grinding against his nose.

Trevor could tell that it had been a minute since Aniyah had an orgasm, she was at the brink already. He loved the way she was fucking his face and taking what rightfully belonged to her. From her taste, her satisfaction and those sinful noises she was making, Trevor was on his way over the edge too. He began to suck on her clit causing Aniyah to cry out in pleasure.

"You eat me so fucking well baby. I've missed you so much." Trevor moaned in response, not letting up. He eased two fingers inside of her, pumping slowly in rhythm with her movements against him. The way she gripped his fingers was unreal.

"I'm—shit—I'm cumming!" Aniyah cried out, at the same time Trevor felt himself cum just from pleasing her. He placed a gentle kiss against her mound before standing to his full height.

Aniyah was still catching her breath leaning against her front door. Her eyes traced over him. Her juices glistening on his face would always be a favorite sight of hers.

"Thank you, baby. I needed that." Trevor said. Aniyah blushed in return.

"You're thanking me when I should be thanking you. I've been wound up for months. Let's get cleaned up." She said moving towards her bathroom.

"Yeah I definitely need to clean up, you still got my extra pair of briefs here?" Aniyah turned to look at Trevor . A sheepish smile crossed his face.

"Pleasing you made me cum, so I need to clean up." Aniyah's mouth dropped open.

"My heavens, my stars. We are never going to make it to dinner with you telling me things like that!" Trevor laughed loudly, he felt so light in the moment. This was exactly what he needed.

"Come on girl! I know you're hungry. Let me feed you."

"That dick?" Aniyah asked slyly.

"Real food." He sternly replied, although dick was absolutely on the menu tonight. They needed to talk first and Trevor would make sure they would.

"We are always going out to eat, greedy asses." Aniyah joked as they sat down at their favorite hole in the wall.

It wasn't crowded, just a handful of couples scattered through the room, the occasional clink of glasses rising above the gentle hum of the speakers.

Trevor noticed when the staff began clearing a small patch of floor near the bar before the first notes of Deborah Cox drifted through the room.

He was already standing before he fully realized it.

Aniyah lifted a brow from her chair, amused. "Are you serious?"

Trevor held out his hand like the answer was obvious. "Come here."

She laughed, that quiet, familiar sound he'd missed more than he realized, but she slid her hand into his anyway and let him pull her toward the open space near the speaker. The opening notes of *Nobody's Supposed to Be Here* rolled through the room as Trevor settled one hand along her waist, guiding her closer without thinking. Their bodies began to sway in rhythm with the song.

Aniyah rested her head lightly against his shoulder, and for a moment neither of them spoke.

Trevor let out a slow breath, the scent of her perfume wrapping around him in a way that felt grounding after the last few months of noise. He hadn't realized how much he'd missed this until now—the simple closeness of her body moving with his, the quiet ease that always seemed to settle between them when the world stopped demanding something from him.

"This song feels appropriate," she murmured against his shoulder.

Trevor chuckled softly, his hand sliding a little lower along her back as they swayed. "Yeah?"

Aniyah tipped her head back so she could look up at him, her eyes catching the candlelight.

"Because nobody's supposed to be here."

Trevor smiled faintly.

"But here we are."

They moved slowly with the rhythm, neither rushing the moment. The music wrapped around them, familiar and warm, the kind of song that had lived in the background of a hundred late-night drives and quiet Sunday mornings.

After a moment Trevor glanced down at her. "You written any poems lately?"

Aniyah lifted a brow, the corner of her mouth tilting. "Of course."

His thumb brushed lightly along her back as he pulled her a little closer. "You gonna let me read them?"

She studied him for a second before that slow smile spread across her face. "If you're a good boy."

Trevor laughed under his breath, the sound rumbling low in his chest. "I'm always a good boy."

He leaned closer, lowering his mouth near her ear, his voice dropping just enough to make the words land.

"I know you remember the last time I was a good boy for you."

The heat that rushed across her face made Trevor grin immediately.

"Aht-aht," she warned, lifting her head to look at him, though the laughter dancing in her eyes ruined any attempt at real reprimand. "Don't start."

Trevor chuckled softly, tightening his arm around her waist as the music carried them through the rest of the song.

When the music faded, neither of them moved right away. Trevor kept his hand at her waist a second longer than necessary before finally guiding her back toward their table. This time they didn't sit across from each other. Aniyah slid into the seat beside him instead, their shoulders brushing while the candle between them flickered softly.

Trevor watched the flame for a moment, gathering his thoughts before he spoke.

"These last few months..." He exhaled slowly. "As hard as it was, you were right. I needed them."

Aniyah turned slightly toward him, her arm resting along the back of the booth. "It was a tough decision at the time, but it needed to happen."

"I had to sit with some things," Trevor agreed, his voice steady but quieter now. "The end of my marriage and Zara losing her mom. The guilt I didn't realize I was still carrying around." His fingers brushed lightly against hers on the table. "I didn't want to drag any of that into whatever this is between us. I've been going to therapy to work all that shit out too. "

Aniyah didn't interrupt. She just listened, her hand staying where it was beside his.

"You gave me the space to do that," he said. "But you never disappeared."

He glanced over at her.

"The calls every day and seeing you with Zara..." Trevor shook his head slightly, a quiet smile touching the corner of his mouth. "You've been a pillar in my life even while we were standing on opposite sides of the room."

Aniyah studied him for a moment before asking softly, "Why now?"

Trevor blinked. "What do you mean?"

She met his gaze fully.

"Three months ago, everything was falling apart around you," she said calmly. "How do I know this isn't just relief from that?"

Trevor leaned back slightly, absorbing the question.

Fair.

More than fair.

"I knew you would ask that question once we ended up here," he admitted after a moment. "I thought about it long and hard.

His thumb brushed lightly along the back of her hand.

"Relief feels temporary," he said slowly. "Like catching your breath after a storm." He looked at her again. "This doesn't feel like that."

Aniyah held his gaze taking in his words.

"This feels rooted," Trevor continued. "I'm not running from anything when I'm with you. When we started this, everything I felt for you was genuine. I know I've said this before but I was not using you because I was lonely. My feelings for you are genuine even back when I was trying to hold my life together by the seams."

He took a quiet breath, feeling the weight of the moment settle between them.

"Somewhere in the middle of all that I realized something..." Trevor turned fully toward her now. "I'm in love with you."

Aniyah's breath caught softly of all the things she expected him to say, that was not one of them.

"I thought I knew what love was, from watching my parents and getting married young. This love feels different," he continued. "It's something we didn't force. Something that grew because we showed up to each other honestly each day. Even when I couldn't have you, you were still there. You're always on my mind and I find myself considering you in every move I make."

His thumb traced slowly along the back of her hand.

"I don't just want to protect you. I want to laugh with you. Travel with you. Experience life with you."

Aniyah blinked quickly, tears gathering in her eyes.

"I thought I was the poet," she said softly. "You have a way with words, Mr. Porter."

Trevor grinned.

"You'd be surprised what love can turn a man into."

She laughed through the tears. "You remember Anthony in *Bridgerton,* the show I made you binge watch with me? He always said he was a man of little words until Kathani came around, then he was vomiting his feelings to her every chance he got"

Trevor chuckled, shaking his head.

"Now look at me," he said. "Fell in love and turned into a poetic ass nigga."

Aniyah burst out laughing.

"I'm serious," he added, smiling at her.

She wiped at the corner of her eye, still smiling.

"I can see that. And let me just say, I never intended on leaving. Yes, that day at my condo where you snapped brought me back to reality. But it did so in a way that I knew if I didn't back off, if we didn't take a break, this would end before it could truly be beautiful." Aniyah looked down at her lap nervously and then back up at him.

"I love you too," she said with quiet confidence. Trevor felt his world go aglow with her admission. There was no way he was letting this woman go.

Trevor barely made it through the door before Aniyah's laugh met his mouth.

It started as a kiss meant to be gentle, something soft to mark the end of the evening, but the second she reached for the front of his jacket and pulled him closer, the careful distance they had carried for the last three months disappeared between them like it had been waiting to.

Trevor backed her toward the couch, his hands sliding along her waist as he kissed her again, slower this time, taking his time like he'd promised himself he would if he ever got this moment back. The warmth of her body against his felt familiar in a way that made something in his chest loosen.

He missed her so much.

Aniyah's fingers slipped into the curls at the back of his neck, her voice quiet against his mouth. "You still thinking too much?"

Trevor huffed a small laugh against her lips. "Trying not to. I know we had a prequel before we went to dinner, but I may die if I don't get inside of you soon."

"Good thing I want you there just as bad as you want to be there," she murmured, tugging him closer.

The rest of the night unfolded slowly after that, like something neither of them felt the need to rush anymore. They moved through the condo together in that easy rhythm they'd always seemed to find with each other, laughter slipping between kisses, touches lingering longer than they had any right to.

When they finally reached the bedroom, Trevor felt the last of the tension he'd been carrying dissolve somewhere beneath the quiet of the room.

They made love without a care in the world, slow motions cementing the confessions of love that hung between them. This was everything he hoped for and more.

Later after two more rounds, the world outside the condo faded into nothing more than the soft hum of traffic in the distance and the steady rhythm of Aniyah's breathing beside him.

Trevor lay on his back with her tucked against his side, one arm draped across her shoulders while his thumb traced slow circles along her bare arm beneath the sheet. The lamplight cast a warm glow across the room, catching the edges of her curls where they spilled across his chest.

He looked down at her, a quiet smile tugging at his mouth.

"I don't know if you needed the reminder since we've been apart for a minute," he murmured, his voice rough from sleep and laughter, "or maybe you forgot because I saw how Mr. Nelson was looking at you the other day at pick up time..."

Aniyah lifted her head slightly, her chin resting against his chest as she studied him.

Trevor brushed his lips across her forehead.

"But once I was in this motherfucker," he said softly, hand moving down to rub her soaked slit, "it's mine."

She blinked up at him trying to decide to pounce on him again or let him get his joke off.

"We go together real bad."

Aniyah burst into laughter, pressing her face into his chest as her shoulders shook. "Don't nobody want Wesley's ass. Boy, you are ridiculous."

"Mm," he hummed, tightening his arm around her. "You love it."

She lifted her head again just long enough to kiss him, slow and lingering, before settling back into the space beneath his chin.

"I do," she said quietly. "I love you too, baby."

Trevor kissed the top of her head, letting the moment settle around them.

"On a serious note, I can't end the night without asking. Aniyah, my Roxanne. Would you do the honor of being my girlfriend?"

"I'd thought you'd never ask, Max. Yes, I'll be your girl." Aniyah let out a yelp as Trevor pulled her on top of him and planted kisses all over her face. They calmed down soon after and just held each other.

For a while neither of them spoke. The quiet felt easy now, the kind that came from knowing there was nothing left to prove.

After a moment Aniyah shifted slightly, reaching toward the small notebook sitting on the nightstand beside the bed. Trevor watched her flip it open, her brow furrowing in that familiar way she got when words started forming in her head.

"You writing right now? You not tired yet?" he asked, amused.

She shrugged lightly, already scribbling across the page. "Inspiration doesn't keep office hours."

Trevor chuckled under his breath and let his hand drift slowly along her back while she wrote.

After a moment she turned the notebook toward him.

"What I'm Not," she said softly.

Trevor read the lines quietly.

I am not the silence
left behind by broken love.
I am the quiet
that comes after healing.
And you...
you are the man
who learned how to stay.

Trevor swallowed slowly, the words settling somewhere deep in his chest.

He looked at her again, his thumb brushing lightly along her cheek.

"Damn," he murmured.

Aniyah smiled softly. "Good damn or bad damn?"

"Good damn," Trevor said, pulling her closer. "Really good damn."

She laughed quietly and closed the notebook before setting it back on the nightstand. When she curled back into his side, Trevor tightened his arm around her without thinking, like his body had already decided this was where she belonged.

Maybe it had.

Somewhere in the quiet of the room, Trevor felt the last of the noise he'd been carrying for months finally settle. The work waiting for him back in the city would still be there in the morning. The premiere coming up soon. The world's response to it. The stories he'd fought so hard to protect and amplify.

But tonight he slept beside the woman he loved.

EPILOGUE

"Now when they say how are you, we say — LIVING LARGE AND TAKING CHARGE BIG BOIII" - *Nesi, B*A*P*S (1992)*

THREE MONTHS LATER

July arrived wrapped in heat and camera flashes.

Trevor stood just outside the theater entrance, the low hum of the crowd spilling out into the street while photographers shouted names from behind the barricades. Flashbulbs popped in quick bursts of white light, reflecting off the glass doors and polished black pavement like a second sunset. It was the release party and premiere of *Making Love: The Art of Us.* They would answer questions from the press, do a two-step on the dance floor and then watch the first three episodes.

He adjusted the collar of his jacket and glanced down at the small hand wrapped firmly around his.

Zara squeezed his fingers once before looking up at him with a grin that felt far too grown for her seven years.

"Are we famous now?"

Trevor huffed a quiet laugh. "Let's not get carried away."

Across the carpet Angelou was already being cornered by a reporter while Nina stood beside him looking effortlessly composed, one hand resting on her hip like she'd been doing this her entire life. Jackson and Mackenzie were further down the line, Jackson's locs pulled neatly behind his shoulders in barrel twists while Mackenzie laughed at something a journalist said.

His dad and Teri were talking to a blogger further down the carpet, Trevor hoped they weren't telling embarrassing stories about him.

The whole Porter crew had shown up tonight.

Family had a way of doing that.

Trevor felt movement beside him before Aniyah slipped her arm through his.

He glanced down at her automatically, the same quiet moment of disbelief still hitting him sometimes when he saw her standing next to him in spaces like this.

Aniyah squeezed his arm lightly, "You good?"

Trevor nodded once, "Yeah, just taking all of this in."

But truthfully with Aniyah by his side, he felt... steady.

Which still surprised him.

The last day of Zara's school year had come with a kind of clarity Trevor hadn't expected. He'd picked Zara up early for ice cream and when they got home he'd opened his phone, stared at the blank caption box for a long time on Instagram, and finally posted the photo that had been sitting in his drafts for weeks.

It was a simple picture.

Aniyah sitting cross-legged on his living room floor helping Zara build a puzzle.

The caption had been his own version of her poems.

What I Am
I am not the man
who mistakes silence for peace.
I am the man
who learned how to stay.
And she...
she is the woman
who taught me what real love looks like.

The internet had exploded within minutes after he uploaded it, which he expected. He was normally a private person. The last relationship status the world got was when his divorce was finalized.

Aniyah had laughed about all the comments for two straight days. She always knew the type of attention came with dating one of the Porter men and honestly, she did give a damn. She was amused by all of it.

Katelyn, on the other hand, was not.

The messages from an unknown number started that night. His phone had blown up with notification after notification. Angry texts. Voicemails that started incoherent and somehow got worse from there.

"You are a piece of shit, Trevor! How are you going to get with that ugly bitch instead of me?!"

Trevor listened to exactly two of them before blocking the number and calling his lawyer the next morning. Katelyn started showing up at his office and then at Zara's school, but not for Zara —to try and pick at Aniyah.

Trevor got the order of protection immediately, which Katelyn violated four days after. She went to jail and promised to get her act together. Of course, that only meant she started seeing another affluent man once she was released. Trevor hoped this one worked out so that he wouldn't have to deal with her anymore.

He was glad she was gone from their lives, even if it was temporary.

It was a hard truth to carry, but Trevor had watched his daughter blossom in the months since. Therapy with Dr. Sanders continued, and somewhere between school mornings, dance parties in the kitchen, and the quiet consistency of the people around her, Zara had started laughing like a kid again.

Kids bounced back when the ground beneath them stopped shaking. He had also been doing better with seeing Dr. Goodwill and applying her sessions into real life.

Trevor felt a tug at his sleeve.

"Daddy," Zara whispered loudly. "The lady with the microphone is staring at us."

Trevor looked up just in time to see the reporter waving them forward.

It was showtime.

The theater lights dimmed slowly as the audience settled.

Trevor sat between Aniyah and Zara while the opening credits rolled across the screen, his knee bouncing slightly in a way he hadn't quite been able to control all night.

Aniyah noticed, of course.

She slipped her hand over his knee and squeezed.

"Breathe," she murmured.

Trevor glanced down at her hand and exhaled slowly.

The screen faded to black.

Then one by one, the artists appeared.

Jackson stood first in his studio, paint streaked across his forearms as he looked directly into the camera.

"Love is creation," Jackson said.

The scene shifted.

Mackenzie stood in a photography studio surrounded by towering light panels, her camera hanging loosely around her neck.

"Love is seeing someone exactly as they are."

The sculptor appeared next. Malcolm Reyes, his hands coated in clay as he carved the curve of a stone figure.

"Love is patience."

Then the rapper, Jason "Verse" Carter leaned against a microphone stand in a dim recording studio.

"Love is truth."

Next came the singer Avery Rhodes who stood beneath stage lights during rehearsal, her voice echoing through an empty theater.

"Love is courage."

Finally, the screen cut to Aniyah. Trevor felt Zara sit up a little straighter beside him.

Aniyah appeared standing in her condo, sunlight spilling across the plants behind her. She looked directly into the camera and smiled.

"Love is you."

The theater fell silent for half a breath before the docuseries truly began.

The credits rolled two hours later and the applause that erupted felt like thunder.

Trevor sat there for a second longer than everyone else. The sound of it washing over him while his chest rose and fell slowly. He had done it. He had released his art into the world and they loved it. This moment felt surreal, but he knew he had worked hard to earn it.

Aniyah leaned into his shoulder and placed a kiss against his cheek.

"You did that," she whispered.

Trevor shook his head softly, turning to look at her. He really loved this woman.

"*We* did."

The headlines started appearing before they even left the building:

A Love Letter to Black Art and Storytelling

Trevor Porter's Docuseries Redefines What Creative Love Looks Like

A Cultural Moment Worth Watching

A week later his agent called with three new offers and a meeting to discuss all of them. One of them came with funding attached, another original screenplay request and traditional release of *A Sunday Kind of Love* to theaters. This was major news and something Trevor couldn't quite wrap his mind around. He accepted the meeting without a second thought.

Summer moved differently after that.

Aniyah leaned all the way into her break from school, trading lesson plans for airport terminals and tour buses while Trevor made appearances across the country promoting the series.

Somewhere between Chicago and Los Angeles she had to fly home for a weekend to be a bridesmaid in Maya's wedding, and two weeks later she helped Stephanie organize a baby shower that involved more balloons than Trevor believed possible.

Watching her move through those moments with her friends reminded him how many lives she had quietly been holding together long before he stepped back into hers.

It made loving her feel even bigger somehow.

One warm August night Trevor stood in the doorway of his living room and paused.

The house looked... different.

For years it had been neat to the point of not looking cozy. Organized in the quiet, functional way of a place someone slept in but never really lived inside.

Now there were throw blankets folded across the couch. Plants on the windowsill. Zara's art taped proudly to the refrigerator.

Aniyah had never announced she was changing anything. She'd simply started doing it. The place that was once filled with cold emptiness had turned into a home.

Trevor walked further inside and found the two people responsible for most of the noise in his life sitting cross-legged on the couch.

"K-pop Demon Hunters!" Zara shouted without looking away from the television.

Aniyah glanced over her shoulder and smiled. "You're late."

Trevor dropped onto the couch beside them.

"I'm sorry there was traffic coming from the city."

Zara scooted closer until she was wedged comfortably between them, her head leaning against his shoulder while the animated movie continued playing across the screen.

Halfway through the film her breathing slowed. Trevor looked down and realized she'd fallen asleep. Aniyah noticed at the same time and gently pulled a blanket over Zara's legs.

Trevor watched their daughter's chest rise and fall before glancing over at the woman beside him.

"I'm really glad you told me to get tutoring," he said quietly.

Aniyah lifted a brow. "For statistics?"

Trevor nodded, smiling faintly. "My dumb ass definitely would've failed that class sophomore year."

She laughed softly, a blush growing across her cheeks. Trevor leaned his head back against the couch.

"I don't know if we end up here without that."

Aniyah studied him for a moment before reaching over to lace her fingers through his.

"Trevor," she murmured, her voice warm with quiet certainty, "We were always going to end up here."

She squeezed his hand gently, "Because we were fate, baby."

Trevor looked down at his daughter sleeping between them,

then back at the woman who had somehow turned his life into something steadier than he'd ever imagined.

"The best fate I could've asked for."

The End.

ACKNOWLEDGMENTS

Whew! Where do I begin?

First things first—to my mom. Thank you for being my number one cheerleader through all of this. For pushing me to reach for the stars, for selling books out the trunk, for making sure people are *reading*. I truly could not do this without you. I love you so much.

Dad, whenever I need to remember that being a Renfroe means being a badass, you're the person I call. Thank you for all the love and all the support. I love you!

To my girls—my girly pops, my Golden Girls—Dri, Jac, and Dee Dee. I love y'all down. I couldn't have asked for better sisters.

To the Hoochies who always hold it down and get me together real quick when I start doubting myself in this author game—Zee, Lee, Nae, Jaleesa, Shawndra, and Candice. There really are no words. Thank you for accepting me into the fold and loving me the way you do. I appreciate y'all more than you know.

To my family—2026 didn't come in gently. We felt loss, but we also felt love in a way that held us together. I love y'all deeply.

Luis, thank you for the creative sessions, for letting me talk your ear off about my stories, my goals, and everything in between. You've been such a steady pillar in my support system, and I'm beyond grateful for you.

To my Eternal Lovers—there is no me without you. The support, the growth, the way you've shown up from *Creative Differences* to now... it does not go unnoticed. This book is dropping a week before my one-year author anniversary, and the difference between then and now feels like night and day. I get nervous. I doubt myself. And every single time, y'all remind me who I am. I love you so much.

I hope you enjoyed this story as much as I loved writing it. Trevor and Aniyah mean everything to me, and I hope you felt that love on every page.

Thank you, thank you, thank you.

With all my love,

DH 🤍

ALSO BY DH RENFROE

The Porter Brothers Series

Creative Differences - A Porter Brothers Novella (Jackson and Mackenzie)

Sky High - A Porter Brothers Novel (Angelou and Nina)

Masterpiece In Progress - A Creative Differences Christmas Novella (Jackson and Mackenzie)

The 2 AM Series

1:23 AM

Substack Erotic E-Series

Lola's Love Chronicles

THE SPIN 'DA BLOCK QUEEN

D.H. Renfroe is a Metro-Atlanta native and indie Black romance author who writes love stories that feel like reverence. A reader first, she has had a passion for fiction and storytelling since she was a little girl—long before she ever imagined publishing books of her own.

Her work centers emotionally rich, sensual romance where Black women are fully seen, deeply desired, and cherished without condition. Best known for her interconnected contemporary romance universe, including *Creative Differences*, *Sky High*, and *Masterpiece in Progress*, D.H. blends intimacy, vulnerability, and grown-folk passion with characters navigating love, grief, ambition, and healing.

Beyond the page, D.H. is one-sixth of the award-winning bookish podcast *The Lit Library*, where she helps foster thoughtful, joyful conversations about Black books, authors, and community. When she isn't writing or reading, she's a proud soccer mom and an avid lover of whodunit mysteries—always chasing the truth, whether it's on the page or on the screen.

Her intention as a writer is simple: *that readers leave her stories feeling satiated, softened, and wrapped in love.*

Instagram: @authordhrenfroe
TikTok: @authordhrenfroe
Threads: @authordhrenfroe
Email: dhrenfroe@dhrenfroe.com
Website: DHRenfroe.com

www.ingramcontent.com/pod-product-compliance
Lightning Source LLC
LaVergne TN
LVHW090551110826
845146LV00001B/102

* 9 7 9 8 9 9 5 6 5 0 1 0 2 *